IN THE CITY

IN THE CITY

Joan Silber

THORNDIKE PRESS • THORNDIKE, MAINE

Library of Congress Cataloging in Publication Data:

Silber, Joan.
In the city / Joan Silber. – [Large print ed.]
p. cm.
ISBN 0-89621-845-7 (alk. paper)
1. Large type books. I. Title.
[PS3569.I414I5 1987b]
813'.54 – dc19 87-25632
CIP

Large Print edition available in North America by arrangement with Viking Penguin Inc., New York.

Cover design by Armen Kojoyian.

For Lee

ACKNOWLEDGMENT

I would like to thank the
Guggenheim Foundation for its generosity
during the writing of this book

1
(Summer, 1924)

Pauline had forgotten about the straw seats on the train.

She had a half hour's ride from Newark to the Hoboken ferry terminal, and the moment she took her seat she was attacked through her clothing by a vicious meshwork of woven bristles; it was like sitting on a hair shirt. She had dressed for the heat – it was August and near ninety – and she wore a loose voile outfit which, even with her slip under it, provided very skimpy insulation against railroad upholstery.

A woman across the aisle from her had spread a newspaper under herself. Pauline had only a book of poetry with her, which she certainly wasn't going to sit on. She was seventeen and not inclined to be offhand about looking ridiculous in public. And she did think the woman looked ridiculous, settling her skirts over the paper like a hen brooding newsprint.

So she sat on one hand and fanned herself with her book. The train hadn't left the station yet, and outside the window she could see across the street to a theater marquee. Below it there was a poster of a couple about to kiss, a man with a pencil mustache and a woman with marcelled hair. Even from a distance the picture of their profiles leaning toward each other made her smile in recognition, as though she were looking at a picture of herself. She had spent several hours the night before in the front seat of a boy's roadster while it was parked behind the playground of a grammar school. She did not think that the boy, whose name was Harry Bitt, was himself important, except as the agent of certain sensations, but she was in awe of these sensations, and she reviewed them constantly.

It was very hot, and it would be worse in New York, with its reflecting pavements and the massed crowds diffusing their own conglomerate body heat. Pauline didn't mind the weather except that she had to pull at her bangs all the time to keep them from frizzing. All summer she had been going into New York as often as they would let her, on the excuse of running errands for her father's dry-goods store, picking up samples of edge trim and dropping off orders for white cotton batiste. Her visits always pleased her and gave her a great feeling of personal superiority, although they involved a lot of aimless walking in tight shoes, and she generally got lost at some point toward the end of the day; once an oily-haired man in a plaid coat had followed her for blocks, calling out, "You want a map, doll?"

The train began to move, jolting forward so that Pauline was jerked across the raspy seat; then it stopped and began again. Outside the window there was a constant dull flow of scenery – flat-fronted brick buildings. Once they were out of Newark these gave way to a bare and marshy flatland, like a giant vacant lot. Along the horizon there were water towers and crows flying. Pauline liked this part, which gave her a sense of traversing the steppes or the moors, some bleak European wastes.

She took up her book, which she thought she should read since she had brought it with her. It was a copy of Baudelaire in French, and Pauline's French wasn't nearly good enough to read most of it without a dictionary, but she knew some of the shorter poems almost by heart, and she moved her lips over the phrases. In her room at home she read them aloud in a languid chant, trying to absorb into her own personality something of the poems' atmosphere of sonorous corruption and rehearsing her own allegiance with ennui and other delicate monstrosities.

She was trying to figure out what *chevelure* meant when the words *luxe, calme, et volupté* started her thinking about Harry Bitt again and sent her back into that smug nostalgia staying on as aftermath from the night before. She did not resist; she intended to keep thinking about it as much as possible. He was a pale, soft-faced boy, smooth and blond, who went in for soothing hugs and fluttery kisses. With encouragement, a more serious and urgent side of him showed itself, and it was the fact of having worked this transformation in him which lingered most powerfully in her imagination. She kept going over the exact sequence of it; she wanted, if anything, more mental repetition, a more insistent record, since the experience had otherwise all the vagueness of the invisible, witnessed, after all, with her eyes closed. It was to rescue all of it from the blurred realm of private evidence that she always reported everything that happened on dates to her friend Bunny, but these were only lists and lacked the audacious nuance of the real thing.

Bunny was wrongly nicknamed; she was a bulky, solemn girl, burdened with *Bunny* by face-pinching parents when she was young and cute. (Her real name which she still hated anyway, was Roberta.) When she listened to Pauline's descriptions of what happened with Harry (in June it had been Ray), her eyes glistened; she asked intelligent and sometimes peculiar questions. Pauline liked explaining, but she felt there was something too soft, too romantic, in Bunny's attitude.

Still they were really friends – outsiders together – egging each other on in their shared scorn for the monkeyish antics that passed for hilarity in their high school. Minna Green played the piano with her feet at parties; Gilbert Markus had eaten eleven sardine-and-egg sandwiches on a dare in the school cafeteria; the captain of the football team had once set a live chicken loose in the auditorium. Pauline couldn't believe the fatuousness of all this, the "rampant stupidity," as she and Bunny liked to say. It made them style themselves as aloof and eccentric by contrast; they both wore their hair in the same triangular bobs, sometimes wrapped with a ribbon across the forehead, and carried the same knotwork bags; in class they rolled their eyes at each other across the room and passed sarcastic notes.

This avowed indifference did not, of course, make them favorites in most crowds. It was harder on Bunny, who looked so mild and blinking in her middy blouse, and who had once had a balloon filled with ink thrown at her back. Pauline was more convincing – she was a trim, nervously pretty girl, with a clear, slightly nasal voice. She had thin, peaked shoulders and carried herself well; she was also quite vain and a little too eager to be original about her appearance (today she had tied a striped ribbon around her hips for a sash, with somewhat awkward results). Older boys were sometimes drawn to her; she had that slyly knowing look when she was being quick and satirical (always flattering when you were not the target) and a sudden, fresh smile.

The train entered a tunnel and everything went dark inside the car for several minutes; Pauline sat upright, watching the rows of lights bob past the windows. The sensation of this got mingled with the constant physical remembrance of Harry, and she was feeling excited and reckless. The train came out into daylight and passed through the Hoboken track yards, where it stopped short. The breeze that had been coming through the windows died instantly; all the passengers were sighing and blotting their faces and plucking at their clothing to let the air in, as they lined up to get off. A conductor on the platform reached up to help her step down; he was a fat, white-haired man, who put his hands under her arms, touching her breasts: on purpose, she thought.

She was startled but not angry, since it seemed to her that anyone might want to do that, and it was over in an instant. She followed the crowd through the station – with its great domed ceiling and its dingy skylight – out to the street, and across to the ferry dock. The boat was already waiting, a boxy wooden hulk with peeling paint; beyond the glare of the water, the skyline of the city loomed flat and close, as though she could swim there if she were dressed for it. As soon as the entrance chain was unhooked, she found a seat on deck.

Pauline stood up when the boat got under way. The light cloth of her dress got pressed flat against her stomach and legs and flapped behind her like a sail. Everyone else was sitting down, blinking as though the wind were too much for them, which made her feel very blithe and sturdy, a spirited young thing braving the elements. Near the railing, her face got misted and wet, and she backed away because of her hair.

When she walked out into the Twenty-third Street ferry terminal, she tugged at her dress to pull it down, and a man who was standing under the clock tower smiled at her. She laughed slightly, to show that she was amused at having been caught grooming herself. He said, "Did you ever think about being a model?"

He was about thirty (too old for her), a tall man in a straw hat and a summer suit.

"You've certainly got the face for it," he said. Pauline said thank you. He was almost good-looking, except that his freckles made his skin appear splotchy and irritated, and his Adam's apple was too large. "I mean a designer's model," he said. "You didn't think I meant an artist's model, did you?"

"Oh, no," Pauline said.

"The designers are hiring ones like you now, brunettes with little faces, not these horsy blondes. You ever hear of a designer Jean Patou?" He pronounced it more or less correctly, with a soft *j* and the last name a twangy approximation, Patoo as in sweet patootie. "My friend is hiring for him now. He should see you. You could make a lot of money."

"I wouldn't do it for the money," Pauline said.

"It would come in handy, though, right?"

Pauline had heard – who had not? – of girls being "discovered" in odd places, of their piquant expressions and unforgettable complexions striking the commercial hearts of impresarios. She would not have said she wanted to be a model; she had pictured something more singular and Bohemian for herself; she wanted to enter, somehow, a circle of people who did artistic and outrageous things, and to be admired by them, to be famous for being with them. It struck her that being a model would have its own seductive cachet even under those circumstances; no matter what people said, they always wanted to know women like that.

"Do you always wear your hair this way?" he said. "We could just comb it flatter – it's a little messed up now, isn't it?" Pauline had tried pulling spit curls down over her cheeks, and she was disappointed that he thought these weren't deliberate, but she stood still while he brushed them back with his hand and said, "Don't want to hide that face.

"It's a clean business," he said. "There's no monkey business in it." Pauline thought it was a bit quaint of him to reassure her about that. She did not, after all, object to monkey business, as he so cutely called it. He seemed a little unsophisticated and hokey in his seersucker suit with the pants rolled too low. His shoes were that cheap leather that looked almost orange.

"My name is Earl," he said.

"I'm Pauline Samuels." There was a little silence as they crossed the street, and Pauline asked him where he was from, which was always a good thing to ask new people.

"I've been all over the world. You won't believe me when I tell you where I just came from."

"Where?"

"Paris, France. It's wonderful there except they make you sit with Negroes in cafes and buses."

"What's wrong with that?" Pauline said.

"You're probably very idealistic," he said. "You're young." She hated arguing with people who were so backward in their thinking. Probably he thought Sacco and Vanzetti were just a couple of hooligans too. Bunny would have given him a whole speech.

"We could go over to my friend's office," he said, "if you're not in a hurry. It's around the corner."

If they were hiring right away, she would have to say no; she wasn't graduating until next January. She walked with him down the block; he stopped in front of an office building and held the door for her to follow him inside. The lobby, which was empty, had a cracked marble floor and brown-painted molding. "Wait, here," he said. "Let me go up and see if he's still out to lunch or if he's there." He went up the stairs and came back again in a few minutes. "He's out. You don't mind waiting?"

Pauline shook her head. He edged her under the stairwell, and then he drew her toward him and began kissing her. He said, "Ah," as though he thought she had been expecting this, which she had not, but she kissed him back by habit since she was proud of not being cold or timid. His tongue was much more forceful and probing than Harry's had been, a technique she did not particularly like but submitted to quietly; his friend would be arriving soon anyway. They went on kissing for a minute; then he drew back and took off his hat, which he put on the radiator. He was balding, with fine, reddish hair, wispy at the top of his head; he smoothed it down as though he were sorry she had to see it. He looked toward the door a moment; then he put his hands down under the neck of her dress, kneaded her breasts, and said, "Ah," again, as though he had found something. She felt suddenly foolish and unprepared, shocked that he was really touching her bare skin, and aware that she was in a public place and that she didn't like him or find him attractive.

He kissed her very hard and eagerly again, and then he fumbled with the buttons of his trousers and pulled her hand down to touch him. Pauline had never done this before, although he seemed to think she had. She was still struck with something like physical disbelief, alarmed now, and frozen into a sort of hardened patience with herself, with her own mistake. It seemed strangest to her that her life contained this now forever; it awed her beyond everything. He moved her hand in a tightened grip, thrusting up against her, and began to shiver all over. "Is it okay?" he said. "Can I put it in?"

"No," she said.

"No?" he said, and he let her take her hand away. She turned then so she couldn't see what he was doing. When she looked back, he was wiping at himself with a handkerchief.

"I have to go," she said. "I have to meet some people."

"Wait," he said, buttoning his pants and tucking his shirt back under his suspenders. "I'll walk you."

He hooked his arm under her elbow, as though they were strolling through the park, and they walked out through the door of the building. The street was full of noise, busy with the stream of traffic that had been going on the whole time they were inside, and very bright in the afternoon sun. Pauline squinted as though she were coming out of a movie theater.

"You believe in free love, don't you," he said. "I like that. I like a free spirit."

There was an El station by the corner, and Pauline thought she could get away from him there. He said, "Meet me here next Saturday, okay?"

"I can't come into New York any more. I'm not going to be able to for the rest of the summer."

"I could meet you in Hoboken, if you want. Your parents wouldn't have to know. They wouldn't like me, would they? You don't think I'm too old for you, do you?" Pauline shrugged.

He took out an envelope and asked her to write her phone number on it. She gave him a number with one digit wrong, let him kiss her again, and walked up the stairs to the El entrance.

There was a moment while she fumbled for a nickel in her purse when she heard someone running up the stairs after her, but it was only a boy in knickers who pushed ahead of her at the turnstile. She waited on the platform with the others, and no one even looked at her or noticed her especially. When the train came, she took the first seat, next to a woman with an infant in her lap.

She got off at Penn Station and went at once to the ladies' room, where she spent time hiking up her garters and washing her face. Her eyes looked terrible – all hangdog and watery like Bunny's – but she put on powder, which made her cheeks less flushed and swollen, and she pulled the spit curls down again. She walked out into the station until she found a lunch counter, and she sat with her purse and her book balanced on her lap and read the menu, but no one came to wait on her. There didn't even seem to be anyone behind the counter, although other people were eating. She felt clumsy and wincing, laughably timid in all her gestures. A counter boy with crooked teeth came over to her finally, and she ordered a lemonade and drank it down quickly.

When she walked outside again, it had begun to rain. It was only a light rain, which cooled the air and made a soothing, rushing sound on the pavement, but she was wet by the time it was over, and she had to walk the rest of the way with great splotches on the front of her dress, which looked lewdly comical, as though something private had leaked through her clothing.

The office of Art Style Trim was on the second floor, and as soon as she opened the door, a man who was standing up talking to the receptionist called out, "It's the orphan of the storm here. What's the matter, honey, your boyfriend doesn't love you enough to buy you an umbrella?"

A tiny leathery man in glasses who was sitting on one of the armchairs said, "What are you, testing the fabric to see if it runs? That's it, right? I know."

They were salesmen. The older man in fact looked like someone she had seen in offices since she was a child, although she wasn't sure. Pauline hated on principle the heartiness of salesmen, their constant bantering to pass the time, but she sometimes flirted with them to show them they hadn't gotten the best of her. Today she just nodded her head at them: let them think she was shy, a sodden, mincing little thing. She could tell already that was what they thought. They had gone back to talking to the receptionist, a beefy woman with fierce eyebrows and shrimp-colored rouge.

Pauline's errand was to pick up an order of soutache braid. This would come rolled on a large wheel, and she had planned to stop for it later in the day, since there was nothing to do but go home once she was carrying it. The receptionist told her to take a seat and wait for Mr. Gittelson, who was out.

She took a chair in the corner, next to a wall papered with silhouettes of black swans holding funereal loops of black ribbon in their beaks. The salesmen went back to playing a game of cards, and Pauline picked up a copy of *System: The Magazine of Business* and flipped through it. She read an article on "Bad Debts and Hidden Losses" and the advertisements for correspondence courses. ("Your future depends on yourself. Will you always be a drudge? A few years hence, then what?") The magazine made her feel vexed and vaguely tearful, and she had to put it down, although the encounter in the hallway had left her feeling leaden and dazed, the opposite of weepy.

She waited for a long time, an hour at least, hearing the slapping of the playing cards against the tables and the salesmen's voices. Once it seemed to her that they were saying, "Woes are wild," which could not be right but she let it pass, another piece of oddness from the crackling surface of the world.

By the time she heard the click of the office door opening, her dress had dried where it was stretched between her knees. "Here he is," the receptionist said, "the man of the hour." Pauline had always thought that Mr. Gittelson was handsome in a stocky way, although the stiff collars made his eyes look startled and over-eager. There was a shininess near his scalp now where the brilliantine had melted. When he saw her, he said, "Paulie," and then, "So did they give you coffee while you were waiting? A glass of water even? Nothing, right?"

"I was fine," she said.

Mr. Gittelson pinched and wiggled the end of her nose. "A sweetheart." Then he went into the back office. When he returned, a boy came with him carrying the roll of braid wrapped in brown paper. Pauline tore one corner of the package to make sure it was the right kind. "Look at this," Mr. Gittelson said. "She looks before she leaps. This is a very intelligent girl here. You could all of you learn something."

"My father would kill me if I didn't look," Pauline said.

"You're a lovely girl," Mr. Gittelson said. "Your kind I would hire in a minute."

Pauline said, "Thank you," and then she smiled a little. She was thinking, with some appreciation of the irony, that it was the second time that day someone had "offered" her a job. Mr. Gittelson, who thought she was smiling with pleasure at being praised, kissed her on the cheek before she left, rubbing his mustache against her.

On the way back she had to sit on the lower deck of the ferry, so her package wouldn't get wet; the air was close and smelled of gasoline from the engines. When she boarded the train, she dozed off almost at once; once she dreamed someone was holding a fur hat over her face and stifling her, and she woke feeling frightened and slightly ashamed.

When she got off at the Newark station, the downtown streets were thick with people going home from work or shopping. She walked for blocks, shifting her bundle, which was heavy and left marks on her arms.

At home they were already sitting down to dinner; from a block away Pauline could see the yellow light of the citronella candles set out on the screened porch at the side of the house, where they took their meals in hot weather. Pauline rapped on the screen door, and her mother called out from her seat, "We gave up waiting for you already." The porch room seemed very bright and tensely cheerful, with the pink glass plates and the ugly metal fruit bowl and the tablecloth printed with drawings of bananas and sombreros. Solly, who was twelve, banged his fork against the juice pitcher and said, "Time and supper wait for no man." There was cold roast chicken and Harvard beets. Pauline ate slowly, with some pleasure in the tastes but no appetite. She felt as though she had been traveling for a long time; her legs ached, and things were dry in her mouth.

Solly, who had gotten a haircut from his father that day, kept licking his finger and dabbing the back of his neck. He was bleeding in spots from where the clippers had nicked the scalp. "Stop already," his mother said. "Don't touch."

Pauline's father went on gnawing his chicken with that private, inward gaze he had when he was chewing. The upper half of his face was always hawkish and worried, but around the mouth the expression was slack and old, and he lapped at his food when he ate. He was quiet at the table. He could sit still for hours, and then, out of his brooding, he would speak out or dart up suddenly. Sometimes even now he would grab the children and hug them until they squealed. Fits of annoyance came over him without warning. When they were little and he was angry with them, he used to shake them rather than hit them – which was worse, Pauline thought, because there was that hideous feeling of your head rolling over and over in rhythm, as though you were helping.

Her mother said, "You got wet in the rain, right? Next time you'll wear a hat." Pauline had a straw skimmer which she wouldn't wear because it looked like a shellacked waffle.

Solly said, "Ease-play ass-pay the ickles-pay." Pauline reached across and passed the relish dish, because she knew she was the only one who would bother to translate.

Her mother was pouring salt now on a spot where beet juice had gotten on her lap. She wore a kerchief tied around her head in a turban, as she did whenever she was in the house. Sometimes she kept it on even when she was in the store waiting on customers. She was a patient but unsmiling salesperson, hauling down bolts of cloth and unfurling them silently for inspection; she could carry out a sale without speaking more than a few words. Standing in front of the shelves of silk chiffons and plaid taffeta ribbons, she was a plain figure in a shapeless dress, short and solidly built, with a high mount of bosom. Her looks were marred by an underbite – a jutting chin like a terrier's – which made her say her *s*'s too thickly. She was cautious by nature – full of warnings about how eating bread in the morning was the only way to avoid getting worms in the stomach, afraid of elevators and uncooked vegetables and drafts in bedrooms – but having come from Europe as a bride of twenty, she had lived for so many years in a state of half-understanding and misapprehension that she had grown shy and hesitant and peevish about her opinions. Her English was not good, and had it been up to her, she would not have gone out of the house at all. Every child on the block could imitate the way she said her own name – Mrs. Shemuels; they would suck in their lips and click their front teeth together. Sometimes Pauline and Solly did it too, beyond her hearing.

Pauline's father said, "Leave the stain on your dress alone. We'll say you were murdered and sell it for a bundle."

Months before, he had read in the newspaper that the clothing Abraham Lincoln had on when he was assassinated had been sold at auction for $6,500, and this had struck him as so fantastical – an example of enterprise carried to extremes of splendidly grim cleverness – that he brought it up at every turn. He would cough into a handkerchief and hand it to one of the children: Here, go sell it when I'm dead.

He said to Pauline, "You got the right ribbon, right?" Pauline pointed to the package, which she had set in the corner of the porch.

Her mother said, "So long as she didn't bring back any rotten berries this time." This was a reference to Pauline's having purchased – on Bleecker Street, two weeks ago at least – a basket of blueberries, which had looked very tempting but which had turned out to be soft and spoiled on the bottom. "Miss Millionaire," her mother said. "So you know to look first, then buy?"

"I didn't buy anything this time," Pauline said. Solly rolled his eyes; they did go on about things. Pauline had been made to eat the berries as an instructive exercise, although she had not really minded. She was used to them at home, the way they were fixed and strict about some things and blindly lenient about others.

Pauline had stopped listening anyway. She was thinking about the ferry slip and how the man had seemed better-looking and more intelligent at first; she still had that preoccupation with going over the details as though she could correct them by thinking about them. Her mother was talking about how they should have reported the fruit seller to the police. It struck Pauline that, for all her parents' suspicions, they were full of ignorance about the way things were (which made her feel rather spitefully sorry for them). At the store her mother was always watching old ladies picking over the notions counter, sure that they were going to steal the needles packets. They understood greed, but the rest made no sense to them. Pauline thought of the man Earl (that was probably not really his name) wiping himself with a handkerchief, desperate and methodical, as though he were following some habit of hygiene repeated often before. This went on all the time; the world was full of this. She had kissed him, which made her flinch back in her chair now.

She sat up straight again, but no one was looking at her anyway. Her mother was complaining about how mosquitoes got through the holes in the screen, and Solly was saying the bugs could eat his beets if they wanted, hurry up, come eat. Pauline did not dislike her family at this moment – she was quite relieved, after all, to be back in the house – but they seemed very distant, and at the same time their voices were very loud.

The phone rang then, a long metallic rattle. Maybe Earl had figured out the right digit, or she had written down the right number without thinking. Her father went into the kitchen, and she could hear him saying "Yes?" (that was how he greeted people in the store too – Yes? instead of Can I help you?). It was for the other family on their party line. When he came back he said, "What did you think, it was your friend Mr. Harry?"

Pauline did the dishes while her parents sat in the living room listening to the radio, to a concert of the Philharmonic Orchestra playing Rimsky-Korsakov. The music sounded stiff and silly, with its swelling rushes and dying falls.

It annoyed Pauline and made her utterly sure that she was on the other side of things, dry and unfeeling and modern. She began swabbing the dishes in time, as a sort of joke to herself, dipping and lifting them out of the suds on the soaring beat. She didn't really mind kitchen work; she had tied the apron, which was much too big for her, with the strings crossed twice around her waist so she looked tightly bodiced like a tavern wench. She had to heat up another kettle when the water got cold; and although she had been hot all day, she put a dish towel over her head and leaned her face over the spout, because she had heard that the steam was good for her complexion.

For a while Pauline was afraid that the man would be lurking in wait the next time she walked out of the ferry terminal, but then this came to seem more and more unlikely, and childish of her to imagine. She could not go into New York any more now anyway; the August sales were on and she was in the store until late every day.

Pauline worked in the stockroom, which was really a hallway under the stairs, lit by one dangling bulb and heaped with bolts of cloth and cardboard cartons. The window was painted shut and there was no ventilation; all the elastic binding went gummy from the heat and stuck to its spools, and the finish on the chintzes had a gluey feel to it. Pauline pulled things out from under piles and then sat on a stool and made lists. She had devised a way of wearing a strip of flannel around her forehead so it was hidden by her ribbon, to keep the sweat out of her eyes.

Bunny was working at the five-and-ten over the summer, and sometimes she came in on her lunch break, and they went out and sat on the steps at the back of the store. There was a dusty yard and some shade from an overgrown hedge. Bunny always brought a ragged-looking sandwich filled with hacked slices of leftover roast, and they ate together, crackling their waxed paper into little balls for the store cat to play with.

Bunny had gotten fatter over the summer, and she had had her hair cut shorter, which looked mannish instead of boyish on her. Harry Bitt said she looked like an otter that way. He had said that to Pauline in a conversation on the street one night, when he had passed her coming home from work and walked her as far as the schoolyard. He had come into the store once since then and tried to neck with her behind a pile of remnants; after that she hadn't heard from him, and by now he was probably getting ready to go back to engineering school in Pittsburgh.

All summer Bunny had been afraid she was going to get fired from the five-and-ten. Her supervisor kept telling her she was sullen. Bunny wasn't the least bit sullen, but she had a crooked half smile on her face sometimes, which was only faltering and incomplete but which looked sly to some people. Pauline thought that if Bunny wore lipstick it would offset this effect, but Bunny didn't take criticism well so Pauline had stopped suggesting it.

Pauline had waited a week before telling Bunny about the incident with Earl in the hallway. Bunny had listened without interrupting or looking too aghast, and at the end she had even made light of it by joking about how Pauline was always looking for trouble. In many ways she was very sensible. But then later she had said, "Dress models don't earn that much; the ones in stores are exploited worse than clerks." Pauline resented her always bringing her anarcho-syndicalism into everything, nosing it into Pauline's private confession, but she had said, "Oh, I know," politely enough.

Bunny was poking in the dirt with a stick; she drew the lines for tic-tac-toe, and they played a few dullish games. Then the two of them together sketched the figure of an anatomically prodigious naked man. Pauline crossed it out right away in case anybody came by and saw. Bunny said, "You could have just drawn a very large fig leaf over it."

"I would not be so philistyne," Pauline said. This was a pun of long standing between them – there was a girl in their class named Phyllis Stein, and they thought this was funny.

Pauline could hear her father from inside the store, groaning as he hauled something across the floor. Already he was hinting to Pauline that she shouldn't count on working in the store after school was over, she should think about getting work someplace else with a salary. She hadn't mentioned Gittelson yet.

She and Bunny talked about whether rents were really getting higher in Greenwich Village. Bunny thought that two girls could share a furnished room really cheaply if there was a Murphy bed and a sofa in it. A lot of Bunny's ideas of romantic experiment were curiously bound up with finding ways to live ingeniously on very little; it was a kind of ethical adventure for her to think how she might invent methods of curbing her own needs.

Pauline didn't see how with Bunny or someone else there, she would ever be free from a certain strain; even in confiding about Earl she had left out details, and not from delicacy really. She was beginning to think about staying alone in a small, bare white room, with a metal bedstead and a ewer basin and one extravagant object, a Chinese rug or a bronze vase, probably a gift from a lover.

Bunny took off her gray smock from Woolworth's and folded it up under her neck for a pillow. She said, "Wake me up if I fall asleep," and leaned back against the wooden frame of the door. Pauline was just almost closing her eyes when she heard a boy's voice humming Brahms' lullaby, quavering on the notes like an Irish tenor. It was Murray Appelbaum; he was gazing at them over the hedge. "Go back to your naps," he said. "And they talk about the wild, restless fervor of youth today."

"We're warm," Pauline said. "Come fan us with your jacket or something."

Murray crossed into the yard, taking off his jacket as he walked, and then he stood in front of them, flapping it in their faces, until Pauline told him to stop.

"How come you're not working at the bakery?" Bunny said.

"Let them eat crackers," he said. "On Mondays I'm off."

"So you just loaf around," Bunny said.

"Get it?" Pauline said.

He sat down on the grass near them.

Pauline said, "You don't look like you've been outside too much." He was always white-skinned like that, too pale and bony; he was close to homely, except for his eyes, which were deep-set and slanted, with fine, girlish lashes.

He said, "I'm very rugged and outdoorsy but it's just too subtle for people to grasp."

"You having a good summer?" Bunny said.

"What does that mean? People always ask that, but they don't really want to know. They should say, Are you having a good gozornplatt? Are you having a good gritzilplick? It would open up conversation."

Pauline could never decide whether he was too clumsily whimsical or really unusual. They had been in the same art class last spring; once she had almost agreed to pose for him in the nude. He was always telling her his sketches were as good as Manet's at his age. He was full of quirky arrogance and then streaks of self-parody; at the bakery he would pretend to gauge the perspective of a tray of rolls, edging back from them with his thumb up, with his white hat mashed down like a droopy beret.

Bunny had taken up the stick again and was doodling something in the dirt. Murray said, "Let me see. I'll tell you if it's good or not."

"Toulouse LaDreck here," Pauline said. "He's so modest."

Bunny said, "Draw something yourself," and handed him the stick.

Pauline said, "Wait." She went inside the store and came out again with a box of tailor's chalk she had stolen from the stockroom.

Murray took it and said, "I'm very touched." He rubbed his shoe over the surface of the cement walk, to sweep away loose dirt, and made a few tentative lines and smudged them out. Then he started making big shading strokes with the flat slabs of chalk, until he had produced a pink triangle floating on two brown trapezoids, which (he was disappointed when they did not guess right) turned out to be a cubist version of the Baptist church across the street, with a series of overlapping green ovals for trees and a scribbled purple sky.

"I like it a lot," Bunny said.

"Genius comes to Peshine Avenue," Murray said.

It looked very splashy and vivid on the pavement, next to the scratchy grass and the discarded cardboard boxes. The best thing about it was the way it transformed the yard.

They were all feeling pleased with themselves. Pauline said, "My father will have a fit if he sees it."

Bunny said, "The rhythm of it is really nice."

Murray was wiping the chalk off his hands onto his pants, very workmanlike and casual. He said, "It *is* as good as a Manet." Pauline was sure Manet himself never would have said something like this. It was not bad, but the purple sky wasn't deft so much as sloppy, and he had made the trees too much like the spirals in the Palmer writing exercise. She began to think it might have been better if he had done something funnier, a witty parody or something. The more she looked at it, the more it embarrassed her a little.

They sat quiet awhile, listening to the voices of people passing in the street. Bunny had pulled up a blade of timothy grass and was chewing it absently. Pauline said, "Are you grazing?"

"She was only a farmer's daughter," Murray said, "but she sure knew her oats." Then he said, for Pauline's benefit, "She was only a notion seller's daughter, but she had me on needles and pins."

They heard a lunch whistle from one of the factories, which meant that Bunny was late getting back to work. She started fidgeting with the laces on her shoes, retying them. She still wore those heavy leather oxfords, even in summer. Pauline herself had on scuffed brown pumps (hardly better than Bunny's) over soiled cotton lisle stockings. She was almost surprised when she looked down and saw them; she always thought of her things as nicer than they really were. She felt that all her own tastes were thwarted now, and that nothing really counted yet.

Bunny left, buttoning her smock, and they waved her off. Pauline yawned and leaned back against the screen door again. Murray stretched over closer to her and pretended to pick a dried leaf out of her hair. He said, "Do you know what a butterfly kiss is?" and then he flicked his eyelashes against her cheek. Pauline thought this was bumpkinish of him and in some way unmanly, but she gave him a flashing smile anyway, out of habit or for practice, with her eyes closed.

2

All that fall Pauline walked to school in the mornings by a longer route, through the park. Since she left the house at the same time she always had, she was almost always late for her first class, but she liked the coolness of the park at that hour – the empty benches and the dusty cement fountains – a landscape that had nothing to do with school.

Sometimes as she was leaving the park she would hear the bell, and then from the next block she could see the schoolyard, already deserted. When she got there she pushed open the heavy, metal-cased doors and walked through the halls, trying not to let her shoes make noise on the corridor tiles. Outside senior Latin she could hear Miss Oughton giving drill and the blurred rumbling of the answers chanted in unison. Sometimes as she slipped through the doorway Miss Oughton would point at her and say, *"Ad principem,"* which meant that Pauline had to go to the office to get a blue slip. Pauline did not see that it mattered how many demerits she got, since it was her last semester, and after a while Miss Oughton didn't bother any more.

In Latin she sat behind Minna Green, who wore beautiful silk-knit sweaters with sappy little piqué collars on them and who got giggly and red-faced when she had to read words like *testis* and *menses*. Once Pauline, without thinking, had actually kicked the back of her seat from annoyance.

Pauline had wanted to take Latin partly, of course, so as not to be left out of knowing what *sine qua non* and *caveat emptor* meant and the phrases that were always interleaved in sentences and used obscurely for titles. She had also been secretly much impressed by the doctrine that through the discipline of Latin the mind attained a certain purity of reasoning and took on classical habits of thought. She had only been thirteen when she'd begun it, and she had liked the idea then of being trained to a sublime and calm logic (she was sorry she was not good at math). It was a kind of whiteness of the mind she wanted, a mental stillness like the sealed expressions on eyeless statues.

She had been disappointed to find that Latin was so involved with military campaigns and letters back and forth from generals, and with learning the idioms for "to pitch camp" and "to lay waste to," and that none of it was useful internally. She still did not hate it; it was too unpopular a subject to feel rebellious toward. It seemed only dull and blockishly masculine, like Miss Oughton herself, and it made Pauline feel wild and futuristic, sitting there with her plastic bangle bracelets and her plucked eyebrows, more ready than ever to slip away from all this.

She had a familiar stock of thoughts which usually occupied her, in the midst of hearing Minna or someone else try to stumble through one of Cicero's orations. She still hadn't done more than hint to her father about the possibility of working for Gittelson. Her father had said nothing so far; it was always hard to know what he thought about things. At times she imagined that he would say no to any job outside of Newark; she could, of course, not ask him at all and just disappear one morning, get on the train and go. She had already looked at the railroad schedule to see how early a train she would have to take to get out with her luggage before they woke up.

At times she tried to prepare herself to be the sort of person who could do this. After school she took detours on the way home, walking by pool halls and weathered woodframe houses where men sat out on porches, so that she wouldn't be afraid of strange neighborhoods. Once in the park she made herself watch a cat mauling a sparrow, to harden herself.

The idea of running away (although she did not always think about it directly) kept her distracted and even a little somber. In school this had the effect of actually making her appear more well-mannered. She sat quiet through class, answering most questions by rote in her clear, singsong voice, which carried well. Even in gym she looked earnest, skittering around in her blue serge jumper playing kick soccer.

She felt that she was waiting, that there was nothing in this time but a kind of unprofitable repetition and a prolonged suspense. Bunny was also graduating in January – they had both been skipped a semester in grammar school – and they often greeted each other in the hall by calling out, "Only a hundred and nineteen more days!" (They had argued about whether they should count to the last day of classes or the last exam day.) It braced them both to hear the numbers shrink, as though the march of time were on their side.

At home sometimes she had fits of restless energy, and she would sit in the kitchen and sew, making underwear for herself out of scraps of fabric – silk pongee step-ins and cotton lawn chemises – working the treadle with fierce, slapping rolls until her father complained of the noise and asked her how come she was so busy all of a sudden. She could hardly settle herself to do homework, but during one week she worked feverishly on an essay for a school competition (topic: "What Price Freedom?"), discussing the death of Lord Byron in terms indicating that she would have behaved exactly the same under similar circumstances, as if she were dragging a clubfoot over the cliffs of Greece instead of sitting at the kitchen table eating an apple; she was so distant from her surroundings that any activity in the outside world seemed more possible and more characteristic of her.

On Saturday night she went to the movies with Bunny, although their tastes were very different, and on the way out they had an argument about whether Pola Negri wore too much black stuff on her eyelids. Afterward they went to the candy store, and they were sitting drinking their sodas, making bubbles with their straws rather childishly, when Murray came toward their table, walking pigeon-toed to attract their attention.

Behind him was a short, heavy-chested boy whom Pauline knew only by sight, someone from another neighborhood. "These girls want to beg us to sit down but they're too shy," Murray said.

Pauline said, "If there's one thing I hate, it's begging."

"You see? They can hardly control themselves. Sit down, Cafferty. This is Jim Cafferty. He knows everything, but he's very understated about it."

"That's a nice change," Bunny said. He wasn't bad-looking, Pauline thought.

"You never believe me any more," Murray said. "Cafferty, what's the capital of Nebraska? Whisper."

Cafferty leaned over and pretended to whisper something in Murray's ear. "He says Lincoln," Murray said.

"He's turning you into a talking dog joke," Pauline said. "You ought to bite him."

"Not me," Cafferty said. "I don't get into fights over state capitals."

Murray took a sip from each of the girls' sodas.

"That's a nice ornament you have on," Cafferty said. He meant the scarf ring Pauline had made for herself out of a fake-tortoise belt buckle. "Very unique."

"Thank you," Pauline said.

"How do you boys know each other?" Bunny said.

"We have history together," Murray said. "He's the only other one who thinks the Mexican War got started purely from greed."

"Thoreau thought so," Bunny said.

"He's not in Mr. Klopmeier's class," Murray said. "Probably he studied with him once, though. When they were both in their prime."

"Let us not make fun of the aged," Bunny said.

"Klopmeier's not so old," Cafferty said. "He's just dried up. It's his mental viewpoint is his problem. He has a prune in place of a brain."

"Don't you feel sorry for him?" Bunny said.

"Sure. Someone should slip him a shot of gin in his Ovaltine to perk up his coloring."

Pauline, who did not like practical jokes, stopped smiling.

"She thinks I would really do it," Cafferty said. "I wouldn't – how could I do it? I wouldn't waste the gin anyway." Pauline went on twisting her empty glass in its saucer. "She doesn't believe me. She's going to ask you, Who was that Irish lower-element type you were bringing around to meet us the other night?"

"No, I won't," Pauline said.

"You won't ask?" he said. "Too bad for me."

Bunny started fussing with her coat and talking about how late it was. Murray said he knew she had another date. Pauline stood up and said, “Bye-bye, boys. Don’t get into trouble when we leave.”

Bunny said, “So long. Abyssinia.”

Murray walked them to the door and waited while they fastened their collars and pulled down their hats. “He’s nice, right?” Murray said. “He’s very good with girls. He’s got five sisters. The oldest sister goes out with a famous gangster, you probably heard about that.”

“Stop exaggerating everything all the time,” Pauline said.

Jim Cafferty came up then, with a rather adult-looking hat on, and said, “You want a ride home?”

“In what?” Pauline said.

“He’s a good driver,” Murray said.

They followed the boys to a black Studebaker parked on the corner, and the two girls got in the back seat. “Ooh, this is nice,” Bunny said.

Cafferty said, “It belongs to a friend. He lets me use it sometimes.”

It was windy once the motor started, but Pauline said she liked riding in the open and it was a nice night, you could see the stars. They dropped Bunny off, and Murray said Pauline should get in the front seat between them. “If she doesn’t mind being crowded,” Jim said.

“It’s all right, we’ve known each other for years,” Murray said, and Pauline settled between them, centering herself so she could just feel the pressure of their knees on either side. She thought Cafferty was pushing his leg against hers on purpose, but she wasn't sure.

Jim said, "Want to go to Philadelphia?"

"I'd rather Miami."

"No, I mean it."

He couldn't really mean it – it was too far, what would they do when they got there? He might have to take them if she said yes (she eyed him as he drove); maybe he was that type. Pauline said, "Not this time." She had only been to Philadelphia once; it depressed her to remember this. She couldn't tell whether she had just failed to be bold – not that she wanted to go – but the whole issue of her personal courage made her panicky all the time now.

While Murray was going on about how they could visit the Liberty Bell and maybe take Ben Franklin out for a drink, they passed her house and she let them drive around the park, just for the ride. At a bridge just past the turnoff to the river, they stopped to look at the view. "There's a new moon," Pauline said. Jim said that was lucky, and Pauline said good, she needed luck, she was trying to talk her father into something.

Murray, who knew about the Gittelson idea, said, "You should try whispering to your father when he's asleep. Induce autosuggestion."

"Very funny," Pauline said. She was thinking about how nasty her father got when anything interrupted his sleep. Once he had knocked Solly to the floor for bumping into the sofa while he was taking a nap.

Jim said she should wish on a falling star and she would get whatever she wanted.

Pauline said, "What do they look like, falling stars?" Not that this would help – nothing would help if her father said no. She could hear how he would say it. She had no plan really for what she would do, and she was afraid of her own capacity for submission.

They waited by the water, listening to the mild lapping of the river and arguing about whether shooting stars were ever seen in October and whether the steady twinkle in the lower left horizon was really a planet. It was pleasant sitting between the two of them. Jim brought out a flask, and Pauline took down a quick gulp. The two boys passed the flask between them, reaching across her while she gazed overhead, leaning her neck back, as though she could see farther into the night that way.

It was very late when they dropped her off. Cafferty patted her knee before she got out of the car. The street was dead quiet and all the lights were off in all the houses. Pauline had trouble turning the key in the lock; it had gotten chilly out and her fingers were stiff. Tiredness came over her all at once, and she was thinking about how grueling it was going to be getting through a day's work at the store tomorrow. She slipped her shoes off in the hallway.

Often when she came in at night there was a whistling growl all through the house, from someone snoring upstairs, and she listened for it now. In the living room a lamp was still lit by the sofa, and then on the stairs she saw something pale moving by the newel post, and she shuddered. It was her father, standing now in front of the stairway. He was in the heavy long underwear he slept in – gray-white and baggy – his eyes were puffed and fierce, and his hair was matted in tufts. "You know what time it is?" he said. "You don't even know, do you?" His mouth was contorted and sunken with his false teeth out, and his words came out thickly. Pauline stared at him with her shoes still in her hand; she was badly frightened, not knowing whether to answer and wondering if Solly and her mother were awake now and listening.

"What are you standing there for?" he said. Pauline moved toward the stairs, and when she passed him, he grabbed her shoulders and shook her, hard enough so that she bit her lip when her head jerked back. He pushed her as far as the landing, hissing, "Go to bed. Go to sleep, what's the matter with you?"

Pauline ran then, and when she got to her room she could hear him go up to his own bedroom and shut the door. She took off her clothes, and she sat on the bed in her slip, afraid to go downstairs to the bathroom and wondering whether she could fall asleep without peeing first. What time was it? She still didn't know. She felt dangerously stupid. Why had she taken the ride by the river? She had thought something was going to happen with Cafferty but then it hadn't; she had made everything at home much harder and nastier for herself, and for nothing. When she shifted her weight, the bedsprings creaked, and she was afraid once more of her father across the hall, leaping out again with his face raw and twisted. This can't go on, she thought, and the phrase gave her blind comfort, as though it were a plan. She was too old for him to shake like that – a rage of protest went through her. Even now she didn't know whether he was angry because he thought she had done something wild and low and shameful, or only because the sound of the key in the door had broken into his sleep.

For most of the next day he did not speak to her at all. He never mentioned the night or her lateness, and she might almost have talked herself into believing that he had passed it off as a dream, except that when she asked him if she should sort remnants in the stockroom or come out and wait on customers, he said, "Go, do what you want. See if I care."

All the next week he was grim and curt with her, not harsh so much as indifferent. In the store when they were both behind the counter, whenever she brushed past him he stepped aside and grunted. At times she thought he had developed a kind of distaste for her presence. Once at home he picked up a stocking she had left hanging in the bathroom and tossed it on the doorknob with real dislike in the gesture. When he came into the kitchen at night while she was doing her homework at the table, he stood at the stove fixing his tea without seeming to see her. But then he had never been a very sociable person.

For a while she took walks in the evening, to get away from the house. By late November the winds were icy, so that when she came back she was chilled, and she would sit in the kitchen with her coat still on, until her mother told her she would get sick from being overdressed indoors. By then Pauline had decided to write to

Gittelson herself. She wrote at some length, explaining her skills in bookkeeping and dwelling on her eagerness to be part of his company. The letter alternated between being very formal and then perky in parts, and in the end she rewrote it so that it was so short it sounded almost rude.

As soon as she sent it she regretted having chosen this prose style. But then that week she found out that she had won the school essay contest, which seemed to prove that even in her simplest utterances she was probably more eloquent than most people.

It was around this time that she had a brief but major quarrel with Bunny. After the news of the essay prize, Pauline mentioned Byron constantly in conversation; his importance as a figure seemed massive and irrefutable now, although at the time she had chosen him more or less at random. Pauline had read in a footnote that Byron had had gonorrhea for most of his adult life – a disease whose effects she understood only vaguely but which she pictured as a sort of glowing decay – and she theorized to Bunny that it had probably enhanced his poetry. Bunny said that disease, no matter who had it, was never beautiful, only ugly and degrading, and that Pauline's attitude showed great shallowness. (Bunny was planning to go work at a settlement house in Philadelphia, and she had started talking all the time about diphtheria prevention campaigns and well-baby clinics and the need for hygiene in tenement neighborhoods.) Pauline said that only trivial people thought that suffering did not have its sublime side and that Bunny was becoming ridiculously prissy and wholesome. Bunny did not eat lunch with her for the rest of the week, and for days she was sulky whenever they spoke.

The essay contest carried a prize of twenty-five dollars, and Pauline bought a New York paper and read through the classified ads for boardinghouses and furnished rooms, trying to calculate how long the money would last her. In magazines she studied recipes for dinners made with condensed soups and canned fish, things that would be cheap to fix in a chafing dish. Solly kept asking whether she was going to buy him some mink long underwear now that she was a millionaire.

Gittelson wrote back that he had been delighted to hear from her; he knew she was a girl who was bound to be a success in whatever she did because she was willing to work hard. He was not hiring any bookkeepers at present but he could find her something as a clerk if she was so inclined.

Pauline's father didn't seem surprised when she told him about the letter. "You like to write letters, I see." He said this in a quietly nasty singsong. "So you'll be a clerk now," he said. Only her mother looked frightened and asked whether any other girls worked at Gittelson's and whether there was a separate washroom for women. Gittelson had not mentioned salary (which even Pauline could tell was a bad sign), but her father didn't offer any guesses about what she would get; perhaps he thought it was no longer any of his business.

They were finishing dinner at the time, and they all went on spooning up their fruit compote. (Pauline's mother had set out a dish for them to put the plum pits in, a sign that she was trying to copy certain manners Pauline had brought into the house.) Pauline began telling them about the rooming house on West Twenty-second Street where a girl cousin of Murray's lived, very clean and reasonable. Especially the rooms at the top in the attic were very cheap, and then if she got a raise she could probably move down to a lower floor. Also she could easily walk to work, which would save extra on carfare.

"He pays you," her father said. "It's your money." Solly wanted to know if she could see the Statue of Liberty from her room, but Pauline told him it was probably too far south.

It snowed heavily during the week when Pauline was taking her last exams, and on the final afternoon she and Bunny came out of the classroom – where they had spent hours answering questions about Eli Whitney's cotton gin and the mercantile theory – into a schoolyard piled with blinding white. They kicked through the uncleared paths, shrieking to each other; the flakes were still coming down thickly, and the wind kept driving gusts of snow up into their faces. It struck them as hilarious that the weather had gotten this wild. Bunny yelled, "Look at it!" and tossed up a few handfuls like confetti, as though the whole thing proved some point they had both supported, an example of elemental excess unhampered by bourgeois restraint. They wrapped their mufflers across their faces so only their eyes showed, which Pauline thought made them look foreign and heroic, breasting the wind. They could barely see in front of them because of the gusts, and the strangeness of this made them more giddy. When Bunny slipped, Pauline said, "Drunk again, I knew it. What a degenerate." The drifts in some places were as high as their knees, and they walked home, skidding and pushing each other.

It was dark by the time Pauline got home, and when she came into the kitchen Solly was sitting on a chair by the stove, holding one of his galoshes in his lap and whining about a hole in the toe. Her mother was trying to fix it by holding a match to the rubber to melt it together, which did not work at all and made a horrible smell. Pauline patched it with a piece of oilcloth and some glue, and later, when her father came into the kitchen to ask when supper was going to be ready, she held it out to show him. He seemed quite pleased with it. "You could go be a shoemaker," he said. "The world is full of holes you could fix."

For a moment Pauline was terrified that he was going to change his mind; he was not going to let her work in New York at all; he had something else in store and had been waiting to tell her. She started to say, "She was only a shoemaker's daughter, but she had me head over heels," to distract him, and to her own disgust a crooked half smile like Bunny's came over her face. But he was already shuffling out of the kitchen.

Her mother was cutting onions, crying and rubbing her eyes – even Solly knew enough to tell her not to do this, it only made them worse.

Her mother said, "It's my eyes, what do you care?" But then she rubbed them again and couldn't open them, so Pauline had to bring her a soaked dishcloth to hold against the lids.

Her mother said, "Pauline, when you go live in New York, don't buy any more fruit from Italians. Maybe they sold you that on purpose before to make a Jewish girl sick."

Pauline said, "It's all right, Ma. Don't worry."

Her mother pushed the dishcloth to the top of her head, like a soldier's bandage, and did the rest of her kitchenwork like that until Solly took it to wipe down the table. Pauline put out plates and they all sat down to supper quietly, with the smell of scorched rubber still around them.

In the end, only Solly went with her to the station to help carry her luggage, although she just had a suitcase and a crate tied with string. "I could carry both," Pauline said. "I carried *you* the whole time when you were little. You were always crying if someone set you down, what a complainer. I could still lift you." She tried to lift him under the arms to show him but she couldn't get him off the ground at all. He squealed, "Stop it, what are you doing?" which made her realize she was behaving childishly in the middle of the station.

She had not slept much the night before, and all the lights along the tracks looked very bright and hotly yellow. The whole station looked different to her, and she was afraid she was going to get on the wrong train. When she finally did take a seat, she gave Solly a nickel for helping her with her things, which surprised him – she had never done anything like that before, and she herself didn't know why she did it. Solly said, "Thanks, I'll get a ice cream," which instantly made her feel jealous and sorry she had given it to him.

She rode the whole way staring out the window; it was bleak skies and stripped trees – everything looked flat and vibrant, the way it did sometimes when she'd been drinking. The river was pearl-gray, a washy streak on the horizon. But it was roiling with whitecaps once she stood at the shoreline, and the ferry pitched and bobbed a great deal, which Pauline liked, although her suitcase slid back and forth and nicked her on the knees a few times.

When she came out into the Twenty-third Street terminal with her luggage, she was hot under her coat from excitement, even in the wind. She walked briskly, brushing past people. She was out on the street before it occurred to her that she had gone past the clock tower without remembering to look to make sure Earl wasn't there. She kept walking, reading the signs on the buildings – advertisements for warehouse storage and grocery supplies – which seemed freshly important.

The rooming house was in the West Twenties – not far – on a block of mostly low, gray stone houses with carved fronts and wide stoops. She went past the right number at first, and then she stood ringing the bell and trying to peer through the curtains at the windows. A very old woman with a mustache shadow on her upper lip answered the door. It was not so nice inside – Pauline could see that already – there was a dark splintery staircase and a purplish-brown flowered carpet. Pauline said, "Mrs. Poganyi?" and was halfway through her speech explaining who she was (Murray's cousin Beatrice was supposed to have told her everything), when the woman said, "Okay. Come, you want the room? Come."

Pauline had only a fleeting impression of the parlor – old plush armchairs and a sepia-toned wallpaper with scenes of shepherdesses – and then Mrs. Poganyi gripped her sleeve to lead her up the stairs. Along the way she said, "Good house, everybody behaves good," and when they got to the top landing she said, "Water is down the hall," and something that sounded like “Do you like windows?” but her chief means of making sure that she was understood was to push and pivot Pauline so that she faced the different features of the room: an iron cot, a framed mirror with a waterfall painted at the bottom, and a set of embroidered valances that matched the dresser scarf on the bureau.

There was a strong odor of mildew in the room, which Pauline tried at first to ignore, and which seemed to be greater once Mrs. Poganyi was gone and she was left by herself. She had not really thought the room would be any better than this, but the sight of it was embarrassing. She was glad no one was there with her, even Solly; she didn’t like the idea of anyone associating the taste of the place with her. Of course it could be described cleverly – she decided already that the plaster molding looked like bird droppings, and she imagined herself repeating this witticism.

She could hear the traffic from Ninth Avenue and the sudden surge of the El going by on its tracks. The rising and ebbing roar of the street made the room seem more still and empty. She got up from sitting on the bare mattress and began unpacking her things; she shook everything out vigorously to get rid of the wrinkles, and this had the added effect of keeping her warm, since the room was distinctly chilly. She thought she shouldn't go outside until she had finished unpacking, and this gave her a pleasantly nervous sense of postponement while she was piling things into drawers. In the end when she put her box of powder on the dresser and her glass beads in the little china dish next to it, the effect was surprisingly artful – sweetly careless – showing she had done much with little.

By then the light in the room had faded. She had already switched on the lamp, which cast rather dramatic shadows on the floor. When she lifted the curtains, a bright blue came through the windows from the early winter dusk. She wanted to go down to walk in the street, and she changed to her wool suit. It was dark when she stepped out the door, and the block was bare and drably quiet under the streetlights.

On Twenty-third Street it was still lively and busy with people, bright from the neon in store windows. A woman passed, wearing a style of Russian boots Pauline thought would look good on her. She peered into the windows of little cheap shops selling ladies' gloves and hosiery, and restaurants where people sat eating supper with their hats on. She wanted to go in somewhere, to order even a cup of tea, but she grew uneasy as she walked farther from the rooming house – she was not at all sure about the neighborhood and she was wary about walking back too late.

After a few more blocks she turned and went back to the house. Mounting the dim staircase, she could hear people moving behind the doors of some of the rooms; she wondered which one was Beatrice's, but she couldn't very well just go around knocking till she found it. So she stayed in her own room and sat on the cot bed eating the two cheese sandwiches her mother had packed for her.

She had a nice sense of picnicking – of living well in a blithely improvised way – but after that she didn't know what to do with herself. She read a little from a newspaper she had bought, but she kept hearing the screech of the El trains and the occasional rattle of a truck going by. A group of men passed under the window, calling out to each other raucously and laughing about something. She did not want to talk to these particular men, but it hurt her that she was shut away from them, and she opened the window, as though she could enter into the quickened atmosphere of the night by watching it long enough. There was a blast of cold air – which she liked at first; she stood it until she began to shiver – and then the room seemed worse to her when she lowered the window shut.

She lay reading her newspaper, but she couldn't concentrate on the news and she wound up reading the Women's Page, which was full of hints on how to freshen old blouses and add years to your linoleum. Possibly Gittelson would be impressed that she knew about washing black lace in ammonia and coffee. She lay in bed thinking of this and listening to the sounds of taxi horns and buses going by without her, until it was late enough to go to sleep.

3

On the first day at work she was handed over to Miss Pfeiffer, the stout, unpleasant receptionist, who Mr. Gittelson said knew the whole business from soup to nuts. Miss Pfeiffer spoke rather fiercely about the special ways that the company did things, much better than some places she knew. Pauline was comparing Miss Pfeiffer's blouse to her own and wondering whether she had worn the right thing. At one point she realized that Miss Pfeiffer was giving instructions and she tried harder to follow, but in listening to each part she forgot what had been said just before.

Then she was led to an alleyway of wooden file cabinets and given a stack of invoices to file. She was already hungry for lunch, but on the way back from the washroom she saw that it wasn't even ten thirty yet. Mr. Gittelson stopped by to ask how she was getting along, which made her wonder if she could be doing the filing right; perhaps there was more of a trick to it. One of the salesmen told her if she had any complaints she should come to him, he was in charge of helping all the pretty girls, and Pauline said she would remember.

Miss Pfeiffer did show up finally to ask her what was the matter, wasn't she going to lunch? Pauline put on her coat and walked outside to the first cheap-looking luncheonette she could find, where she ate a bowl of soup sitting at the counter. After lunch she was put to work addressing envelopes, using a horrible little contraption called a stamp affixer. It had a metal plunger that had to be slammed down with the palm of the hand, so that she had a welt from it by the end of the day. She knew that it was the newness of the office routine that made everything go so slowly and seem to take so much time; nothing in the work was harder or more monotonous than what she had done in her father's store, but still it filled her with dread to think that there were four more days left in the week, and weeks after that of five days together.

When she got home there was a note on her door from Murray's cousin Beatrice. The note said: *I'm in the bedroom at the end of the hall on the second floor. If you would like to go eat supper someplace not too pricey, let me know.*

Beatrice was very dark, with large, sleepy features set in a small face, and she said, "Oh, you're here," in such a flat voice that Pauline thought she wasn't very glad to see her, but then it seemed to be her only way of speaking. She was older than Pauline had guessed, twenty-five at least. She wore a dress with a jaunty bow on the shoulder, stylish in a way that Pauline thought was maybe a little overdone but admired nonetheless.

"Your room is bigger," Pauline said, for lack of something else to say. Beatrice said she'd had it for three years, although it looked as bare and unadorned as Pauline's upstairs.

Beatrice warned her that they were only going to a chophouse nearby and it wasn't exactly the Ritz or anything. Once they were outside, Pauline kept trying to guess which it was, and when they walked into the steamy dining room, with its odors of beef and frying onions, she said, "Oh, I could eat a whole cow, couldn't you?"

Beatrice said, while they were looking at the menu, that she worked for a company that packed olives and pickles; she was a typist in the warehouse, and even the elevators smelled of brine. Her boss was always trying to give her bottles of the stuff to take home; he liked to think of himself as wonderfully generous, although he was a petty person who cheated on his partner. Pauline said, "That's terrible," trying to echo Beatrice's outrage, but Beatrice laughed and said, "Everybody does it."

They both ordered stew, which was the cheapest thing on the menu; Beatrice picked out all the fatty parts, but Pauline, who was used to her mother's cooking, ate everything in hers. Beatrice told a long story about a man who had taken her out dancing; the point of the story was his shabbiness in some things and his nervy freshness in others, but Pauline didn't understand all of it and said the wrong things in a few places.

After supper they walked back along the side streets. A man passing them called out, "You're two gorgeous girls. Probably the most beautiful girls in New York." Pauline couldn't help smirking a little, but Beatrice didn't change her expression at all, and it wasn't until she cursed under her breath that Pauline saw she was bitterly annoyed. Pauline thought that she was really a much better sport than Beatrice, and that people probably found her more likable because of it.

After the first few weeks at Gittelson's the work did get less horribly slow. She stopped feeling dazed and unsteady, and one of the stock boys made her his confidante and came to discuss his problems about his fiancée, and this also helped break up the time. Mr. Gittelson always asked if they were working her hard enough, and Miss Pfeiffer said this was wonderful training for her. Mostly everyone was on the other side of the office and she didn't see them.

What was disappointing was that after she came home and had supper – sometimes with Beatrice and sometimes not – she read or did crossword puzzles and then she went to bed, so that there was nothing much between one day and the next. Once, after she had learned to keep bread and cans of fish and fruit in her room to save money, she went to the movies by herself. She liked watching the picture alone, and she found she concentrated better than she ever had before. But when the lights came on she felt awkward and sorry for herself.

On the way home she saw a man on the street with a blondish mustache; she stared at him without meaning to, and he smiled at her when they passed. She felt that she excited the interest of men wherever she went, but she was never in a position to meet them. She had walked so much through her own neighborhood – and farther south too, all the way down to the harbor – and still there was nothing in it but looking.

She missed Bunny at times, and she wrote her a letter which was full of sarcastic references to herself as the poor working girl heaven was protecting all too well, and in which she described Mrs. Poganyi's mustache and got in the line about the molding in the room being like bird droppings. She had a feeling she was putting in too many laboriously arch expressions, like "I daresay" and "fancy my surprise when," but after she wrote it she felt better.

Beatrice was also impatient with the way things were going in her life – which seemed as uneventful as Pauline's – but it was hard to tell what she was really waiting for; she seemed to want most of what was around her to disappear. She ate her listless dinners with Pauline, complaining that no one in New York ever said anything worth hearing, in a way that Pauline found distinctly unflattering.

Once Beatrice did confess that she would really seriously like to move to Florida, and she brightened when she talked about beaches and cheap bungalows and lucky investments. She already knew Pauline's enthusiasms, and she sometimes teased her and asked if she didn't want to save her dinner roll to bring to some starving artist in a garret who was shivering over his easel by candlelight.

Pauline said, "Not really." She was actually touchy on the subject. She knew better than to ever say anything to Beatrice about the "hunger for freedom" or the "cravings of the spirit," although she and Bunny had used these expressions with perfect sincerity and with a shared sense of their exact meaning. There was no way to voice her ambitions with enough delicacy to avoid sounding precious, but in fact she was full of cravings of the spirit all the time. Beatrice had shown her sketches in the newspaper parodying Village girls as overearnest and ill-groomed – Bohemia was apparently a well-worn cliché to everyone but her. That it had become all too common only made her feel left out.

Once at night while they were eating supper together, Beatrice said, "Listen, if you really want to, we can go to Vera's sometime and just sit at a table. That's where they all go, those people."

Pauline did not believe that Beatrice could really know this. Probably it was one of those tearooms that fleeced tourists. "What is it – it's a restaurant?" Pauline was finishing a piece of gristly meat loaf, and she kept twirling her fork in the gravy without looking up.

"Sort of. Or you can just sip a cup of something and draw pictures on the tablecloth, they don't care. It's cheap enough. The tea tastes like stewed brooms, but that is only my personal opinion. I'll take you now if you want. I don't mind, it doesn't bother me."

"I love a nice broomstraw taste in my tea," Pauline said.

During the long, chilly walk down to Washington Square, Pauline tried to keep up a brisk conversation about Mrs. Poganyi's eccentricities, and even Beatrice was getting more animated by the time she stopped on a side street and said, "Oh, yes, here it is." They went up a narrow staircase – Pauline could hear the hum of voices, a kind of tinkling monotone – and then they were walking past a tiny kitchen where a black cook stood at the stove with his back to them. They went through another corridor, past a row of coats on pegs; Pauline put hers next to an opera cloak with a ripped lining. There was also a man's sheepskin overcoat, of a kind she had never seen before.

In the main room, small tables had been set impossibly close together. It was crowded and warm and thick with noise – men with longish rumpled hair were sitting with pale, sleek girls, a fat woman with a shrieking laugh was being thumped on the back, and in the corner two old women dressed in identical men's suits were playing chess. There was a log fire, which made the light reddish and intense at that end of the room, and a grouping of copper pots over the mantel, a rustic effect Pauline had not expected at all.

The only seats left were right by the fireplace, and they had to edge their chairs away to avoid roasting their spines. A man near them said, "It kind of gives you an idea of how Joan of Arc must have felt, doesn't it?"

Pauline said, "Do you suppose if we confessed they'd tamp down the flames or something?"

"If you have anything really good to confess," the man said, "I could speak to the management."

Pauline said, "Wait a minute. I'm searching my conscience."

"I'm dying of thirst," Beatrice said.

"It takes days to get served here," the man said. "I knew a man who keeled over from dehydration and the waiter just stepped over him."

The waiter showed up at their table just then – they both ordered Russian tea with lemon – and the man said, "Adolfo is only human, contrary to popular opinion. Pretty women get faster service."

Beatrice complained of its being smoky in the room. The man said smoke was excellent for digestion, most people got too much oxygen, and then a ruddy-faced blond girl swooped down on their table. "Is he telling you all about mapmaking?" she said. "That's all he ever talks about now."

"Actually he hasn't said a word about it," Pauline said.

"He must be bowled over by your beauty. Normally he goes on about how maps are what we should all be looking at, they're the true distilled vision of the world. Isn't that right, Peter?"

"Don't say anything about distilled too loud," Peter said. "The whole place'll be rummaging through our pockets to see if we brought anything."

"I like maps," Pauline said.

"I just think it changed people's sense of quest once they could see where they were going. It made everything much more concrete and modern. The modern world really begins when they figure out how to gauge longitude."

"Don't listen to him," the girl said. "It just makes him more fanatical. His paintings aren't bad at all, really."

"You've never seen my paintings," he said.

The girl ignored this and asked if any of them read tea leaves and whether they were superstitious.

"I'm sort of skeptical but open-minded on the subject," Pauline said. This was not true at all; her mother had a whole collection of bad-luck-avoidance rituals, all of which disgusted her. The blond girl decided that they should get Rose to come over and read their leaves. "Oh, yes, we need to know our fates badly," Pauline said, "we're about to go astray any minute," and the girl got up from the table and brought back a tall, fine-featured woman with strands of premature gray in her hair.

"You don't look like a gypsy," Beatrice said.

"Oh, I just learned it from someone one time," she said. "I'm not really very good." Pauline would have liked to know how she had met whoever taught her, whether she had traveled or was just the sort of person for whom these contacts were commonplace. The woman poked in their teacups and told Pauline she was going to live to be very old, she had a strong constitution; she told Beatrice she was going to have three children and marry a man she could look in the eyes, which Pauline thought was a nice touch.

Several people had gathered around the table to watch while this was going on. Peter seemed to be a general favorite – he wore icy-looking spectacles and he had soft, boyish cheeks, but he did get more attractive as you looked at him,

Pauline thought – there was an outbreak of groaning and clapping when he was told he was going to die rich. A very smartly dressed couple began talking about whether you really drank tea in a way that showed your personality, and they all ordered more tea and a few people burned their tongues demonstrating their sipping techniques. Pauline was wedged between Peter and a dark-haired man who kept suggesting they should really read the imprints left by women's lipstick on the cup rims. He held up Pauline's cup for an example, interrupting Peter, who was telling her about leaf tracings in fossils. Pauline felt that they were both vying for her attention, and she talked at some length about auguries in ancient Rome, so that she wouldn't lose either of them into another conversation. Her voice in her own ears didn't sound altogether like her – she had caught a lilting, slightly petulant way of speaking from the blond girl, and she used bits of slang like "Don't I know it?" and "Tell me another" which were not really native to her – but she liked all this, and there was no one to know it was new except Beatrice, who was on the other side and couldn't hear anyway.

The blond girl announced that she was going to a party at Mickeling's and if anybody wanted to go over with her, this was their chance.

Someone wanted to know if Mickeling was still seeing that woman who had thrown the couch cushions out the window the last time, and someone else began imitating the way he hummed arias to himself when he was drunk. Pauline had, of course, no idea who Mickeling was – she gathered, after a while, that he was also a painter – but people seemed eager to recount things they had seen him do; there was a general desire to employ his name familiarly. Peter and several others were already standing up, getting ready to go.

Pauline leaned over to Beatrice. "What do you think?" she said.

"Oh, I'm going home to bed," Beatrice said. "Go on without me, you'll be fine."

It occurred to Pauline that no one had invited her directly, but then Peter was leading her along and the blond woman was chattering about how Mickeling was going to drink all the decent liquor if they didn't get there soon. Pauline got separated from Beatrice while they were all fishing for their coats. She felt that Beatrice disliked her now (just when they'd been getting friendlier), but there was nothing to be done about it; she was probably thinking, quite correctly, that she'd glimpsed Pauline in her true colors.

In the taxi the blond girl and the dark-haired

man – who turned out to be the owner of the sheepskin overcoat – kept up a conversation about whether parrots could be taught to whistle two tones at once. When they got to the party, the blond girl was still croaking *Polly want a cracker* in different experimental pitches while they pushed through the doorway. This seemed to amuse the man who had answered the door, who went at once to bring her a cracker, which she nibbled at neatly with little beaklike movements, quite a skillful mimicking of a bird.

A record was playing – something bouncy, with a lot of wailing violins and saxophones – drowned out in places by the din of voices. People clustered in small, bobbing groups, slouching against walls and nodding into each other's faces. A fat man in baggy tweeds pretended to box Peter's ears by way of greeting. A woman in a celery-green dress came by with a tray of drinks. "They look frivolous, I know," she said, "but they're extremely good for cuts and bruises."

Peter sniffed one and gave it to her. Pauline sipped a little and said, "Oh, yes, that was just what I needed."

Across from her, a man teetered and slid against a woman, who pulled him up and said, "I wish you would stop trying to prostrate yourself before me." The woman was wearing a large speckled lily in her hair, and the man leaned forward and nosed the petals. "You'll sneeze," the woman said, rather gently.

A collie was eating some salted almonds off a woman's knee. There were some astonishingly beautiful girls – pretty in clever and interesting ways – in deft makeup and cunningly arranged outfits. Pauline was at once thrilled to be in their company and worried that she looked like some prim office miss in her drab gabardine. But sometimes a neutral appearance was striking in its own way.

"That dog," Peter said, "is the reason no one is dancing."

"He doesn't allow it?" Pauline said.

"He herds people – nips at their ankles and starts yipping and running in circles."

"It's in the blood," the man in baggy tweeds said. "That dog leads a terrible life. Every time the doorbell rings he waits for a sheep to arrive."

A man behind them thought this was extremely funny. He had an awful, high, hiccuping laugh, and he went on for some time, trilling and hawing. The blond girl, who was standing with them again, said, "No more wit, Walter. You see what it does to people."

"That dog," Peter said, "is the proof of nature over nurture. In the middle of Manhattan he still wants to tend a flock. He has to suppress his instincts constantly."

"Oh, that's so bad for you," the girl said.

Walter decided suddenly to introduce himself, and the blond girl, whose name was Nita, said, "Oh, we've known each other for hours already," and shook Pauline's hand, a thing Pauline didn't even know women did with each other.

"Pauline, Pauline, theme of a dream," Walter said. Pauline smiled. She had downed most of her drink, which tasted far less medicinal than anything she'd gotten drunk on in high school, and she was feeling numb around the mouth and pleasantly warm. The room, which she hardly noticed before, seemed to be all white and gray and embellished with oddities – a foot-shaped ashtray made of blue glass, an old puppet hung on the wall, a votary urn used to hold cigarettes; she had never seen furnishings that were funny on purpose (even Mrs. Poganyi's were dead earnest), and it struck her that something had been missing from her aesthetics. The drink had made her a little sentimental, and she felt sorry for her self of the day before who had not understood all this; she pondered the arrangement of the things in Mickeling's apartment with a great feeling of personal satisfaction.

Nita had dragged over a tall, poker-faced boy, and they were all talking about whether an instinct to drink was natural to all humans. Peter said, "Suppose you just put some people on a desert island. Don't you think if you came back in a year you would find them all fermenting passion fruits or distilling wild roots or something?"

Pauline said, "Only if there was a law against it."

This was received with such a chorus of knowing chuckles that Pauline felt she had gotten off a remark that probably bordered on being a stunning paradox. Walter said, "Hear, hear," and patted her on the shoulder.

"In the country, people drink more," the poker-faced boy announced. "I had a friend from boarding school whose parents lived on top of a mountain and they were blotto all the time. The mother used to giggle all through dinner."

Pauline thought fleetingly of her own mother and the timid, sour expression she always had when she stood in her apron and her kerchief, dishing out their supper; she could not be imagined as gaily tipsy. It was true that Solly's ear-wiggling tricks sometimes struck her as funny, but her laugh, when she laughed, did not resemble giggling at all – it was hoarse and hissed through her underbite.

Peter offered a toast to rural life, and Walter went and got them more cocktails. The record had changed to something slow and syrupy – a man's voice singing in a lachrymose tenor – and Nita made faces and sang along in a mocking vibrato. "Let's go tell them we can't stand it," she said to Pauline, and she took her hand and led her across the room. A bald man in evening clothes was by the victrola, and Nita plucked at his sleeve and said, "My friend here is just getting over a very tragic love affair and she can't stand to hear anything too dreary. She's been trying so hard to be brave – but this music –"

Pauline said, "I'll be all right, really. I just need some jazz to make me laugh and forget."

"Oh, in that case," the man said, and he took off the record so quickly it sounded as though the tenor had been throttled. "It's awful, isn't it, how cruel the world is to young girls," he said, giving Pauline a long look. He was apparently not sure whether he was being teased or not, but he wanted them to stay with him. Nita found a louder record, and they bantered for a while about what cads all the men were now. "Oh, not all, don't say all," he said.

"All right, I won't say it then," Pauline said. This made Nita go off into giggles, and Pauline, who was in the midst of sipping her drink, laughed as she was swallowing and sputtered some of it on the man's feet.

"You see what a state she's in," Nita said. "I'm going to take her into the kitchen and feed her dry soda crackers until she calms down." And she took Pauline's hand again and they went back across the room, sliding against each other.

"I missed you terribly," Peter said. "Even the dog wouldn't talk to me."

In the corner near them a group of people was having what was apparently a hilarious discussion in a language Pauline recognized happily as French. A woman shrieked, *"Oh! C'est juste!"* Pauline was so pleased at having made this out that she almost translated for Peter, but he wanted to talk now about why he had red paint under his fingernails and about color values in maps and why Canada was always pink. Pauline let the conversation drift around her. Peter seemed full of extraordinarily strong opinions about the color red and its importance in the underlying scheme of almost everything. Pauline did not follow all of what he said, but it made her feel inwardly content to think that there was some latent meaning overflowing even from the colors of things, and she had only to sharpen her own understanding to catch it. She began looking around the room, to check for bits of red in what people were wearing. Nita made them get another round of Manhattans, in honor of the color. Pauline sat down on the arm of a chair, which fit comfortably under her, as though her body had gotten very pliant and light. She heard Nita say, "Oh, look, Garrett's out cold," and she looked up and saw a figure slumped on the sofa with his eyes closed – it was the boy who had been talking about drinking in the country – and a woman was draping a silk shawl over him for a blanket.

"Getting about that time, isn't it?" Peter said. "I'll see you home if you like."

"Oh, yes," Pauline said, getting up. "I've got work tomorrow, isn't that peculiar to think of?"

"Mickeling says his liquor never gives you a hangover, but you know how men lie," Nita said. Pauline said she knew. Nita murmured, "Till next time," while they shook hands good night, and then Pauline and Peter made their way over to the door, where there was a great crush of people in the hall. A sharp-featured man (Bunny would have said he had a Greek profile) came over to ask if she was lost and if she wanted something to drink.

"Too late, Ernest," Peter said, coming up from behind.

"Till next time," Pauline said, shaking hands.

She was a little sorry now to be leaving so soon.

"No use trying to say good-bye to the host," Peter said, and he guided her down the stairway.

"I never got to meet him," Pauline said. "I liked his apartment, though. And his dog."

"You did meet him. You made a big hit with him. Walter can be very rude to women sometimes. He's got a nasty streak in him."

"Walter is *Mickeling*?" Pauline said.

"He's got a low opinion of women. He thinks they're all after his money. He behaved awfully well with you."

"I guess he did," Pauline said.

It was a still, icy night, quiet now except for the sound of ferry whistles hooting from the river. They had both drunk too much to feel the cold, and Pauline walked looking down, watching the mica in the pavement glittering ahead of their feet. Peter put her hand in his coat pocket, and they waited at the corner while a bus went by, lit up from inside and ghostly at this time of night. When they got to the block near her rooming house, the buildings looked fatefully familiar, and she felt a great rush of affection for her neighborhood, where she lived at this time of her life.

In front of her doorstep he kissed her fully on the mouth. He pressed her to him, but he wasn't sudden about it (she was used to boys reaching for her as though they had to take her by surprise, before she changed her mind), and there was something hearty and friendly in his passion. Pauline had the passing, exultant thought that all night she had been with people whose assumptions about things were like hers, only in surer form, and this accord made everything simple and natural. He watched while she went up the steps, and they waved to each other before she slipped inside.

When she came home from work the next day, there was a note by the phone in the hall. One of the boarders had taken down the message with a splotchy fountain pen – it was not Peter who had called her, but Walter. He sounded a little gruff when she called him back; he wanted to know whether she would meet him for dinner at a certain Italian restaurant, and he seemed surprised when she didn't know where it was.

Pauline didn't change clothes before she left; she wanted the feeling that this was her regular evening outing and not something she dressed up for. She brushed her hair until the static turned the bangs wispy, so she had a sense of being very rushed and careless. When she got to the restaurant, Walter was sitting at a table with Nita and the boy who had passed out on the sofa the night before.

"And so we revelers meet again," Walter said. "Don't expect much. You're sitting with a bunch of symptoms here."

Nita said, "What we all need is some food to convince our stomachs that we're sweet people really."

Pauline had felt fine all day, only a little strange and disembodied, as she might after any dense and startling experience. Nor did she think that any of them sounded dull, although they apologized for it all through the spaghetti and while they were downing tumblers of what Walter called blood tonic, which turned out to be sour red wine, inky with sediment, brought by the waiter in an unlabeled bottle.

Pauline, to her own surprise, began a long and giddy description of two boys she had seen having a fistfight on the way over; she was overstimulated and full of nervous brightness. Walter said, "I couldn't stand to walk in the street and see people today. They all looked so god-awful. Some days my dog is the only one I can tolerate being around. My dog and certain rare women. Sweet honest ones like you girls."

Nita said, "Angels of mercy," and snorted, but Pauline was interested in his degree of disillusion and her apparent powers of refreshment. Garrett, who remained wan and expressionless, repeated a long and dirty piece of gossip about a writer's wife. They all made references to people they were sure Pauline knew, and Pauline wasn't sure whether by not saying anything she was pretending she did know them. Nita talked about her job – she worked as a violinist playing for tables at lunch in a midtown restaurant – and about one businessman who danced with a chair whenever she played "The Blue Danube Waltz."

They stayed until very late, when Garrett and Walter started arguing about whether they should go to Vera's or to some cafeteria called Anselm's for coffee. Nita tried to get Pauline to agree that Anselm's was too greasy and noisy. For a moment Pauline wondered whether they had really confused her with a girl seen at these places – people did sometimes mix her up with other wispy-haired brunettes – but it was only their habit of regarding these spots as sites, like the Statue of Liberty or the Paramount Building, too famous and unavoidable for anyone not to know. Pauline would have gone to any of them, but in the end Garrett passed out again, and Walter stayed with him while she and Nita walked each other home.

After that, she almost never stayed in during

the evenings. She was often tired and sluggish at work, but as soon as she had come back to her room and eaten her cold, makeshift supper, she felt restless and full of steady energy, and she would walk to Vera's or to Anselm's, usually stopping to pick up Nita from her apartment on Twelfth Street on the way downtown. Pauline liked Anselm's because it was big and open, like a banquet hall, and there was that sudden rush of noise as they walked through the door and the long vista of crowded tables so that they could see who was there as they walked to the back. There was a table by the back wall where they liked to sit and where people sometimes waited for them.

Pauline had let her bangs grow longer, and she had copied Nita's way of wearing a long, flimsy scarf with everything. Peter said she looked loosely gift-wrapped. She and Peter had a brief spell of seeking each other out at large gatherings as though they were bound together romantically, but then they settled instead into a temperate friendship, still marked by certain gallant attentions on Peter's part. It was Mickeling who most often paid for things at the end of the night (although Pauline did frequently pay her share too – she thought Nita was too much of a gold digger the way she always looked around for a man to sit with just before she was ready to leave). Anyway, it was never very much; they did most of their drinking at parties, unless Walter dragged them off to one of the seedy speakeasies he liked, with spotlit pianos and drab girl singers. Walter said it ruined your health to go to bed too early, your blood got slow. And it was true there was never anything wrong with Pauline's health, despite the fact that she was sleeping so little, and Mrs. Poganyi kept the rooms so cold Pauline could see her breath when she got up in the mornings.

Except to sleep, Pauline was scarcely in her room at all now, and no one ever called for her at the rooming house. The tassel fringe she had tacked around the mirror, part of a plan for refurbishing with small, skillful touches, came undone on one side, and she left it to dangle and get dusty. For a while she was afraid that Mrs. Poganyi was going to speak sternly to her about her late hours, but the landlady apparently slept like a top, and she beamed and nodded when she passed Pauline in the halls.

Sometimes, when Pauline came home from work, she saw Beatrice on the stairway. Beatrice was never rude, but she was decidedly chilly. Pauline would ask her how she was, and Beatrice would say, "Fine, thank you," as though she doubted that Pauline believed her. Pauline wondered whether Beatrice didn't harbor, if not envy, then some admiration for the change in Pauline's prospects. She was not a stuffy girl really; she liked dance music and the idea of travel, she was fearless about a good many things and certainly outspoken. She would not have wanted for herself the sort of social life Pauline was leading, but perhaps she respected the liveliness of it. Pauline would have liked to know if she ever talked about it at all when she saw her family, and whether she ever said anything to her cousin Murray about it.

4

When the weather grew warmer, Pauline would sometimes walk down to Nita's apartment on weekend afternoons. Nita lived in two high-ceilinged, underfurnished rooms in a building that had once been luxurious. There was still a marble fireplace and – the apartment's best feature – a tiny balcony that overlooked a small courtyard. Nita, who generally had a hangover on Sundays, believed in the curative powers of fresh air, and she would drag out the kitchen chairs to the balcony and sit there drinking cups of Horlick's malted milk.

There was a single tree in the yard, overgrown and sprawling, with big elephant-ear leaves and – for a few weeks in April – hanging clusters of purple blossoms. Neither of them knew what kind it was. Nita was from Wilkes-Barre, which Pauline had thought was in the middle of farmland or cow country, but Nita said only someone from Newark would think that. She said Wilkes-Barre did not consider itself at all socially backward; there were a lot of tea dances and a local nightclub that featured an all-girl orchestra, which had given her the idea that she could earn money playing the violin.

By her own account Nita was nothing special as a violinist. It was the homeliness of the girls in the orchestra that had inspired her. She had felt an immediate indignation that girls who were so bovine in their flounced dresses with those silly bertha collars should be paid to do something she would look so much better doing.

She was always reasoning in this way. When they saw newsreels of the young Duchess of York waving to a crowd, Nita was personally affronted by the dowdiness of her hat, and for a week she went around saying it was too bad that one of them hadn't met the duke first. It wasn't so much that Nita thought herself beautiful – by her own estimate she was merely pretty, with her high coloring and her sandy hair. It was only that she believed in a natural ranking that accorded all privileges to the most gloriously attractive, and it shocked her whenever she saw evidence of this order violated.

There were great advantages to this belief; according to this scheme, Nita, whatever her minor lacks, was certainly in line to deserve quite a lot, and it gave her an almost innocent confidence at large social gatherings. Even at the stiffer, dressier parties Walter sometimes took them to farther uptown (where Pauline felt somewhat out of her element), Nita was certain that strangers would welcome them by right.

With all this, she was not vain or apt to fuss unduly over her appearance, and on the afternoons when she stayed out on the balcony with Pauline she wore a faded old cardigan sweater and sat over her malted milk red-eyed, with no face powder even. Pauline admired her forthrightness.

"I bet Peter would know what kind of tree that is," Nita said, as they were looking across into the courtyard. "He knows lots of little useless bits of information like that."

"Doesn't he ever," Pauline said.

"Now Walter, on the other hand, knows nothing. It makes him very restful to be with."

"Walter is not restful," Pauline said.

"I think it's nice for a man to be like that, not always smothering you with information. Walter blusters but he's not boring." She had obviously thought this all out before. "He's really one of my best friends. When I was sick last year, he had the waiter from Tony's bring over a whole pot of soup and a chicken and everything. He's getting kind of soft around the middle now, but it goes with his height; it's more portly than fat. Do you think he's fat?"

Pauline had a fairly good idea where all this was heading. "I think of him as a largish medium in weight," she said.

Nita wanted to know what Pauline thought of her new idea that friends could really make good boyfriends because you knew them already and could tell what you were getting into. "Walter's not a skinflint, for instance," she pointed out. As far as Pauline could tell, Walter hadn't made any passes recently or said anything out of the usual – the idea was strictly Nita's – but there seemed to be no doubt in her mind that Walter would leap at the chance. Pauline thought she was probably right about this.

"Did you ever notice Walter has wonderful shoes?" Nita said.

"You can tell a lot about a man from his feet," Pauline said. "Fallen arches are a sign of weak character."

"I absolutely always check their insteps first," Nita said.

Inwardly, Pauline was appalled that Nita would want to talk herself into a romance with Walter. Imagine having to work yourself up into an attraction instead of having it overtake you by its own force: it made Pauline's flesh crawl; there were things she was quite purist about. It seemed wrong, a betrayal of the higher instincts. Lately she had been thinking rather constantly about Ernest, the man with the Greek profile, who was of course not Greek at all; he was Middlewestern and Protestant, as almost everyone she met now seemed to be. Nita said he was really humorless, and it was true that he was never exactly playful and often hard to talk to, but Pauline thought that this would change on knowing him better, and there was something she definitely liked about his austerity; men who were clownish lacked sex appeal. He wrote poems – once she had talked to him about Byron but he had said Byron was glib and facile and that had stopped the discussion.

Whenever she saw him at Anselm's, he was attentive enough so that she knew he considered her good-looking – and their conversations always had the flavor of mild flirtations, very promising and yet so far short of the full ambitions of her longing that, when she thought of them, there was a feeling in her chest as though she were really bleeding around the heart.

This was not a thing she talked to Nita about.

For all her apparent impulsiveness and flighty reasoning, Nita could not be imagined entering a situation where she was not at an advantage, and she always talked as though Pauline were just the same. This gave their speech when they were together a special crackling brightness – she always felt very good after seeing Nita – but they never wavered from that style, and Pauline had no way within it to talk about her bleeding.

Nita said, "I bet Walter's been married."

"You think so?" Pauline said. "Why do you think so?"

"Oh, the way he talks about how women are. Also one time we passed a baby carriage on the street and he went into a song-and-dance about how all infants do for the first year is smell cheesy and throw up all over you. The Irish don't divorce, you know."

Pauline pictured some hefty Mrs. Mickeling in curling papers chasing Walter with a rolling pin. The wives she knew were not like that at all; they were lively girls who had nicknames for their husbands and who arrived at parties with long stories about how they'd washed all the silverware in bluing for a joke. They treated the details of household routine as things that could be described only with irony but which they were obliged to mention often; you could see they were pleased with themselves. It was not sex that Pauline was curious about in marriage – she was curious about that too, but she felt she was closer to knowing about that: she was so used to thinking of herself as advanced and initiated that it seemed to her that the final knowledge must be an intensification of what she already understood. What seemed harder to imagine in marriage were the domestic arrangements, the constant surveillance of having someone see you at all moments. Nita in her tatty cardigan was obviously not afraid of this.

"I can't picture Walter as a groom," Nita said. "He would look like a black walrus."

"He must have been boiled to the ears at the time," Pauline said. Ernest would look very good in a black morning coat; he was long-waisted and wore clothes nicely.

"You know who looks *boiled* when he drinks?" Nita said. "Garrett does. He turns bright red, and then when he starts to turn pale again, it means he's going to pass out."

"At least he's quiet about it," Pauline said.

"He fell off his chair at Tony's the other night, just like a drunk in a play. Tony was mad; he told him not to come around for a while – go away, go home, dry up."

"Not us too – do we have to stay away too?" Pauline said.

"Of course not us. You think Tony would keep us out?"

Pauline never understood when Nita was going to get snappish like this. She didn't like being on the receiving end, but she admired the trait in Nita.

For a while there was a fad that spring and summer about taking the ferries all the time. Nita would walk over to Walter's, where there were always three or four people playing cards and drinking shots of peach brandy (Walter's idea of the perfect pick-me-up). Nita would come in and harangue Walter about how he was getting etiolated from lack of sunlight, and then she would coax them all into the great out-of-doors. At first the Staten Island ferry was a great favorite, but once they got to Staten Island there wasn't much to do except eat hot dogs in the station and wait for the next ferry to leave, and so Nita inaugurated other routes, for variety and comparing views – one to Brooklyn and one to Governors Island, a great find because it was free.

Nita had decided not to develop a romance with Walter after all, but they tended to direct so many of their comments to each other that they ended up paired together anyway on most walks. Ernest never went on the ferries with them (he and Walter didn't much like each other, for one thing, so he wasn't likely to be hovering around Walter's kitchen on Sunday mornings). But often as they were pulling out from the dock Pauline was lonely for him, as though his not being with her were unusual.

Nothing in this made her unhappy; on the contrary, she felt very buoyant and hopeful. A friend of Peter's, a sculptor who wore his hair brushed back like a German student's, told her she was eupeptic, a word she had to look up. Later she told him all ax murderers looked that way to the untrained eye. It amused her to think that she was getting a reputation for having a good temperament, a faculty people apparently found desirable and rare.

Frequently they all ended up at a saloon off Greenwich Avenue that everyone called the Elephants' Graveyard. In the summer weather Pauline stayed out as late as possible. Her room at Mrs. Poganyi's was extremely hot, and she kept hoping that it would cool off if she stayed out further into the night. There was some truth in this theory, but it meant that it was harder to get up in the morning to go to work at Gittelson's, and twice she had her pay docked for coming in late.

Then she found that if she took a nap as soon as she got home from work, she could stay out till whenever she wanted and still get up the next day. She thought there was something very efficient in dividing her sleep into two shifts. It did make her feel a little unstrung at work; she didn't have to be very alert to file things, but she thought her conversation probably sounded strange when people spoke to her, and the office itself seemed flat and oddly lit.

When Pauline went home in July for one of her rare visits, she was amazed at how cool and green Newark seemed. In front of the houses there were maple trees all down the block, a thing she had never taken much notice of before, except when she and Solly had stuck maple pods on their noses when they were little.

For supper they gave her boiled fish with carrots and potatoes. She ate two portions, and her father said, "That's the big fashion in New York now, to eat like a horse." Solly wanted to know what she ate now for all her meals (Pauline lied about this) and what they cost. "She doesn't look like she's starving," her father said.

"Like what does an average banana cost?" Solly asked. He was chewing while he talked, and he reached to get at the plate of bread, leaning sideways so that his elbow stretched across the corner of the table by his father's place. His father gave him a sharp, chopping slap on the back of the neck – very fast and sudden, with the side of the hand. Solly yelped and jumped back in his seat; Pauline thought she heard him whimpering, but then when he looked up he was trying not to smirk.

Her mother, who was standing up as she always did when they ate, came over to bring more fish. She moved much more slowly than usual, and she spoke in a kind of whisper around Pauline, as though she were cautious of her. She made a face when Pauline asked her about the store, but then she went on at some length about how they couldn't get enough glass buttons in stock this year, there was a big shortage, customers kept asking, they acted like she had them but she was hiding them.

"I saw a girl wearing a beautiful dress with glass buttons in a big slant across the skirt," Pauline said. "It was at a dance I went to at the Lafayette Hotel."

"When you don't have what people want in a store they get like animals," her mother said. "They behave like pigs over buttons."

Her father wanted to know when Gittelson was going to make her a full partner so he could retire already. Solly said she should be careful her scarf didn't fall in the fish broth. It was true that her outfit, which was the same thing she always wore to eat out in New York, was overdone here, too carefully put together. She had not spoken Yiddish since the last time she was home, and she thought there was probably a discordance between it and the way she looked, like those jokes about how Rudolph Valentino was really someone named Rudy Valensky, and that this was why she felt stilted and foolish.

At night she slept in her old room. They were using it for storage now, as a place to keep the off-season fabrics and the old ledgers and invoices, and the floor was all piled with cartons and rolls wrapped in brown paper. The room, which had never been big, was crowded and had a dusty smell – what was oddest about it was that while she was lying in bed with the light still on, looking out at the mounds of packages, she could hardly remember ever staying anywhere else, as if she had made a mistake or dreamed the room at Mrs. Poganyi's.

The first time Pauline read a poem of Ernest's, she was sitting at a table in Vera's drinking tea with Peter and Nita, and someone passed around a little magazine printed on pulpy paper with a dark blue cover. The poem was different from what she would have expected – full of black parrots and metal landscapes – but Pauline thought she liked it. Nita said, "Oh, them," when she saw the magazine. "They're always holding benefits to get more money. Now they want to put on a wild, madcap revue to express their great ideas. They asked me to play the violin in one part – I have to do Chopin's Funeral March. I told them I haven't played it in years. All I know is those slimy Strauss waltzes I play in the restaurant."

"You could practice," Pauline said. Nita said she hated to practice, it gave her rashes under her chin; that was why she had started wearing scarves in the first place.

"I can play musical water glasses," Peter said.

"Well, I'm sure they'll ask you," Nita said, "they're that starved for raw talent."

In the end it was Pauline they asked to do something. Ernest had probably suggested her, or maybe someone else on the staff had been eyeing her. The revue was mostly a series of attacks on literary enemies and stylistic opponents, with a lot of court-martials and hangings in effigy and mock burials. The editor, Dean White, a man she knew from Walter's house, said she only had to stand still dressed as a flame in one scene while someone else did all the work of writhing and perishing.

Pauline went to one rehearsal in the basement

of a meeting hall, where she sat smoking cigarettes and flirting with some of Ernest's friends. Ernest came in later. There was no more room on the benches so he sat on the floor, leaning his back against Pauline's knees. The editor gave a speech about old forms and new forms. He said all belief was a disease. "I don't want to even know," he said, "if there have been other human beings before me." Pauline, who knew perfectly well that he had not made all this up himself and had copied it from someone you were supposed to have read, was nonetheless stirred to hear him. What she really liked – what she found truthful – was the coldness in it. It took her own private moments of repudiation and suggested (as she had always suspected) that they were the road to purity.

Ernest looked attentive during the speech – there was an atmosphere of fraternal agreement in the room. At the end he and a few others called out heckling remarks. Pauline would've liked to think of something to call out with them.

The rehearsal was very noisy. People in the middle of the room went through a series of stylized pantomimes, and then someone else practiced an oration in pig Latin. There were references Pauline didn't follow, burlesques of writers she didn't know, but she liked most of it. She had nothing to do until the end, when she stood in a certain spot and someone flashed different lights on her, which she was told would ripple and glimmer over the shiny surface of her costume once it was done.

Ernest said the scene she was in was crucial – the ending was always the most important part of anything. Pauline agreed – she was noticing the shape of his nose, guessing whether it was what you could call aquiline. He left her to go argue with Dean White about how one of the sketches was being directed.

It wasn't until the night of the performance that Pauline saw the costume she had to wear. One of the writers' wives had taken her measurements in a brusque and cursory way, and Pauline had been secretly afraid they were going to give her something that made her look terrible. The costume was really very clever, though; it was a cloak with the sides sewn to drape into sleeves, made of a cheap gauzy red fabric that someone had streaked with gilt paint, and there was an underlayer, an amber taffeta slip that showed through. Nita, who was bustling around backstage in her own black crepe day dress, said, "You look good in that. Probably hell is very flattering to brunettes."

"That's a relief to know," Pauline said. They sat while the writer's wife put makeup on them. Nita got white face powder and silver glitter in her hair. Her eyes were very blue behind the mask of white and her lips were wickedly dark – it was odd to see her smile normally. "You look dangerous," Pauline said. Pauline got gilt greasepaint and red pencil in very fierce-looking flames around her eyes. When she saw her face in the hand mirror she kept looking at it sidelong to try to catch it without seeing herself look. Glimpsed that way, the forked eye was like an animal's markings, brindled and severe.

For most of the performance she was backstage and could see only a small part of what was going on. She stood with the other actors, crowded close next to some men in black tights. It all happened very quickly: the pantomime troupe simulated the motions of a giant typewriter while there were shrieks and the sound of gongs in the background; parodies of certain authors were read; a trial was held in incomprehensible languages. Ernest had written the trial scene – he watched from the wings, nearer to the front than Pauline was. She saw the dark back of his head, blue-tinted in the lights, and the tense angle of his profile. The sharpness of her physical longing for him distracted her; later she realized she had forgotten to watch his scene.

During scene changes, people came out and did card tricks or played tunes on a pocket comb wrapped in Kleenex while staring deadpan at the audience. In the last act a hugely padded green figure meant to represent a dollar bill came out and tried to crush a child by sitting on him. The child (really Bertha Goodwin in short pants) was rescued, and the dollar bill was put in chains and forced to confess his crimes. And then he was condemned to die while Nita played the violin and Pauline stood with her arms upraised under flickering spotlights. She had been afraid that she would start to giggle or smirk onstage, but it all had the opposite effect; her features got very still and solemn – it was almost horrifying to see the rows of faces – she felt incredulous and then flushed and elated, prickly with exhilaration.

When it was over, everyone gathered in the hall upstairs. The editor had originally wanted to have a banquet on the floor with tubs of punch ignited in blue flames, but instead there were barrels of beer on trestles and trays of sandwiches. Most of the cast were still in their makeup and costumes; Nita said if you stopped for cold cream you'd never get anything to eat. The editor was very excited and went around with a gloating expression, and there was a general feeling that things had gone well.

Pauline saw Peter talking to Ernest, and when she brushed past them Peter said, "Here she is, in a literal blaze of glory."

"You were very good," Ernest said.

"I thought your trial scene was really excellent," Pauline said.

"I've heard of red-hot mamas, but this was beyond the pale," Peter said.

" 'Nature red in tooth and claw,' that's what you look like with that makeup on," Ernest said.

"We need more of that sort of thing nowadays," Peter said. "Girls with a little fiendish streak in them."

"I'm wild but I'm not violent," Pauline said.

Peter said, "A likely story," and he asked what she wanted to drink after all that sizzling. Pauline said a dainty glass of beer would cool her off nicely, thank you, and she was left with Ernest while Peter went off to get it.

"The attack on MacIver's prose was very good, I thought," Ernest said. "He deserves it. In spades."

"Oh, yes," Pauline said. That had been one of the parodies she had recognized right off; it was an easy one to spot because it had lines like "He held a cigarette carefully between his upper and lower lip," which really did have the overwrought preciseness of MacIver's style. "No one will ever be able to read him again without thinking of it," Pauline said.

"Writing like his is really pestilential. It's a kind of mental corruption to read it."

People – men especially – were always getting extreme like this, ready to beat into the dust all sorts of art that outraged them. Pauline sometimes thought there was something wrong with her that her opinions weren't so impassioned, although she still didn't see that a bad prose style did any harm really.

"I've heard he's very nice," Pauline said. A friend of Nita's went out with someone who knew MacIver, and Pauline was looking to work this into the conversation, but then she thought better of it.

"Oh, nice," Ernest said. "What does nice matter?"

"That's true," Pauline said. "Baudelaire wasn't known for being nice. And Byron was a cad, he kept deserting all his women. And probably giving them gonorrhea."

Nita's friend Rose came up to hug Pauline, just as Pauline was remembering that Ernest didn't like Byron. Rose said, "Everyone loved you in that last scene. A memorable moment." Peter returned with her beer, and with him was the sculptor with the brushed-back hair, who told her she was perfectly cast in the part, a model flame. On the other side of the room someone made a toast to Dean White's magazine and its fiscal serenity. When she looked around again, Ernest had been drawn into another conversation; he gave her a little quick wave when he caught her eye.

A very small band had been hired for the event; the players were all holding glasses during the toast. Pauline didn't want to begin dancing right away, and she stood watching for a while. Peter was talking about which couples on the dance floor looked as if they were really sleeping together, whether you could tell by how they danced. Rose said, "You can't ever tell." She said this very mildly, her voice just audible over the sound of the music, which made it especially convincing.

Pauline didn't dance until later in the evening, when she was fairly drunk and a tall man in white flannels led her onto the floor. The room was crowded now – full of couples swerving and sidling around each other, women in limp, fluttery dresses and men with their jackets flapping. One joker went around picking the men's pockets, pulling out handkerchiefs and fountain pens and handing them to the other dancers. Pauline's partner called out, "Watch out, bozo," and "Look out, it's two-left-feet White," when they passed people he knew, and the editor yelled back at him, "Go bury yourself in fertilizer, Dewey. Excuse me, Pauline."

"Old friends," the man explained. "We go back a long way."

"How long?" Pauline said.

"Before he could write worth beans. Those first poems were pathetic. He had to bribe Bertha Goodwin to print them in that rag she had then. Well, not a bribe really. More like your basic physical persuasion."

Pauline asked if he was a writer too. "I write plays. Are you an actress?" Pauline said no, not really.

"Too bad. I have a play where there's a girl onstage who has to jump from a ten-foot ladder. You'd be great, you look very agile."

"I think you're going to have a little trouble casting that part," Pauline said. This apparently struck him as very funny – he let out a loud, hawing guffaw – until Pauline recognized the long hiccuping laugh she had overheard at that first party last winter at Walter's. The laugh made him seem oafish, but he was good-looking enough otherwise, Pauline thought. Actually, she wasn't sure. He had gaunt, slightly pitted cheeks and spaniel-brown eyes, so he looked weathered and very young at the same time. He had a tattoo on his arm just above his wrist, a small blue anchor, which he said he had gotten in the navy. Pauline asked him how the navy was, and he said it was dog's work but you got to see good places; Tierra del Fuego was a very good place to see.

They sat out the next dance; they were near the door talking when Pauline saw Ernest coming toward them with his coat over his arm, on his way out. He took her hand and kissed it by way of good night, and Pauline said, "Till next time." Her voice was husky from drinking. She thought it was quite adroit of her to think of saying this. It seemed interesting and somehow richly gratifying that this was becoming a sort of joke between them, a friendly conspiracy of acknowledged undercurrents. He looked rueful as he left, and she was very animated and bright when she turned back to hear more about Tierra del Fuego.

"Is Patagonia in your play, is that what it's about?" she said. Dewey – that was his first name, it had taken her a while to get that straight – said no, his play was a modern retelling of the story of Romulus and Remus, how they were raised by a wolf. "I have a lot of respect for the Greeks and Romans," he said.

"They gave good parties," Pauline said. He laughed his braying laugh again.

It was nice that he thought she was so witty; he was a peculiar mixture, with his spots of intelligence and his mannered roughness and his lapses into showing off. They danced more – he was very supple in his dancing, if not altogether natural – and then Nita came over and whispered that they were all going to Anselm's for breakfast. "About time someone thought of that," Dewey said.

They made a noisy entrance into Anselm's. There were nine or ten of them, all blinking in the sudden bright light; Walter was singing one line of the "Anvil Chorus" over and over, and she and Nita were still in their makeup, with their costumes showing under their coats. Walter complained that he couldn't read the menu, and Nita ordered them all waffles and scrambled eggs.

"Fuel for the machines," Walter said, when the waiter brought the plates. Dewey said, "Grub for the starving crew." They all grew quieter as they ate; Pauline was suddenly tired, and the warmth of the food made her drowsy. She looked down at her waffle for a while – it had a very regular pattern of little diamond grids interlocked – and then she leaned on Dewey's shoulder and let her eyes close. "Baby's gone bye-bye," Dewey said.

It was raining when Pauline got out of the cab in the blue early morning light, and when she woke up the next day it was still raining outside her window. She was lying on top of the covers in a nightgown she had put on backward. The first thing she remembered was walking up the stairs, carrying her shoes and being afraid that Mrs. Poganyi was going to wake up and come out and see her in her flame makeup. This seemed funny even now, and she got out of bed smiling to herself about it.

Pauline never got hangovers really – what she got instead was a rush of recalled scenes from the night before; her own theory was that she was still a little drunk in the mornings. She had a running picture in her mind at the moment of a man with red hair waving his shoe during the dancing and of Nita eating waffles in Anselm's in her dead-white powder and glitter. Pauline was slightly sorry about having spent so much time with Dewey. She didn't think now that she much liked him – he mispronounced words and he had a habit of echoing phrases people had just used. Peter's friend the sculptor would have been better at least, after Ernest drifted off, if she had stopped to think about it. But there was an element of chance in who you ended up with sometimes.

She walked over to Vera's that night, thinking that Nita or Walter would certainly be there, but when she stepped into the room the first person she saw was Dewey, beckoning to her from his table. Out of politeness she went over to him, and he said, "There's the girl. Didn't stay home very long, did you?"

"A few hours," she said. "That's a lot."

"You're like I am," he said. "Don't fence me in."

When the waiter came to their table, he pretended to hit his head when he saw Dewey and he said, "Oh, no, the poor man's Shakespeare is here again." Pauline had never seen the waiter so jolly before. Dewey called him "Adolfo, you dumbbell." Afterward Dewey said, "We're writing a play about his life, Adolfo and me. He used to be a boxer."

A couple Pauline didn't know – a swarthy older man and his painfully thin girlfriend – came and sat with them, and Dewey told stories again about the navy and South America. They were good stories, with grimly comic punch lines, and he cocked his head and looked genial when he told them. He winked at her once while someone else was talking, and he kept patting her hand and trying to buy her more tea. "Tea makes you strong as bull," he said. By the end of the night she was used to him.

It was raining again when he walked her home, and he held his jacket over her head. He said, "You walk like I do. When did you hurt your knee?" She had noticed that he walked with a rolling gait – not a limp exactly but a rocking to one side, very appealing in its way – but she hadn't known she was imitating it. She lied and said she had a stiff muscle from dancing. In front of Mrs. Poganyi's stoop they necked a little in the rain; he had a slow and thorough way of kissing, undulant and persuasive. She was pleased now that all this was happening, although after it went on for a while she was afraid someone was going to look out the window and she began to mind getting wet in the rain.

Later that week, when she came home from work, Dewey was waiting for her in Mrs. Poganyi's parlor, ready to take her to supper as though they had agreed on it. Afterward they went to the Elephants' Graveyard for drinks. Pauline thought she could feel a certain faint surprise from people at seeing them together, although Walter seemed to like him well enough. The two men had a contest about stacking matches, which involved buying each other drinks, and Dewey cawed and clapped when Walter started singing.

She had told Dewey she often had just a tin of sardines and a banana for supper, and in the following weeks whenever they were out having dinner, he always said as he handed her the menu that it was time for her to get some nourishment and fatten up. He was noisy in restaurants, although waiters sometimes seemed to like it. He had a way of arranging at the end of the night when they would meet the next time, so that their times with each other were hooked together.

Once he asked her in a light, teasing voice if she had come into Vera's that Sunday night looking for him. She said, "I was kind of interested in a sandwich actually," and he said, "Oh, I know. Never ask a lady." It was a great issue with him that she was ladylike; when she wore a certain deep-brimmed hat with a velvet band, he kept saying, "Look at the duchess."

She didn't mind spending so much time with him, but she still didn't feel that he really counted. Privately she and Nita called him the Lounge Lizard of Literature, and Pauline would describe with groans his habit of buttonholing strangers to tell them the plots of his plays. Sometimes when he was talking to people, she rolled her eyes so they would know she knew better. He did not seem to notice this; on the contrary, he liked to refer to "Pauline's favorite character" or "the scene Pauline thought was good." He liked to tell her how glad and contented he always was being with her, and he would often look at her as they walked with a grateful, beseeching gaze.

Sometimes he phoned her at work and he would talk a kind of baby-talk lover's slang over the phone, trying to get her to answer in kind. When they saw movies together, he was always comparing the sweetheart couples to themselves. Once he brought her a present – a painted fan he said he had gotten in South America. She put the fan on the dresser in her room; it reminded her of the sort of thing a gently bred child might play with. It lay folded in the china dish next to her beads, a placement that made it look more sentimental than it was, and in the end she was touched sometimes by the sight of it, as a sign of his devotion to her.

5

Dewey liked to try to make light conversation with Mrs. Poganyi when he came to see Pauline. He would stand around the living room saying things like "It's raining cats and dogs and goats outside" or "Sure and begorra, 'tis a dreadful night out there in the peat bog." Pauline wasn't sure what Mrs. Poganyi made of this; she never spoke more than a sentence at a time, except to scold the maid in a language Beatrice had identified as Hungarian. Dewey's opinion was that he brightened things up for Mrs. Poganyi and that she was probably secretly a little sweet on him. Pauline thought that she looked tense and worried when Dewey went on for too long. Perhaps it was only from the effort to understand, but it made Pauline uneasy, and she frequently chose to meet him outside.

Once when he was supposed to meet her in front of a movie theater, he kept her waiting for so long that everyone else in the ticket line went inside and the picture began; she could hear the music. She was afraid he was waiting for her in another place, impatient by now, or even that he was paying her back for being late so often herself. She tried to read from a newspaper she had brought, and that confused her more about how much time had passed, and when she saw him coming toward her, she called out, "Oh, you're here, I'm so glad." He said he had gotten all delayed trying to see a friend about something important, and then they went into the theater and she forgot about it while she watched the film, a comedy with a chase scene and a car falling apart, not her favorite kind of movie but very funny in parts.

Afterward when they were having drinks at the Elephants' Graveyard, Dewey said, "Helene would have screamed bloody murder all over the street if I was late like that." Helene was his old girlfriend; she lived in Chicago now and always sounded like a shrew in his descriptions. "I would've heard about it for months after," he said. He seemed to think that Pauline had shown a fineness of character and also a deeper appreciation of him, a trust in his better side, by waiting. Pauline had a feeling his standards were low – she didn't believe she had really demonstrated anything so substantial as all this, but she was pleased that he thought so.

She did feel loyal to him in some way, and when Nita called him a lout and a clodhopper, Pauline said he was really surprisingly courtly sometimes. She always stressed to Nita how fervent he was in his attentions and how fixedly he had attached himself to her. He did do things like carrying her over puddles in the rain, although she didn't altogether like being hoisted like that in public. With Peter and Walter she emphasized his time in South America or his friendship with Adolfo the waiter. She liked it when Walter called him a tough customer – praise for a side of him Pauline found strongly attractive – although it was possible Walter meant this as a slur against Dewey's "background." Walter always laughed about him in a way Pauline thought was probably affectionate. And Peter wavered – for a while he seemed to think of Dewey as a decent enough person who had for some reason adopted a boorish facade – but then later Peter got very stony and cold whenever Dewey's name was mentioned.

In a way Pauline liked it when people asked her what she saw in Dewey. For one thing, it showed a certain offhandedness on her part in settling herself on an admittedly odd choice. That it was not what she or anyone else would have expected only proved how extensive the possibilities were; she was not, at the moment, in a hurry for anything better. She felt, when people expressed too much puzzlement, that there was something lazy and stubborn in her that mocked their earnestness. Peter gave her speeches on how she was getting in deeper all the time. Sometimes it struck her that this was the nature of a great love, that it drew you against all sense on the least foreseen paths.

Dewey's way of earning money was to work at times as a court reporter. He met her in the evenings still dressed in what he called his working-stiff uniform, a blue suit and a shirt with a high collar. Pauline liked the idea that he was tapping away at a stenotype machine with his anchor tattoo hidden by his shirt cuff, and he looked gratified when she mentioned this. He said someday he was going to throw a stink bomb in the judge's chambers just to see everyone's faces. He would do it now except he had to pay the rent. Pauline rubbed the joints of his fingers to relax them; she didn't know whether this could really help but it pleased him.

He had switched from writing plays to working on short stories. On his urging, she brought home pads and a new fountain pen from Gittelson's. She had never really stolen anything before, and the ease with which she simply walked out with it all under her coat was thrilling in its way. "A little larceny in your soul, my dear," Dewey said, cackling and rubbing his hands like a stage villain. Pauline thought he was overdoing it – she said a small batch of office supplies did not constitute larceny – and this made him hoo-hah more fiendishly; he kept patting her cheek and saying, "Fine work, my pretty."

Dewey lived in a railroad flat, with a curtain in the archway between the two main rooms and a kitchen that always smelled faintly of unlit gas. Sometimes Pauline cooked suppers for them – scrambled eggs or lamb chops. They were cheerful, savory little meals; Dewey called them campfire cookery for wasted youth.

His typewriter was on a table in a corner of the kitchen; possibly he really used it, it wasn't thick with telltale dust or anything. She had never seen a real page of anything he had written and she was hoping not to. She supposed that it would be overdrawn, a copy of things not well understood. As long as he didn't press her about it, she didn't think she cared what his writing was like. She already knew people who were well known and good at what they did – Walter was probably the closest to being truly famous – and her connection to them seemed permanent and settled. But even Walter, who was so forthright and expansive and so maniacally sure of himself in certain ways, did not have Dewey's physical sureness. In that sense, Dewey, with his rolling walk, was from another element. The way he carried himself made him seem very resolute – Pauline was aware that it was not real confidence, but the lack of it in other people seemed unappetizing to her now.

On the nights when she was home alone, she stayed in her room and ate her suppers of sardines and soda crackers with a sense that this was a custom she had invented in a much earlier season; it made her feel her time in New York as very long. Once in the evening she went outside to buy a magazine, and when she came back in the house she saw, on the second floor, that the door to Beatrice's room was open. Beatrice was standing over an open trunk, folding clothes into it. "Hail and farewell," Beatrice said. "You can have my room if you want to. It's bigger."

"You're leaving?" Pauline said. She thought Beatrice must be getting married. She felt unobservant not to have guessed; there must have been signs.

"I can't wait to walk out that door for the last

time," Beatrice said. "It's heaven to think of never waking up in that bed again. I can't tell you." She was moving to Brooklyn – a girlfriend of hers had an apartment and was renting her a room in it.

"Moving to the wilds of the outer boroughs, huh?" Pauline said.

"Here it's the wilds," Beatrice said. "It's noisy from the El and it stinks. The mice have a smell. It's worse in warm weather, but I can smell it all the time."

"You'd think Mrs. Poganyi would put out traps," Pauline said, although she didn't care herself; she had only seen mice a few times, and they didn't bother her.

"Oh, Poganyi's a witch. You can see how she walks around shrieking at that girl who's the maid."

Pauline didn't see that any of this justified a move to Brooklyn – the rooming house wasn't so bad for its kind. It seemed wrong that Beatrice wasn't going to be there any more. "I wish you the very best of luck," Pauline said and hugged her.

"Oh, thanks," Beatrice said. She looked happy.

"I'll miss you," Pauline said. "You were my friend when I moved in and I didn't know anybody, and you helped me." Pauline wondered if she had gotten the habit from Dewey of being a little cheaply false once she got going.

"Oh, I was a saint," Beatrice said.

On Friday Pauline went with Dewey to a dinner at Walter's. Walter's own theory was that he was an inspired cook, not good at everyday meals but gifted at fixing certain stylish and highly seasoned foods. There were about a dozen guests, and they all got very noisy over the punch while Walter was puttering in the kitchen. Dewey kept saying, "Mickeling puts dragon's blood in his punch," and pretending to breathe fire on people. No one minded – in fact, for a while they all went around breathing and hissing at each other. Pauline said, "I love these smart Village soirees with a lot of urbane conversation." Nita, who was passing nearby, made a face and gurgled bubbles into her punch glass. Pauline said, "Same to you," which came out sounding more cutting than she meant it. She had had a long and dispiriting day at Gittelson's, and she was not in a boisterous mood. She watched for a while and then she went into Walter's bedroom to find her cigarettes.

A girl Peter had brought was standing at Walter's dresser, powdering her face. "Getting rambunctious in there, aren't they?" she said. She was a small, child-faced brunette, and she used the powder puff with great energy and system, tapping over her chin and neck. It made Pauline worry that she looked too shiny, and she went to the mirror to check. "Use some, if you want," the girl said and held out her vanity case. When Pauline put the puff back, she saw, next to the little sieve-covered wells of powder and rouge, a small square envelope – it looked like a packet of Alka-Seltzer or some headache powder until she read the brand name, familiar from jokes about it, and she understood that it was a condom.

She had a secret desire to ask to unwrap it so she could see it – the woman seemed candid enough. It reminded Pauline that she was still a virgin and that in her own sexual experience a line of distinction still existed, faint but absolute, a border she almost pretended to herself that she had crossed although she had not. She sat on the bed, lighting a cigarette, and when the girl finished combing her hair, they went back into the living room together.

The dinner, when they finally sat down to it, turned out to be veal kidneys – a food Walter said was underappreciated because most people had never had them fixed properly. The kidneys weren't bad, only a little rubbery and close-grained. Dewey was in an especially affectionate mood; he kept nuzzling her neck and calling her Peach of Peaches. An older man, a collector who was a friend of Walter's, told her she looked radiant lately.

Rose said, "She does look good these days, doesn't she?" Pauline wondered if Rose thought she and Dewey were sleeping together. Rose had said you couldn't tell from appearances, but did anyone believe that? Pauline looked over at Peter and the brunette, trying to guess. The girl, spooning her dessert, had a bright, settled look; whatever she was doing she was confident about it. Perhaps it was just the dessert that brought on that expression, a chocolate sponge pudding which everyone agreed had rescued the dinner. In high school Bunny and Pauline had had their discussions about the truth of the senses – philosophically they were both empiricists. Pauline had come up with the formulation that a knowledge of absolute truth was possible in the fullest extension of the senses, probably in sex. Once reasoned, this was a sacred belief of hers. Already she had outgrown some of its earnestness – it meant that in most adults of any experience there had been this contact with the blaze of bare reality, and she wasn't willing to concede this as common to other people. She did feel nonetheless that the brunette's eyes had unusual lights in them, a quickened depth.

Under the table Dewey had his hand on Pauline's knee.

They stayed until late; in the end they all took the dog out to the park for a run. Dewey, who was good with dogs, threw sticks for him. Rose led him to the fountain to drink some water. Garrett climbed a low branch of a tree, which made the dog get very excited and circle the tree, yipping. Nita said, "That's the most excitement Garrett's caused in anyone for years."

Dewey was singing when he walked Pauline home. He sang "Yes! We Have No Bananas"; he only knew a few bars and he kept singing them over and over. He had gotten this from Walter – the idea of singing when he was drunk. A couple passed them, looking amused, and the man tipped his hat. "They admire your beautiful baritone," Pauline said. This made him sing louder, which was not what she wanted.

"Everybody said how good you looked tonight," he said. He was slurring his words on purpose, and he began singing, "Believe me if all those endearing young charms/ Which I gaze on so fondly today."

"People are sleeping," Pauline said. She knew she sounded like someone's mother, but they were on side streets now, moving past quiet half-lighted buildings.

"Were to change by tomorrow," he sang, "and fleet in my arms/ Like fairy gifts fading away."

They were on her block now, and she shushed him outside the house. "Afraid I'll wake the dead, aren't you?" he said. "This is the street of the dead." He kicked a garbage can, which clanged horribly and fell over. Somebody's household garbage – glass bottles, carrot peelings, old newspapers, coffee grounds – spilled out into the gutter. "You jumped," he said, and kicked the can again, banging it against a metal grate.

Pauline stood quiet, trying not to jump, since that seemed to goad him further. "I scared you," he said. "I didn't mean to." He used the can's lid as a shovel and scooped some of the garbage back. He got the largest pieces back in and then he kicked the rest into a more compact pile by the other cans. "No one will know," he said. "They'll think a dog did it."

"There's a dog on the block that does that," Pauline said.

"I didn't mean to scare you," he said.

"I know that," Pauline said.

"I don't mean anything when I get rowdy," he said.

"I know that," she said.

"You know a lot," he said. "I've never met anyone like you." She thought at first this might be sarcastic, but then he moved forward to hold her and he kissed her neck, he rubbed his cheek against her shoulder. They stayed clasped that way for a while; he rocked her back and forth. She felt awkward but interested at something this stagey happening to her; she stroked his back.

"Go to bed," he said.

The next day was Saturday, and when she first heard knocking at her door, she thought she was dreaming that she had to get up for work and she struggled to shake off the dream and go back to sleep. The knocking went on longer, so that she woke up still hearing it. The door opened while she was tying on her wrapper. Mrs. Poganyi stood on the threshold. "Why you sleep so late?" she said, and she put a piece of paper on Pauline's dresser – a phone message – and left. DOOI IS SICK, it said on the paper. CALL DOOI.

Pauline felt she should be concerned, but there were times when she had to rest from being with Dewey, and he didn't seem to feel that she ever needed this. When she called him from the phone in the hall, the number she reached was the candy store on his corner and she had to wait while a kid was sent to find him. She stood, listening to blurred voices and crackling sounds in the receiver until Dewey came over the line. He said that he'd been in bed all morning with a stomachache – he thought it was from the kidneys at Walters; he'd been worried that she was sick too. His voice sounded thin and sad, and she ended up offering to come make him some tea and toast.

When he answered the door, he was half dressed, in pants with suspenders over an undershirt. "It's the Visiting Nurse Service," she said. "I'm here to lay my cooling palm on your feverish brow."

"I'm not feverish really," he said. "It's just a slow death from poisoning."

"The coward's way to assassinate," Pauline said. "Who are your enemies? Think."

"Many," he said.

She offered to make him milk toast as a sort of joke, but he liked the idea. They ate a bowl together, spooning up the crusts of buttered bread in the scalded milk. "Hits the spot," he said. He kissed her on the forehead and said he was going to lie down on the sofa, if she didn't mind.

"Want me to read to you?" she said. He thought this was a good suggestion, and she found the funnies section of the paper and read through an episode of Mutt and Jeff.

"Lie down next to me," he said. "I'm lonely."

She settled alongside him on the cushions; it amused her a little that he thought he had to lure her in this way. He was probably not sick at all, only hung over and lazy. She liked the way he looked now, with the leanness of his neck showing and his arms bare. There was less clothing between them than usual – she was wearing a light sweater, which he slipped off almost at once. His mouth tasted of cigarettes and boiled milk. When she opened her eyes, his expression was blurred and slackened, and he looked at her with a fixed sheen in his eyes, reverent and watery. They had shifted so the weight of him was on her; she liked the pressure of it, blanketing and steady. She had a sudden passing remembrance of Harry Bitt, who had liked to lean her against doorways and car seats.

Dewey was stroking the fabric of her slip as though it were her skin; her skin under it seemed eager and thin. They were rocking in place. It reminded her of someone's definition of infinity: constant motion, constant rest. She made a small moaning sound as though she had become as intense and concentrated as the plainest syllable. By degrees they were moving toward the unfamiliar. She said, "Oh," again, more wildly helpless this time. She was quite awed at herself. She thought how the phrase "going all the way" implied something absolute – the part that had been beyond imagining – although the forms of longing within her own body had perhaps been a pantomime, a kind of physical imagining. Dewey was murmuring to her, an endearment she couldn't quite hear; she wanted to say something back. She wanted to hear her voice outside herself, overreaching.

She unhooked her own stockings. She wondered if he was going to ask if she was willing, to ask permission. For a moment, while he was fumbling with the buttons on his pants, the whole thing seemed too personal. Then he was lying on top of her again, he had begun – at first she was startled, not by pain (although there was something like pain), but by the fact that he seemed to be taking himself away almost as soon as he had entered – he had changed his mind, withdrawn for fear of making her pregnant – until she understood that this repetition of leaving and returning was the thing itself, and not a hesitation before the single consummate sliding she had imagined.

Her own confusion humbled her. She lost track of things somewhat; he went on, intent and purposeful.

Afterward they fell asleep, and it was late afternoon or early evening when they woke up;

the room was almost dark. Dewey got up – she could hear him putting on his pants – and then he brought her back a glass of water from the kitchen. She sat up, sipping it. "You look like a siren," he said. "Like the White Rock girl."

"She's not a siren, she's a nymph," Pauline said.

Dewey laughed his guffaw. "You said it, I didn't." He stroked her arm. "You're terrific," he said.

He smoothed her hair. Did she want a cigarette? She was groggy and quiet, waiting to be more alert so she could think; it seemed odd to have him in the room at a time like this. He asked if she were hungry, and when she told him yes, he said he would make supper for them. "Don't move, stay where you are," he said. She leaned back with her arms folded over her breasts, and when he went into the kitchen, she put on her slip.

He made them toasted cheese sandwiches, and he brought out a pot of tea and some whiskey to put in it. "That looks so nice," Pauline said.

She ate eagerly and quickly; there was a kind of blank excitement in her stomach that made her feel hollow and ravenous. Afterward she said she would go wash the dishes, but he said no, they would wait, and put out his hand to keep her from getting up from the couch; he seemed afraid to let her leave the spot. He told her a long story about how in the navy they washed the dishes with cheap soap that made everyone sick at first, and she drank more of the tea with whiskey, and while she was listening she fell asleep again.

When she woke up, he was lifting her off the sofa, starting to walk her toward the bedroom, through the curtained archway. "What time is it?" she said.

"A hair past a freckle," he said, pretending to look at his wrist. She wondered where her shoes were; she would have liked to be back in her room at Mrs. Poganyi's without the labor of getting there, but to leave would be to break away, to make things fall short of what seemed to be their normal sequence. And she was interested, too, to sleep with him literally, to spend the night, to go to bed with him – all the euphemisms that bonded the idea of sex with lying together unconscious. He had tried before to get her to take naps with him, but the notion of it had seemed too sloppy then.

She wanted to brood; she still felt a certain shock in the tissues. Now she would fall asleep before she had a chance to commit the particulars to memory. She had almost forgotten that it was an act she would be repeating.

In the morning, while she was padding around the kitchen barefoot, making breakfast, Dewey told her she was crazy to think of going back to the rooming house now. Poganyi would be waiting for her with a battle-ax. "She knows where you were, she's no fool," he said.

"She doesn't care about anything, she doesn't notice," Pauline said.

"You can't keep sneaking back there in the mornings," he said. "It's a rat-hutch anyway."

"I don't mind it," she said.

"What about me?" he said. "Think about me." He sucked in his cheeks to show how undernourished he was getting on his own cooking. It was his way of suggesting that they live together; she could see he was very tickled with himself at being so offhand in bringing it up. It annoyed her that this was his idea of artful coaxing. She wondered if he had left the phone message yesterday on purpose, a calling card of her whereabouts.

But what struck her more forcibly was that it would be so easy to do it, to move in. She did not fully recognize herself in the person who would do this – it was too sweeping a maneuver, too simple and probably even too bold for her, and it presupposed all sorts of sureties she did not pretend to have – but it bore an irresistible similarity to a hopeful thought. She had a sense of wanting to drive herself to it, to do it over her own objections.

For weeks she brought the more crucial items – toiletries, blouses for work – over in batches, in little paper-wrapped bundles, so that nothing was handy in either place when she wanted it, until the end of the month, when she changed addresses for good and brought the rest over in a taxi.

Pauline's story to Mrs. Poganyi was that she was moving to Chicago – a completely unnecessary lie – which Mrs. Poganyi accepted without comment; her only bit of sullenness was to insist at the very last minute on charging Pauline for a ripped window shade. Dewey said Pauline was a sucker for paying.

"Flapper file clerk vanishes into Village den," she told Nita. Nita alluded to a definite consensus that Dewey had changed, he was much better since he'd been under Pauline's influence. Pauline took this as Nita's version of manners, an attempt at suitable enthusiasm; Pauline could feel her trying to be nice, which was not altogether flattering but did have a kind of loyal tact in it.

The apartment was small and cluttered with

both of them in it. Pauline was always hitting her hip against the chairs when she moved around the kitchen. It was messier than she had kept her room at the boardinghouse, but the tumble of things left lying around – newspapers and clothing and shoes – seemed to her to be the effects of movement and abundance and family activity, better than the stillness of a rented room. She got very careless right away, leaving stockings and wrinkled pullovers draped over everything, as though she wanted them to commingle with the background and put their own mark on the look of the apartment.

In bed at night she worried about waking him if she moved when he was asleep. In the daytime she was sometimes stiff in the shoulder from where she had lain cramped and motionless. At work she sat at her desk rubbing her shoulder blade – she liked telling the stock boy she had premature rheumatism.

She would have liked to write to tell Bunny, but they hadn't exchanged letters for a long time and it seemed clumsy to suddenly issue an announcement. There were things she didn't get to tell – passing details, half formulated into thought, dissolved and were forgotten. In a way this seemed right, less girlish. She felt that she lived now in a denser realm, in which events went on continuously, without postponement and without opinion. In her current life her daydreams were more physically graphic – bright with detailed sex – but at the same time more repetitious and formless, less tellable.

In the evening when she came home from work, Dewey was always sitting over the newspaper – he seemed to read three or four papers a day – and she would sit on the sofa with him, taking a section, while they half read and half listened to each other. Pauline found this soothing and companionable, except when items in the news made Dewey angry, and then he would rage in sudden bitterness – it was a joke between them that he swore like a sailor.

By and large he was easier to live with than she would have thought. He told her how lucky he was and how much better she was than any woman he'd known. When they went out at night he tried to neck with her in restaurants; Walter said they were so sweet they made his teeth hurt.

They were only irritable with each other occasionally – about money, which surprised Pauline, since she considered herself unusually free from pettiness on this subject. But on their nights out she noticed now that in restaurants he couldn't seem to order anything but the most expensive dishes, almost on principle; he would pretend to debate, considering pending bills or rent, but he always switched at the last minute when the waiter was there.

His other irritating trait was that he had bouts of being playful in mocking ways – he had pet names for her like Sadie Snob or the Jersey Jewess – and he wouldn't stop, he got more noisily amused the more she protested, so that she had to learn to try not to rise to the bait.

In general, though, it wasn't at all bad to be in his company so much. He could get surprisingly interested in small household matters; he liked to bring home kitchen gadgets – cheese slicers and rubber bottle stoppers – and he liked to recite the recipe for an elaborate cocktail he had invented, based on a bottle of green Chartreuse someone had given them.

Peter had told her that she was playing house (a phrase meant as a dismissal of living together unmarried). And it was true that she had a sense of imitating something, of following out a borrowed form. It was only in the mornings that she felt this as a kind of strain. It bothered her getting dressed when he was there, and there were things she waited to do until he was out of the room.

6

Dewey's block was full of families – groups of boys who raced around, chasing each other and shrieking, and young girls who brought chairs down from upstairs and sat in front of their doorways watching the street. Dewey had lived there for a year, and he occasionally showed off by using what he said were curse words in Italian, although Pauline wasn't sure he said them right. He also brought home wine from the grocery store on the corner or sometimes from the newsstand; he said everyone on the block was busy fermenting it in their kitchens; in the fall you could see all the mash dumped in the gutters. Pauline had a secret grudge against the wine because it stained her teeth and made her look ghoulish when she drank it, but she was in favor of keeping reserves of it in the house, since it was Dewey's one real effort at buying cheap.

They did not have many visitors, but one

night when she came home from work, Garrett was in the living room with Dewey. They were playing cards and drinking the wine out of jelly glasses, and they looked up, dark-lipped, when she came in. "The woiking goil is home from the mines," Dewey said. They were both tipsy in a hazy, convivial way. Garrett had that reddish look that Nita said he always got when he drank.

"I hope you boys aren't wagering sums of money on a game of chance," Pauline said.

"Oh, no," Dewey said. "We would never do that, would we, Gar?"

"No, ma'am," Garret said. He had a flat-voiced, hollow way of speaking, somewhere between politeness and plain listlessness. Pauline thought he was a funny choice as someone for Dewey to take up with. They went on playing cards while Pauline fixed supper. Dewey did all the work of conversation, crowing and snickering and firing off rhetorical insults while Garret smoked cigarettes and mumbled.

When the food was ready, Dewey said, "Well, eat something with us, you miserable card-sharking bastard," and Garrett went to the table with them. He ate very little – Pauline was afraid he didn't like her cooking – but he said the juice of the grape gave him all the vitamins he needed.

After dinner they went back to their card game. Pauline sat near them, reading. They played for hours – Pauline got sleepy over her book and went into the bedroom. There was only the curtain in the archway between the two rooms, and she could hear them, Dewey's braying laugh and Garrett's swearing when he lost. It annoyed her that she couldn't fall asleep at night in her own house; she was angry that they didn't have a better apartment with separate rooms, a thing she usually didn't think about. She was afraid, too, that Garrett might pass out and have to stay the night. But after a while she heard Dewey walking him to the other end of the apartment, and she could hear their good-byes and the door clicking shut.

"You have fun?" she said, while Dewey sat on the bed, pulling off his shoes and kicking them onto the floor.

"Sure," he said. "It was a bloody massacre. Some people don't have a feel for poker at all. It's like an instinct some people don't have."

"He stayed late," Pauline said.

"He likes us, he likes to be here. He doesn't like people that are phony, like Peter and that whole crew."

"What's wrong with Peter?"

"Garrett thinks I should write that book

about Adolfo. He thinks it would be a very powerful story."

"He's probably right," Pauline said. By the time she settled the covers over her again, Dewey had fallen asleep, so she didn't have to hear about it.

Pauline had trouble imagining that Adolfo had ever been a boxer. He seemed much too loose-limbed and shuffling for an athlete – although age might simply have crumpled him: he was close to fifty. Now that Dewey had gotten interested in him again, they had taken to stopping at Vera's very late, just before Adolfo finished his shift, and they would sit and wait until he changed into a clean shirt and different shoes and came out from the kitchen, ready to go drinking with them.

Pauline couldn't tell whether Adolfo really believed Dewey was going to write anything about him. Sometimes he would say, "Did you get that down, scribe?" or "Here's one for the records," but he had a vaguely leering tone when he said this. He could be quiet for long stretches of time – Pauline thought he might be uncomfortable in a place like the Elephants' Graveyard – but then, under Dewey's prodding questions, he had spurts of reminiscence and opinion.

Adolfo's favorite stories were about obscure fights held on barges in the days of his youth before boxing was legal. If Garrett was there, he always made Adolfo talk about Battling Levinsky, Tunney's old rival; it was the name that amused Garrett and he would murmur to himself, "Battling Levinsky, oh, my, heaven save us." The idea of a Jewish contender struck him as richly humorous, although there were plenty of them, Pauline thought.

Pauline had no interest in boxing anyway, and she would edge over to other parts of the bar, if anyone else she knew at all was there. This gave her a chance to see people she didn't get to talk to otherwise and to have conversations without Dewey.

Nita was there one night, very stirred up, the way she got when she was drunk sometimes. She said, "Oh, it's you, Paulie," and threw her arm over Pauline's shoulder when she saw her. She had just been out on a date that had bored her and put her in a defiant mood – with a stockbroker who had bought a lot of paintings from Walter – and she was full of invectives about skunky old men and how money made people vulgar. Pauline said yes, it was wonderful how poverty was keeping them both so pure and refined, and they went on for a good while about how they weren't getting fat from overrich dinners or drying out their complexions with too many trips on yachts. Pauline said, "Or getting sweaty necks from those nasty furs." The bartender liked this one, and they heard him chuckle from across the counter. Pauline gave a small smile; she was never quite as good at speaking this way as when she was with Nita.

Nita was still stuck on the subject of how she couldn't stand most men with money – a complete turnabout of her usual position – and she got several people around them involved in a debate about whether money ruined character.

"I'd like to get ruined a whole lot more," the bartender said.

"No, you wouldn't," Nita said. "Not if it meant you turned into some odious toad."

"That's not character then," Rose said. She was standing near them at the bar, draped in a silk shawl with an enormous stringy fringe. "Character's the factor that doesn't change," she said. "That's the whole point."

"Why go out of the house if you're not going to change ever?" Pauline said. "Why let anything happen to you at all?"

"I often ask myself that question," Rose said. She laid her hand on her heart for effect. She had a sweet expression naturally and with her shawl swirled around her she gave a good imitation of a D. W. Griffith heroine.

"I'm talking about ruin, not change," Nita said. She could get quite petulant when she got stuck on a point.

The argument had turned silly again by the time Dewey came to look for her. People were voting on their favorite kinds of ruin; dissolution and natural disaster were favorites. Peter was there, with the brunette Pauline had talked to in the bedroom at Walter's, and he was acting out the way they would all look if they got suddenly buried in volcanic ash like the Pompeiians. "Well, not in this hat," Pauline shrieked. "I'm not getting turned into a statue for all time with this hat on. I've never liked it on me."

"You're drunk," Dewey said.

Pauline, who was still gesturing with her hands on her head, said, "Well, that isn't news to anyone." But she was flustered.

Peter said, "I suppose you never are, Dewey. Not you."

"Let's go home," Dewey said. "Let's get out of here."

"I'll go quietly, officer," Pauline said. She was trying to think of a line about how he was the new convert from the Temperance League, but she thought that anything she might say would just be ineffective and sputtering. She kissed Nita and Peter good-bye while Dewey started walking away. He was outside the bar before she caught up to him.

"You're soused," he said.

"That's a new thing for you to comment on," Pauline said. "No one's ever said anything about my behavior. I don't dance on tables or start drooling or anything."

"Let's just get home," he said. "Go to bed."

"Well, that's what I'm doing. Where do you think I'm walking to?" She walked faster, to get ahead of him, but he kept pace with her, so they moved along the street that way, rushing and hovering at each other's heels.

In the morning, when Pauline got up, Dewey was still asleep. She had an unpleasant sense of smarting under an injustice, and she felt bleak and low-spirited. She thought of calling in sick to work, but there was no phone at Dewey's house, and if she was going to walk to the corner to call, she might as well go to work. And it did freshen her a little, to be up and moving around; she was fine really once she was at Gittelson's.

Sometimes she thought it was an advantage not to have a phone. For one thing, it saved her from the complication of having to explain too much to her parents. They had never called very much anyway. At Mrs. Poganyi's they had always had Solly do all the speaking; he would ask questions relayed by Pauline's mother about how she was doing at work and what she was eating. Pauline told them now that she was sharing a flat with her friend Nita and that this saved money. They didn't believe her that the neighborhood was better, but they liked the idea that she was with another girl. Once when Pauline went home, her mother gave her a length of remnants to take back for both of them to make slips and underwear from.

Dewey thought this was hilarious when she told him, and he paraded around with the fabric wrapped around his hips. He offered to write her mother a note thanking her for adding to his lingerie collection, but Pauline said that was going a little too far.

Most of the time she didn't get much of a chance to feel that living with Dewey was any kind of illicit secret. Occasionally kids on the street ogled her and tittered to each other when she went by, but they did that to anyone dressed like her who was new in the neighborhood. At a party once, someone had introduced her by Dewey's last name – Pauline Franklin – and that had seemed half true in a general way.

The man at the grocery store on the corner had a sales patter that involved pitches like

"You bring home this bacon for your man, you going to see a light in his eye," and Pauline found it pleasant to shop in this guise of eager bride. The phrase *my man* – which was both like a popular song and like the readiest term in Yiddish – covered, more or less, the particular, agreeable feeling of being in the house, standing at the sink or setting out food on the table. She had a sense of labor carried out for some natural purpose and of skills flourishing in her, made brighter through use.

One of their quarrels came, in fact, on an evening when she had made fish for supper, and Dewey picked at it and said finally that he didn't like fish. "You don't like any kind?" Pauline said. "You could have told me, I wouldn't have bought it." Well, no, especially this kind, he said, it was the way she cooked it with onions – she was always putting onions in everything. It was true that she used them extensively in cooking; the smell of them in the house was cozy and nostalgic to her. She felt a kind of violent aggravation with him, a thorough and indelible disappointment. She said something sharp and curt, and then she sulked for a long time, bristling when he tried to tease her.

Afterward it was a habit with him to make humorous complaints about her being a novice in the kitchen, and he groaned to Garrett about her charred potatoes and oversalted peas. "The price of nuptial bliss," Garrett said. Only Adolfo told him he was a moron for complaining, he should try being an old man living on restaurant leftovers sometime.

Pauline had gotten to like Adolfo better, just as Dewey was beginning to spend less time with him. Dewey shrugged when she asked him about the book. He said, "Another great idea that'll never see the light of day." Pauline had expected him to bluff or to make more of an excuse – he was quite appealing, looking rueful and raising his eyebrows in that way.

Dewey was apparently used to this sort of thing. He had a whole web of anecdotes about different projects abandoned at the onset of success, and there were people who figured largely in certain episodes he told and who then dropped out of the stories altogether. She had trouble keeping track of the sequence of it all. She could never, for instance, get it clear whether he had served on a ship off Panama during the war or after and on which trip he had been bitten by a pelican.

In Baltimore at some point he had been in business with a friend – selling Addressograph machines – and his stories were sketchy but consistent about how well they had done for themselves. He mentioned always a certain dove-gray linen sports suit he had bought. But then there had been some trouble with the friend, some blowup or betrayal.

Once he said to her that what he liked about Adolfo was that his stories were mostly just lies, that was the reason they got along so well. It was a habit you got into in bars, he said; he used to make up some real fables when he was younger. Pauline was aware that at times she herself altered stories for different tellings and that incidents seemed to change in her memory, edit themselves for later tastes, but to actually invent a falsehood from scratch seemed eerie to her. But really nothing in Dewey's talk was more outlandish than things she saw every day – possibly a few stories were suspect, only because he told them once and never cited them again. It was more likely that he left things out. Once he had been in the midst of telling about Chicago and he'd used the words "my wife" to refer to Helene, and then he'd had to backtrack into telling about the marriage (very brief and her idea) and the annulment (easy because she'd been under twenty-one).

What surprised Pauline finally was that in all his ventures he could stop and begin again so readily. The waste in this bothered her. She thought it was wrong: to have nothing stick, nothing accumulate. There was something chilling in this kind of discontinuity. She assumed, in her own life, that even mistakes and failed experiments accrued toward a purpose, an eventual composite that was not random, and that everything had its later use.

Pauline did miss – even now – the old practice of entering a room and striking up a certain kind of beaming, animated conversation with new men. She was out with Dewey a lot, but it was duller without the potential of winning people to her in that way. Dewey still flirted – he would sidle up to Nita and ruffle her hair – but Pauline had a feeling that it would only be troublesome if she led someone on.

When she was out, people still greeted her as though she were a welcome and decorative arrival (a local sweetheart, as Peter said), although Pauline felt that her looks had declined; her hair had grown out of its cut and she was holding back parts of it with hairpins. She had gotten very penny-pinching lately. In bars she talked mostly to Nita and Rose and Walter or to Peter, who was usually with his brunette friend.

She was at the Elephants' Graveyard one night when Walter announced suddenly, "You know what the problem is?"

"Oh, God," Rose said, "he's going to tell us."

Walter had decided they were all losing their health from ingesting cheap alcohol. For a moment Pauline was really worried – she thought her pallor had somehow evoked this idea – but it was just Walter's way of insisting that they all go to a place he knew where you could get real absinthe. Dewey said, "Lead on," but Pauline was uneasy about spending more money. It was already late. Living with Dewey was more expensive than she had initially calculated. On the other hand, she had never had absinthe. Peter assured her that this was actually Baudelaire's favorite speakeasy they were going to.

They had to walk for a long time in the cold to get there. Peter had a flask which he passed among them. "This stuff is rotgut," Dewey said. "I'm saving you people from slow death by taking it into my own system."

"That's friendship," Peter said.

The place was on a side street, in a building Walter said had been a stable; there were no windows on the ground floor, and there was a high, narrow door that swung open very slightly when Walter knocked. A woman with a loud, peppy voice was singing inside. Walter and Peter both had cards from the time they were there before, and they fished them out of their wallets and passed them to a man inside the door. Walter beckoned them all to follow him in. "Hold it, hold it," the man said. "Four only." No guests without cards: Peter and Walter and their lady friends could go in, but not the others.

"It's all right," Pauline said. "I'm ready to go home, I have to work tomorrow anyway."

"I'm fine, I don't care," Rose said. "It's just as well really."

Walter put his hand on the man's shoulder – he seemed to be trying to offer him money; the man shook his head. "It's all right," Pauline said.

Walter turned back to her and shrugged. "It wasn't this way before," he said.

"Well, go on in," Dewey said. "What the hell do you care, go on in and get so soused you fall flat on the street and freeze to death."

"I think I'll use that as a toast," Peter said.

Nita said, "You don't mind really, do you?" and she hugged Rose and Pauline good night. Pauline waved to Walter and the others and said, "Tell us all about it in the morning," while they went inside.

"I'd like to punch Walter's face in," Dewey said. "He did this on purpose."

"Oh, he did not," Pauline said. She was feeling left out and disappointed herself, but she thought it made it worse to dwell on it too much.

"Let's get out of here," Dewey said.

Dewey started to walk, leaving behind not only Pauline but Rose. Pauline quickened her steps, looking back. "I'm coming," Rose said.

"Walter didn't mean anything," Pauline said. "He considers you a really good friend."

"People like that don't know what they mean," Dewey said. "You know how many times I've helped him get his drunken carcass into a taxi when he was too stewed to see his way home?"

"That was nice of you," Pauline said.

"I didn't do it to be nice. I don't expect much from people, except a little basic human courtesy."

"Don't think about it," Pauline said.

"You know why he's doing this?" Dewey said. "Because I owe him thirty dollars. You make an arrangement with someone and they have to get petty about it." A lot of Dewey's finances had to do with juggling loans. Usually Pauline paid their bills and he paid her back some of the money later.

"Your friends are real rat-fucks," Dewey said.

"Stop it," Pauline said. "I don't want to hear that."

"I'm freezing," Rose said. Her shawl was blowing across her face; she had put it on over her coat.

"Me too," Pauline said.

"At least it's not wet out," Rose said.

Dewey kept moving at a fast clip. He was leaning sideways as he walked – his limp came out more when he'd been drinking. Rose fell behind them again, and then she yelled to them that she had to turn off at a corner to go toward her street. "You have to go?" Pauline said. She was sorry that Rose had seen Dewey like this, and he had been rude to her too.

"It's late," Rose said. "Sleep well, take care, I mean it."

They were near the Square when Dewey said he wanted to go to Vera's, just to get warm before they went home. Pauline thought this might calm him. But when they climbed the stairs to the restaurant, there was a sign on the inside door that said *Closed due to fire. Nothing serious. Will re-open soon.* "I don't believe it," Dewey said. "I hear them moving around. They're in there. You hear that?"

"Probably cleaning up," Pauline said. "You can smell that burnt smell."

"Adolfo," Dewey said. "Hey, it's me. It's okay. Let me in."

"They're closed," Pauline said.

"I know you can hear me," Dewey said. "You fucker. It's cold out. You know that?" He shook the door to make it rattle.

"Let's go," Pauline said.

Dewey was kicking the door. "I know he can hear me. He doesn't goddamned care."

Pauline started to go back down the stairs. She was surprised when Dewey followed her.

"You know what I've done for that creep?" he said. "The favors I've done? I just can't stand it. He could've given us a cup of coffee, you'd think. It wouldn't have hurt him. You do favors for people, you jump through hoops for them, and they don't see it, it's nothing."

"I know," Pauline said.

"It's nothing to them. If they just appreciated it, I don't care about anything else."

"We'll be home soon," Pauline said.

His voice sounded choked and Pauline saw that he had tears in his eyes; she could hardly believe it. "I can't stand it," he said. As they walked, she put her arm around him, and he stopped where they were and nestled his head against her. "I just can't stand it," he said. He was weeping and sniffling now, and she held him and patted his back.

He was like this for the rest of the way home. He would be quiet for a while and then he would break into speeches that made him stop in the street when he got tearful. "A simple cup of coffee," he said. "You'd think anyone would do that." She kept putting her arms around him, since that was so clearly what she was required to do, but she was horrified that he could sink so readily to this, and for nothing really; she was sickened by all of it. His face, with its pocked cheeks and its gaunt bone structure, got crumpled and red like an infant's. He seemed grateful enough; he burrowed against her shoulder and kissed her neck as they were walking.

For a long time after this, Dewey, in time of affection, seemed to think that one of her great merits was the way she stood by him; she was loyal, that was one thing about her. She wasn't loyal at all; she spoke against him to anyone whenever she could, and she was scornful of any idea that had the least taint of his judgment on it. And yet they were more familiar, more used to each other. He was home almost all the time that she was in the house – he was working less now – and they quarreled easily. She quarreled about how much it cost a month to leave the bathroom light on at night, whether the neighbor below them was Rumanian, whether dogs could be taught not to fight. She had once been more hesitant and more patient, but now she argued readily and sometimes stupidly, not caring if she sounded sensible since he was the only one who heard her. At times she worried that she was becoming less intelligent. There was a low-keyed pettiness that rose up in her. The last time she had been this contrary was a certain stage early in high school when she had picked on Bunny a lot. She felt now that she was speaking out of a reflex that being with Dewey called up in her, and that this was something temporary and artificial, a masking of her actual character.

Dewey didn't seem especially dismayed that she lapsed out of civility so much. He himself was frequently abrasive, full of autocratic pronouncements and menacing sulks. What surprised her was that he had no embarrassment about any of this; he assumed it was common enough – the hidden order of normal things – the "awful truth," to use one of his regular expressions.

She felt that she had declined in certain outer ways too, that she had lost a facility in arranging her appearance. She was down to her older pairs of stockings, and she had gone back to sewing arrow designs on them to cover the runs, a thing she and Bunny had done. At the end of the winter she bought one good new skirt which she wore with everything, so that sometimes when she was out she would find herself in odd colors or strangely paired shapes and she would wonder then why she had thought they matched.

She had toned down her makeup. With her hair in a less definite style, she was afraid that the plucked eyebrows and the dark lip rouge would just look cartoon-like, and it seemed to her that her main chance now was to attempt being handsome in a pale, artless way. It was Dewey who had first made fun of her gravity-defying eyebrows, but he didn't much admire the change in her now either, and he said she looked like she had a skin disease with her stockings that way.

It disappointed her to think that she had failed to keep whatever skill she'd had for displaying herself properly. It seemed to her that it was the sort of pure knack that couldn't ever be regained on the same footing, and that whatever future improvements lifted her out of this spell of plainness, there would always be a gap in her own history, an advantage lost. It hurt her to think that her time of sureness had been so short.

She tried to encourage Dewey to go out at night without her. She had begun reading again, a thing it was hard to do with him in the house. Her tastes ran now to historical novels, gentle epics with plots involving kindly squires and lost wills and sickly nieces. She was aware that if she was going to read junk, she would do better to go in for reading detective stories, as Walter did, but she had tried them and found that even the mildest murder was too harsh to read about, no vacation from the world at all.

Sometimes she remembered living at Mrs. Poganyi's with surprising fondness; she missed the luxury of going out with people and then being alone at the end of the night. She did think at times about what she would do when she wasn't with Dewey any more; she thought she might want to try living in a hotel for a while – Rose had lived at the Walpole for years, and she liked it; she had a room with a nice view. It seemed apparent to Pauline that she was living out the duration of a certain sequence with Dewey and that the conclusion could come of itself, as the term expired.

If Pauline was still reading in bed when Dewey came home, she would sit up and listen while he talked. He was spending a lot of time with Garrett; they had discovered a speakeasy on Eighteenth Street with a poker game always going on in the back, and Dewey would explain in detail the better moments of the night's playing. Garrett was still a rotten cardplayer, he said. Pauline didn't understand about Garrett – what did he want and why didn't he do a better job of having a good time? "He's an odd bird," Dewey said. "He likes to just sit back and watch everything. But the mind is ticking away. When you get to know him, he has a very active mind, but he only shows certain people."

"Well, he talks to you, he likes you," Pauline said.

"You could say so. We're going to start a literary magazine, him and me, I think."

"Another one?" Pauline said. "When did you decide this?"

"Anything would be better than that crap Dean White publishes."

"I like that one."

"If the pages weren't so stiff, you could use it for toilet paper."

"All right, all right," Pauline said.

"We've been talking about it. The first issue's going to be basically about machines. Anything anybody wants to write about the Machine Age."

"That's good," Pauline said. It was better than she would have thought – a copied idea certainly, but not awful. She was relieved, but then it occurred to her that she was worrying for nothing anyway, since it was unlikely that there was ever going to be any magazine.

Dewey did talk about it a lot, as she might

have expected; he brought it up all the time in bars. People who didn't know him so well got interested. Twice he actually got submissions addressed to him in the mail – a set of poems and a scene from an obviously horrendous play. These had the effect of making Dewey act as though the magazine were already in print, and he talked about paper stock and mailing costs. Once he came home from the Elephants' Graveyard complaining that it made him sick the way everyone was trying to get on his good side now that he was an editor.

When they were eating at Anselm's one night, Nita sat down with them while Dewey was holding forth. Pauline gave her a weary, knowing look from across the table. Nita asked Dewey why, if he understood machines so well, he didn't get a machine to go out and raise all the money for the magazine. (Nita could be too rude at times, Pauline thought – she depended too much on her intonation to make everything sound clever.) "Very funny," Dewey said. "You'll eat your goddamned words soon." Pauline had to launch into a plaint about the thinness of the roast beef sandwiches at Anselm's to get everything calm again.

The alarming part, as far as Pauline was concerned, was that the magazine did have some money. Garrett's father had sent a check –

possibly he liked the idea of his son being a helpmate to the arts, or perhaps he was just the sort of father who wrote checks when asked. Dewey said the amount from Garrett's father wasn't enough – printers in this country were highway bandits, you wouldn't believe what they charged – but now they were talking about how one good fund-raising party would bring in the rest. (For a while Dewey had wanted Pauline to ask Mr. Gittelson to be another backer – he kept saying it couldn't hurt to ask – but he had finally given up on that.) Dewey wanted to use the hall where Dean White had held the party for his magazine. Pauline tried to tell him it was much too huge, and he got very nasty with her about it. But then Walter, who liked parties and who for some reason had been a fan of the whole magazine scheme from the very beginning, suggested that they use the back room of Tony's restaurant. The room rented cheap and had a small, open floor for dancing.

Pauline was pained every time the idea was mentioned. She kept waiting for the plans to collapse by themselves, and when they didn't, she began to think about how she could escape, how she could break up with Dewey before the event. She picked one fight, an argument about the rent money. She was perfectly sincere; she came home from work one night and complained, with real bitterness of feeling, about how she had paid all the last month's rent and he still hadn't paid her back for his share. Dewey said, "You know I'll get it to you. You know but you just want to rub my nose in it. You see I'm working day and night to get this magazine going. You think this is just the right time to get on my back, don't you?" She held her ground well; she was sullen and hard all through dinner, and she said nothing at all when he finally went out.

But when he came home very late, he sat on the bed and he was so broken-voiced and contrite, he kept talking about all she meant to him and how there was no one like her, that she couldn't think how to answer him cuttingly: it seemed too inhuman, too incongruous a thing to do. For a moment she felt quite angelic in her forgiveness. He got very happy and playful then, and she let him make jokes about how the whole fight was probably based on indigestion from the cauliflower she had made for supper. He said he thought that this was the sort of arguing and making up that would just make the bond between them stronger – which seemed true enough in a general way, if not really true of them. And yet she felt coarse and falsely sweet, mouthing endearments.

Her idea, after that, was that no one really had to think that the fund-raising party – or the magazine itself, for that matter – had anything to do with her, and there was no need to apologize for it. She did occasionally make disavowals, to the effect that it was Dewey's brainchild and all inquiries about it should be addressed to him. She was counseling herself to a state of coolness about the whole thing, and she would sometimes remind herself that everyone had stories about parties that turned out to be fiascoes, and some really legendary flops were recollected very affectionately by those who'd been there.

At times she thought now that she was waiting for the fundraiser to be over so that her time of breaking up with Dewey could begin. She had a sense of the current time not counting, really, and of something disagreeable being put off till later.

At other times it seemed to her that she was already living the way she was going to continue to live, that her present life with Dewey was permanent, that she had gotten settled without really knowing it. There were women like that – always a little surprised at the impractical nature of their own alliances – initiates of a knowledge improbable even to themselves; perhaps she had passed into that state.

7

On the day of the party, Pauline decided that if she was going to get through the evening at all she was going to have to make an effort to be a better sport about it. She spent the last hours of the afternoon trying on things in her closet; she trimmed the little sidepieces of her hair and stuck them down with lacquer. In the end she looked quite nice, she thought – she wore an old black crepe dress with a yellow glass brooch at the bosom, very classic and impeccable. Dewey had finished dressing and was sitting in the kitchen, fingering the knife pleats in his trousers. She nudged him and said, "How do I look?"

"You look okay."

She kissed him on the back of the neck. "Do you still think I'm pretty?" She was horrified as soon as she heard herself. "I don't know why I asked that," she said.

"Yes, why did you?"

"I sound like we've been together for ninety years, don't I?"

Dewey was putting on his topcoat, smoothing down the muffler. "Only eighty, my dear," he said.

When they got to the restaurant, musicians in dinner jackets were unpacking their instruments, looking listless and bored in advance. Three or four people were hovering around a glass punch bowl set out on a table next to the piano. "Look who's here already," Dewey called out. "It's the starvation army, drinking up the profits."

Pauline recognized one of the writers who had sent poems to the magazine, a bald man with puffed cheeks. He held out his glass and said, "First come, first served. You learn that in life." He pretended to keep Pauline from filling her glass. "It's too strong for the ladies. They'll misbehave."

The back room of Tony's, which Pauline had never seen before, had a décor of potted plants and empty wrought-iron bird cages. On one wall there was a brownish mural of a landscape with hills and Roman ruins. Dewey got busy dragging a table over near the entrance. He seated himself at it and yelled out, "Okay, you deadbeats, pay up. Nobody stays without forking over the admission fee."

"Well, don't threaten them," Pauline said, but they were filing over to Dewey's table, pulling bills out of their wallets. Garrett came through the doorway then, and there was some joking between them over whether he had to buy a ticket or not. Dewey pretended to bend back Garrett's arm to make him pay.

"Pauline, my little pigeon, you know what you can do?" Dewey said. "Go find Tony and see if he'll give us a cashbox or something for the proceeds here."

Pauline went back into the main room of the restaurant, where customers were sitting at tables, eating plates of food and drinking wine; the room smelled of garlic and cooking oil. Pauline envied them all their spaghetti suppers and their conversations. They looked up, annoyed, as groups of people edged past them, heading for the back room.

Tony was standing by the kitchen, drinking a tiny cup of espresso. "What now?" he said. When Pauline told him, he went down to the basement and came back with a black metal box, the size of a Kleenex dispenser, dented and ominous looking. "Tell your boyfriend I'm sorry we don't have a Brink's truck for him," he said.

By the time Pauline went back to the party,

clusters of people had gathered in parts of the room and the musicians were tuning up. Garrett tried to introduce her to two men in striped wool suits who he said were the thieves who bilked him at cards every night. "He flatters us," one of the men said.

Pauline kept looking for someone she knew. She waved to Nita's friend Rose across the room and went rushing toward her. "What a great room," Rose said. "I love that mural, don't you? I'd like to hack it off the wall and take it home."

"Perhaps we could leave with it right now," Pauline said.

"Nita's coming later – she said to tell you she would be late. You want some punch? I'll get you some punch."

Rose led her by the elbow – quite gently, Pauline thought; she had never noticed how soothing and maternal Rose was. A noisy group had gathered around the punch bowl, and it was hard to push through. Someone brushed a lit cigarette against Pauline's arm and she cried out.

"Did you get burned?" Rose said.

"That hurt," Pauline said. She held out her arm somewhat childishly to make sure Rose saw the red spot and the smear of black ash.

"I'll get you ice," Rose said. She ladled ice

out of the punch bowl and filled a cup for Pauline. The ice was sticky from the punch but it did take the sting out, as Rose said.

"It's so noisy in here. It's like a barnyard. Company included."

"I've seen worse," Rose said. "In my time."

"The punch tastes like paint remover, doesn't it?"

"You'll get different people later," Rose said. "The crowd always changes. Don't worry."

"Oh, I'm not worried," Pauline said.

The music had started and people were bobbing on the dance floor, smiling open-mouthed at each other or looking foolishly severe and intent. A man came walking across the floor to Pauline – she was afraid he was going to ask her to dance, and she tried to edge away until she saw that it was Ernest.

"I thought that was you," he said. "You've got your hair different." She let him steer her onto the floor. She was startled at being at such close physical range, up against the scent of his Wildroot Cream Oil, feeling the shoulder pads in his suit. She was stiff and not at all light-footed, but he seemed not to notice. He bantered with her about how the literary magazines were all multiplying so much New York was going to be all buried in printed matter soon. "The whole city'll just be submerged under paper," he said. "Like an Atlantis under pages."

"We'll all just have to learn to breathe under paper pulp," Pauline said. Ernest probably thought she still talked this way all the time; she felt as though she were obliged to keep up an impersonation, but the effort made her lively and more cheerful. They tilted and swayed in a slow fox-trot, and then they sat out the next dance at a banquette under the mural. He was still so good-looking, she thought, in that beaky, sharp-chiseled way, although he did seem weaker now. She might have been with him instead of Dewey, if he had been less dilatory, if there had been a little more force in him.

She had a small spot of resentment in her for what had happened because of his hesitation. It was quite possible, of course, that she was going to be with him sometime later on, after she wasn't with Dewey any more. At first this seemed like a satisfying thought: she would be retracing her steps, going back to where she had made a wrong turn before. But wouldn't this be the same as losing ground? She wanted to think that she was weathering everything with Dewey as a price for something better (something less faulty than Ernest). She had the idea that once she was through being tried by a little adversity, she'd be tempered into a subtler understanding that made possible a refinement of happiness not available to her before.

She danced another time with Ernest. A blonde in smeared makeup was waving a coat hanger, lifting her skirt with one hand as she danced and yelling the words to the song the band was playing. From across the floor Pauline could see Dewey, sitting with his cashbox and smiling about something with Garrett. She waved at him and said, "How's it going?" when they danced past, and he pinched her on the bottom.

Ernest had a glass of punch thrown at the back of his pants when they went past an especially rowdy corner of the room. "Who did it?" he said.

A group by the wall was convulsed with laughter. "Hey," one of the men said, "you need diapers?"

"It doesn't show much," Pauline said.

"Yes, it does," Ernest said. "It's a huge stain, isn't it?" He stopped dancing and stood by a pillar. "Christ," he said, looking back at himself. Pauline kept telling him it wasn't bad, but he said she should go dance with someone else, and he left not long afterward.

Nita and Walter arrived very late, just as the blonde with the coat hanger was trying to throw her shoes into the piano. "I can see we're here for the wild, impetuous part," Nita said.

"It was better for a while," Pauline said. Nita wouldn't dance, but Walter found them a table and they all sat watching the dancers on the floor. Adolfo went by, doing an overstated but graceful waltz step with Rose; when he passed the band, he flipped up the blonde's skirt as she leaned over the piano, exposing her garters so that she shrieked.

Dewey whistled through his fingers to get Pauline's attention. When she went over to him, he said, "It's the host's turn for a little sport and frolic," and he led her onto the floor. He was always a good dancer, but now he hammed it up and did a lot of stylized dips and turns that were hard for her to follow. She kept laughing, since people were looking. Then the lights in the room started flickering on and off, which was Tony's way of telling them all it was time to leave. The band stopped playing at the end of a verse and the musicians began packing up their instruments at once.

In the cab on the way home Dewey was in a gleeful mood. He had emptied the contents of the cashbox into his pockets, and then, when he ran out of space, into Pauline's pockets, as well, and he kept patting and squeezing the lumps of bills at her hips and saying, "Not a bad night's work." He sang "Good Night, Ladies" into her ear, a song the band hadn't actually played although he seemed to think they had.

For days afterward he kept trying to retell her things that had happened at the party, although she was pointedly not interested and only answered dully. At the time the party hadn't seemed unbearable – she remembered being afraid at every minute that it was going to get worse and feeling reprieved as the night went on – but now the mention of it made her shudder and the thought of it was mortifying to her.

In general now she avoided talking much to Dewey, as far as she could. After dinner she would take her book into the bedroom and read. Garrett was in the house a lot; he sat drinking with Dewey in the kitchen until late, and sometimes he stayed over and spent the night on the couch.

Dewey had taken up Garrett's habit of smoking little cigars; they talked about their "venture" and referred to each other quite seriously as business partners. Pauline was at work the afternoon they took the ticket money and Garrett's father's check to the bank; they had been talking about this for days, arguing about which bank to use. ("Just go to any bank," Pauline had said – she didn't like Dewey keeping so much cash in the house.) In the evening when she came home and there was no one in the apartment, she assumed that they were probably still out celebrating. She waited awhile, and then she ate a piece of leftover roast for supper and read until midnight. She liked the calm and the ease of being in the house without Dewey. In the morning, though, it was confusing when she woke up and saw the bed still empty next to her, as if Dewey had somehow been gone for years without her noticing and her life had long since sealed around his absence.

He came in just as she was leaving for work; they passed each other on the stairs. "It's the old wanderer returned," he said, "making his weary way homeward." He made a sheepish face – he seemed to be waiting for her to scold him, which she had no urge to do.

She said, "There's coffee left if you want to reheat it."

Afterward he was always grateful for this, for the flatness of her modern attitude. He seemed to think she had behaved quite beautifully. They had fewer fights about anything now; they avoided each other, which made for less friction, and Pauline was less prone to bursts of irritation.

They did have one battle at the beginning of the month, when the rent was due. Dewey was hardly going in to work at all now; he claimed that the magazine took all his time and that he was too busy having meetings with Garrett. He did, however, buy himself a wristwatch. He came home one night, pulling back his cuff with great flourishes to show it off. He had picked a simple, rather handsome style – his taste was good, she thought. He said he had gotten it because she was always yelling at him for being late, and she agreed that a watch was a good thing to have. He seemed so foolishly pleased with it; it occurred to her that he got more enjoyment out of objects than she did.

On the dresser later she saw the plush-lined box the watch had come in and the price tag still on it for thirty-five dollars. Thirty-five dollars? That couldn't be right, their rent wasn't that much. How could a watch cost more than shelter for thirty days? Maybe he'd bought it some other way, gotten it hot or at a discount. She didn't really believe this, and secretly she envied him his obliviousness to price and budget, his spurious freedom.

A day later, when he admitted that she was going to have to pay all the rent herself again because he was short on cash, she actually wailed in rage. "I don't have any money," she said. "I make half, less than half, of what you make, and you think I can pay for everything." And then there was a bitter satisfaction in her; she had been proved right about him. She liked the sense of accumulating reasons against him; it made her feel hopeful, as though her leaving were more imminent.

Later in the week, while she was unpacking the groceries in the kitchen, he came over to her and dangled a sheaf of bills in front of her face, flicking them against her nose. "Here it is, the fucking rent," he said. He set the bills on the table. "You want to count it? Why don't you count it?" Pauline took up the money and put it inside her purse; she felt that she looked greedy and coarse as she did this, and yet the money was rightfully hers.

Even so, there were moments, not long after scenes like this, when he would turn to her in bed at night, sometimes waking her out of a sleep, and he would ask, as he moved toward her, before he started taking off her nightgown, if it was all right with her; the asking always seemed poignant to her, and there was a feeling of concord and old bodily understandings between them.

Sometimes, even in the daytime, he showed

signs of being about to change for the better. He announced that he was going to look for another job; he hated being a court reporter, that was why he never went to work any more. He had always really had more of a head for business, that was where his real abilities were. His old ventures in Baltimore were on his mind a lot now. He was especially sorry that he didn't have some of the clothes he'd had then – it made a crucial difference in the way people treated you in business. Pauline never understood what *had* happened to his clothes. She herself had garments she'd owned since before puberty; they were a final reserve against really having nothing to wear, although she was always sorry when she resorted to wearing them.

The suit that Dewey bought for himself now was gray with a blue tint, made of a light worsted. Pauline admired the tailoring and the fabric, but beyond that she didn't see what there was to get excited about in men's clothes; they seemed like uniforms to her, subject to only the most minor variations. It didn't surprise her that Dewey was so vain, although it galled her that her own outfits all seemed to center around the same crepe skirt she had bought in the spring, which was getting shapeless from being worn so much.

Dewey wanted to delay the job search until

after the summer was over; serious hiring, he said, went on in September. His idleness seemed to make him even more itchy to spend money. She had to stop him from buying a Persian kitten he saw in a pet store window. He did bring home a big, heavy piece of exercise equipment – a rowing machine – which took up most of the floor space in the bedroom.

It was August when Dewey bought the machine, and he would sit in it in his underwear, grunting and sweating; the sinews in his arms looked glazed. Garrett had gone to the country, to a lodge in the Adirondacks that his family had. Occasionally he sent postcards complaining of the boredom and berating Dewey for not writing. "Poor baby," Dewey said. "Never worked a day in his life. And he's getting worn to a frazzle from those brutal croquet matches. My heart bleeds."

With Garrett gone, Dewey had less company in the evenings. He went out by himself to the usual spots and later to the place on Eighteenth Street with the poker game in the back. Once on a Sunday morning when she woke up he had set out a tin of caviar with toast for their breakfast.

She wasn't sure how much the caviar had cost, but she knew he had bought it to spend money. He was training himself in the sport of expenditure. He gave himself missions – forays and retreats of varying boldness.

She had guessed for a while – it was daily more evident – that he was draining money from the magazine's account. She wondered if he assumed she knew. She had a feeling he didn't expect to be questioned about it. To accuse him directly would be like asking to see him with his teeth bared. At best, she would just get taunted for her priggishness.

She wondered if other people had suspicions – perhaps everyone knew – perhaps they weren't outraged but only mildly disgusted. It was such a shadowy kind of embezzlement, to filch from a nonexistent magazine. Some ticket buyers had been misled, and a few mediocre writers had had their hopes raised for nothing, but the real injured party of course was Garrett, who had signed over his father's check. There was a real ugliness in that, in that buddyship milked for profit. But Garrett was so smooth and unmarked, so sleepy and waxy and removed from the pressures of circumstance – wasn't there a kind of payment for being in the world that he hadn't stood the cost of yet?

In the days when she had worked in her parents' store, her mother had always been sure that people were going to pilfer things like the packets of needles or the embroidery floss.

Pauline had considered this a ridiculous fear: who would want to make off with a skein of thread? To take a thimble without paying seemed like such a violation of normal pride, an admission of the most pitiful kind of greed for something justly withheld. Pauline would have professed indifference rather than stoop to this sort of cringing grabbiness. But for Dewey the whole matter of pride was reversed. He liked the idea of overcoming refusals and getting things by ruses, of gaining consent without the will of the consenter.

It was so unlike her to be linked with anything like this. That a simple romantic attachment – however misguided – could have led her to this still shocked her beyond everything. She had a grudge against the unfairness of it, that she was tainted with a mistake that wasn't her own, a stupidity completely different from any she would have committed herself.

As it was, she ate the caviar when Dewey brought it for breakfast. Plundered goods, she thought, but there was no ethical ground to be won by leaving it on the plate: you couldn't put the fish roe back in the ocean. He showed her how to squeeze lemon over it; he talked about how "concentrated" the taste was and how a part of the pleasure in eating it was the texture of the eggs popping against the roof of your mouth. Dewey was not normally so eloquent about food, and she thought he must be repeating this from somewhere. She had not expected a luxurious food to be so salty, but she ate it with considerable interest and mentioned the meal later to Nita.

The day Garrett came back from the country, he and Dewey went out drinking, to celebrate what Garrett called his return to civilization as we know it. At midnight they came back to the apartment and insisted that Pauline come out with them to Vera's. "Back from the hinterlands," Garrett said. "Back from the bush, never to return."

Garrett had a faint, biscuit-colored tan, and he complained of a case of poison ivy. Vera's had reopened with no apparent changes in its furnishings except new, noticeably clean tablecloths. While they were sitting there, Garrett kept reaching under the starched cloth to scratch his shins. "It's our own Nature Boy," Dewey said.

"Maybe I'll write a nature poem for the magazine," Garrett said. "An ode to a horse turd."

"Never get through the mails," Dewey said.

"We forgot mailing costs, didn't we?" Garrett said. "In our budget."

"Don't ask me," Dewey said. "I forget."

"You know what's the worst thing about the country?" Garrett said. "You can't sleep. The birds wake you up."

"And the mosquitoes. Piercing your tender flesh."

"Don't remind me," Garrett said.

"And the wolves," Dewey said. "Weren't there wolves howling at your windows?"

"No wolves," Garrett said.

"Bears? Any bears trying to raid your provisions?"

"They didn't have bears," Garrett said. He was pouring whiskey out of a flask into their teacups, and he looked slightly grumpy now.

"Probably spiders and worms, though," Dewey said. "I don't know how you got out alive."

"He looks alive to me," Pauline said.

"Just barely," Dewey said. "Worn to a shadow after his days with the spiders and the worms."

"Oh, don't talk about worms," Pauline said. "I hate worms."

"Don't move," Dewey said. "I think one's crawling on you now, down your blouse. Just kidding." He got very interested then in describing in grim detail how to dig for night crawlers and the proper way to hook them for bait. He had these little bits of rural knowledge he could call up at times – actually there were two versions of his growing up: he had been raised in a rough section of Baltimore, but then he had really spent most of his time on an uncle's chicken farm in eastern Maryland. This gave him a range of expertise convenient in most discussions.

Garrett said fishing was the world's dullest, most pointless activity, and he and Dewey got into an argument about whether it took any intelligence at all to catch fish. Pauline thought they were muddled and tedious in what they said; they had both been drinking all day and they were on the verge of being excitable. It occurred to her that she might leave by herself right then, but she knew that Dewey wouldn't want her to go and she thought it wasn't a good idea to cross him now.

"Where's Adolfo?" Dewey said. "Ask an Italian if he thinks fishing is for the feebleminded."

"For the jingle-brains of the world. Strictly," Garrett said.

"Adolfo," Dewey yelled. "Where are you?"

"Don't shout," another waiter said. "Where Adolfo is he can't hear you. He fell off a ladder; he's home in bed with a broken leg." After the fire in Vera's Adolfo had volunteered to fix the stove in the restaurant kitchen so it didn't start a fire again – he had been measuring for putting in a new exhaust pipe when the old one, which he was leaning on, gave way. "Mr.

Clever," the waiter said. "Who asked him to show what a great handyman he was? You can see what the kitchen is like. An antique, a relic of former times."

"How bad is his leg?" Pauline said.

"He has to have a cast for a couple of months. Pegleg Pete, you know. Also, he knocked out a front tooth when he fell. But he can eat all right, he says."

"He's home by himself?" Pauline said.

"He can hobble around okay. His problem is you can't wait tables with a cast on."

"He should sue," Dewey said.

"They paid for his bandage, big deal. Vera sends him food, but you can't exist on that."

"Sue," Dewey said.

"Who told him to go on that ladder?" the waiter said. "Nobody told him." He moved away from them to serve another table.

"You think he was snockered when he went up that ladder?" Garrett said. "You think he'd had a few when he took that dive?"

"Who knows?" Dewey said.

"Old people shouldn't drink," Garrett said. "That's what I think."

"Thank you for your opinion," Dewey said.

"I had a broken ankle once," Garrett said. "I broke it ice skating." Garrett lifted his pants cuff, he pulled down his sock and showed them his scar. Dewey said nobody wanted to watch Garrett waving around his hairy ankle in public, and if people really wanted to see scars, Dewey had a few he could show them. He had taken a few falls on shipboard that would make Adolfo's little jump look like the nothing it was. How high up could he have been on that ladder?

Pauline was woozy from the whiskey in her tea. She heard them talking, and she sat until she was almost asleep. Every so often their voices got louder, and she shifted in her seat and opened her eyes.

By the end of the night Garrett had turned sentimental; he wanted to have another party so they could raise money for Adolfo. Dewey said all the guests could come dressed in white like doctors and dentists. "White flowers, white wine," Garrett said. "White suits for the boys, white dresses for the girls."

"The Moby-Dick Cotillion," Dewey said.

"We give great parties, don't we?" Garrett said. "How much did we make at the other party?"

"A mint," Dewey said. "But we still need another whole mint to put out the first issue."

"Fuck the first issue," Garrett said. "Excuse me, Pauline. What is this magazine that it should eat up all our money? That's what I say."

"It's our gift to posterity," Dewey said.

"Do we need posterity? That's what I say. Adolfo's hobbling around with one leg, he doesn't have a goddamned nickel. Let's dump the magazine and just give the money in the account to Adolfo. Give the old codger some relief in his old age."

"He's not old. He could get another job," Dewey said. "There's things he could do. He's not sick."

"There are not."

"Buy him a keg of brandy. That's the only medicine he likes," Dewey said. "Let him get pickled, he'll forget he has a leg."

"He won't forget," Garrett said. "What's the matter with you?"

"Not everyone can be a great philanthropist like yourself," Dewey said. "A paragon of the higher virtues."

"A broken limb is no joke. I don't suppose you can understand that."

"Don't tell me about understanding broken *limbs,*" Dewey said. "You little piss-ass fairy. Mr. Milk of Human Kindness."

"I won't be baited," Garrett said. "You think that'll provoke me, but it won't."

"I think I'm going. If I stayed, I would start to puke from listening to you, and the waiter would just have to clean it up. Some of us think about these things." He got up and left the table. Pauline didn't catch up with him until he was on the staircase. "Why don't you go back and talk to that little shit?" Dewey said. "You like having fascinating discussions."

All the way home Dewey talked about how Garrett was going to get his face punched in if he wasn't careful. Pauline had nothing ready at hand that she could murmur even as background, although she was afraid Dewey would be angry with her for not showing assent. He was quiet for a long time, and then he said grimly, "I'm very disappointed in him."

When she came home from work the next day, Garrett was sitting in their kitchen drinking tomato juice, his favorite hangover remedy. He and Dewey seemed to be talking peaceably. Pauline went into the bedroom to change out of her work dress, and when she came out again, Garrett was gone. She said, "He didn't want to stay for supper?"

"He's out of his mind," Dewey said. "I can't stand it. He hears someone whining about Adolfo, and now he thinks he can just take the magazine money and throw it away on him. You know what it is if you raise money for one thing and then use it for something else? It's fraud. I told him he'll go to jail if he tries something like that."

"He doesn't care about the magazine any more?" Pauline said.

"I would personally see to it that he went to jail if he tried something like that," Dewey said.

Pauline said maybe they could reach a compromise between them eventually (it was the sort of thing Bunny would have said). Dewey said he hadn't busted his ass over that goddamn party so he could make any compromises with a little shit-pants like Garrett. Anyway, Garrett couldn't get to the money without him. "I'm the treasurer," Dewey said. Pauline thought this was funny; he had never said this before – he must have just made it up – but he was serious. His mouth was set in a tight, frowning line; he looked like a cartoon of a scowling baby.

"It'll get settled somehow," Pauline said. She didn't believe this for a moment; it seemed to her that things were getting worse by the instant and that something uglier was going to happen fairly soon. She wasn't sure how much Garrett could do – he would probably lose if it came to just a battle of wills – but he could rage and complain and make the whole dispute very public.

It mortified her to think of this: to have

everyone know what Dewey was. Of course she had always been critical of him behind his back – probably no one would assume she was his collaborator – but they would wonder why she lived with him and why she still went home to him every night. She didn't think people would blame her but she would seem inexplicable to them, foolish in a tawdry and senseless way.

All through the next week, Dewey went out at night as usual, and he came home late. If Pauline was still awake, he would go off into long, muttering speeches about certain people who thought they could tell him what to do and how they would be sorry they hadn't shut their mouths. Rose had told Pauline that lots of people were asking Dewey why he didn't want Adolfo to have the money. Dewey said it was a matter of artistic principle, the integrity of the magazine. Peter had hooted very loudly at this idea, and Dewey had threatened him, told him that he was very likely to get jumped and beaten up on his way home some night. Dewey also had pretended to hand Garrett the bankbook – "Looky here, Gar, I changed my mind" – but it turned out to be only an empty pay envelope he gave him. There had been a general outcry then; people booed, and someone from the bar threw a pickled egg.

Dewey said the whole thing was a lesson in how people didn't even have the decency to mind their own business and how a rich kid – even a little fruit like Garrett – always had flunkies around to be his friends.

"I guess that's what happens," Pauline said.

"A lot of labor went into that magazine. Labor and dedication."

"It's too bad."

"There's one thing I didn't want to do but I'm going to have to. It's all over for our friend Garrett," he said. "I'm getting a lawyer. I didn't want to do it. You know how long he'll last in jail? I've seen some things from working in the courts. He'd lose his mind in a week, he'd just be a broken piece of a person. He has no idea. His lovely family won't be any help to him either. With their high ideas."

He's ranting, Pauline thought. She wondered how much longer he was going to stay awake and whether he was going to keep on talking and get worse. She was aware of how late at night it was and that she was shut up with him in the apartment. She had a fear of being drawn into his web of thought, of being held hostage so that she couldn't ever get back to the solid world.

It took him a long time to get to sleep; in

bed next to her, he gripped her tightly each time he changed position. Pauline lay looking out at the room. The light was still on; the light fixture in the ceiling was chipped and the string that hung down from it had a pocket comb tied to the end for a weight. Under the window she could see the looming metal frame of the exercise machine. It seemed to her that these were the signs of something dismal and wrongly planned, and that this was a room where unsound people lived.

Sometimes she wondered why Dewey still persisted in going out to the same places at night, since it was clear that the people he knew either avoided him or pressed him now to listen to Garrett and give over the money. Maybe Dewey showed himself in these places out of habit more than defiance, like a job he still reported to. It didn't surprise Pauline, but it seemed stubborn or oblivious. She wouldn't go with him, but she missed seeing people.

Once she called Nita from work – she thought of Nita as the sort of person who was unfazed by things – and they went to an early movie together. Nita said, "*You* look fine anyway," when she hugged Pauline outside the movie theater. They went inside and saw a movie about a nurse in the Crimean War who was in love with a dying soldier. Pauline got very absorbed in the movie; it seemed to her that the expressions on the actress's face were lifelike and complex, and the hot mistiness of the love scenes was an accurate version of a truth everyone in the audience knew. She still felt, despite everything, that sex itself was the purest of wishes. She cried when the soldier died in the movie, not just out of pity for the heroine but out of a general sadness for the bleak endings of things. The nurse put a sheet over the soldier's head and went on making her rounds, rolling men's arms in bandages. She had milky skin and her eyes shone; she seemed to have been ennobled by her ordeal. Pauline wondered what it would be like if Dewey died and how she would behave. The soldier in the film had of course been simple and brave and uncomplaining, not like Dewey at all. And yet Pauline thought she was equal to whatever strength the nurse showed. She felt cheated that all her own tribulations didn't amount to this sort of testing. And the nurse hadn't known the man very long; they had acted out of the same impulses, she and the nurse, only with different consequences.

"Oh, my," Nita said, when they left the theater together. "A three-hanky heart-wrencher. My mascara was in puddles."

"And we pay good money for this," Pauline said. "You'd think we could stay home and be miserable for free."

"It's never as good at home," Nita said.

They had drinks at a tiny, overdecorated speakeasy where the customers were mostly women. Pauline said, "I'm paying this time," as soon as they ordered. She was eager not to have Nita think that she was the kind of person who would be stingy about a check. She wasn't like Dewey: she wanted to make sure Nita knew. She supposed Nita did know, but people couldn't help having suspicions.

Nita talked about her job, how she was getting sick of sawing away at her violin in front of these fatso businessmen. She was cautious about bringing up Dewey's name; Pauline was grateful for this but it made her nervous. She was afraid the blouse she had worn was too prim, and she had a great desire to be home with no one looking at her.

Nita said, "Peter sends you his love. He said to be sure to tell you."

Pauline tried to think why she had decided that Peter wasn't someone she could ever really be attracted to; she had been awfully arbitrary and spoiled in the early days. She had a passing thought of how she might find refuge now with Peter, how they might have one of those autumnal romances of reunited old flames. But there was still something not believable about this, something falsely soft about the two of them together.

"You know what Peter thinks?" Nita said. "He thinks Dewey's going to run away and disappear. There's a rumor now that he's planning to ship out to sea with his ill-gotten gains. Sail off into the horizon."

Pauline was surprised that no one could follow the real logic of Dewey's obstinacy; the single principle to which he held fast was the simple idea that he wasn't budging. "He's not going anywhere." Apparently she was the only one who understood; it was too hard explaining.

"Are you all right?" Nita said. "You seem all right."

"I'm okay."

"I was going to ask if you wanted to come stay with me." Pauline almost got teary again at this – Nita was really a good sort of person, she thought, in all the ways that counted. But if she began staying in Nita's apartment, it would mean that every day there Nita was being nice to her, and the bright hardness she had when she was with Nita would be ruined and lost. What Pauline wanted, in any case, was to leave Dewey at a time when she could slip off quietly, and now there would be torrents of opposition and accusations of betrayal. She told Nita she would stick it out for the time being. Nita walked with her to the El station and they rode downtown together, without trying to speak over the screech of the train.

When Pauline got back to the apartment, Dewey wasn't home. She heated up a can of soup for herself and she read until she got sleepy. She was dozing in a chair in the living room when she heard the key in the lock. The door pushed open abruptly – she thought from the sound that Dewey must be angry (angry at her, maybe, for not having been home to make dinner). Through the door behind him came Garrett and the bald verse writer who had been one of the first guests at the fund-raising party. Peter was there too, and for some reason he had Walter's dog with him. The dog ran into the room at once; he sniffed Pauline and then he walked through the apartment sniffing at the different pieces of furniture. The others – except for Dewey – were standing around the entrance. "Shut the door, for Christ's sake," Dewey said. "You want to get everybody in the building out here yelling?

"Well, go on," Dewey said. "Search the house. Look in the icebox, open all the books. Get up, Pauline, they're going to want to look under the cushions. See, nothing there. Maybe you want to search Pauline. She's probably got something sewn in her drawers." Dewey groped at Pauline's backside as though he were frisking her there.

"Nobody's making any searches. What's the matter with you?" Garrett said. "I thought you were just going to give us the bankbook if we came over."

"I can't remember where I put it," Dewey said. "I used to know but I forgot."

"When did you forget?" Peter said.

"I'm drunk," Dewey said. "Who got me so drunk?"

The bald man had actually started shuffling through the sofa cushions. He lifted a throw rug to check underneath it. The dog followed, nosing at everything. "Stop it," Garrett said. "What are you doing?"

"This is ridiculous," Peter said.

"I'll sue you for trespassing," Dewey said. "Get your hands off those things. You hear what I'm saying?"

"You better give us the bankbook, Dewey. We want to see what's in there," Garrett said. "Right is right."

The dog was barking. Dewey had smacked the bald man on the back of the neck and he held down the man's head as though he were ducking him in something. "I should throw you out the window," Dewey said. "I'm thinking about it. If I were a certain kind of person, that's what I'd do." He let go his hold and the man stood upright. "I'm sick of this," Dewey said. "You're lucky I don't drop all of you out the window. Nobody leaves me alone. I can't even go to my own house and be alone." (Pauline wondered if he meant her too.) "Look at that dog," Dewey said. "That dog is upset. Here, boy. It's okay." The collie didn't move. Dewey went over and patted its head.

"You won't even think about Adolfo," Garrett said. "You're supposed to be his friend. You don't want him to have whatever's left in the account."

"He can't have it if I say he can't have it," Dewey said. "Poor baby fell off a little ladder. You know how far I fell off a roof one time? I broke a lot more than a shinbone, let me tell you. And I didn't go taking up any charity collections to sponge off people. Don't tell me about poor Adolfo." Dewey spat on the floor (a thing Pauline had made him promise never to do in the house). "Nobody can touch that money unless I say so. Go try. I'd like to see you try."

"Garrett's father wrote a check for two thousand dollars," Peter said. "Remember that? You better give up the bankbook, buddy."

"You tell me how much you need, I might think about going to the bank and getting it."

"You see what it's like talking to him?" Garrett said. "I don't know what to do any more." His voice was getting high and shaky.

"You really want it?" Dewey reached into his jacket and pulled out his wallet. He took a dollar bill from it. "Is that enough?" Pauline had a terrible desire to giggle. She made a faint snorting sound, and Peter gave her a look. "You want more?" Dewey said. He took another bill out. "Not enough?" He shut his billfold. "I'm keeping the rest. You want to see something though?" He opened the wallet again. "See this photograph?" It was a picture of his mother, or so he had always said – a tight-lipped young woman in an 1890s shirtwaist. "You know what this photograph does? It guards the portals, it guards things that belong to me." He reached behind the pocket in his wallet where the photo was, and he pulled out a square brown envelope with NEW YORK SAVINGS printed on it. "See this?" he said, and he threw the bankbook down on the floor. "Why don't you just shove it up your ass?"

When Garrett stooped to pick up the bankbook, Pauline was afraid Dewey was going to kick him – she would have been careful not to turn her back if she had been Garrett. But Dewey only said, "Now, will you please leave?" Pauline felt a great surge of relief that it was over; when the others filed out, it seemed odd to her that she wasn't leaving too.

"What a bunch of pansies," Dewey said, when they were gone. "I don't want you speaking to any of them any more. I mean it. Don't let me see that. Ever."

Pauline walked to the bedroom and began taking off her shoes. She was afraid she would have to answer him if he came into the room and she was frightened that she would say yes, she would swear never to speak to them; she would have to hear herself say it. "Fucking pansies," he said.

She was almost asleep when he got into bed. He reached for her, pressing against her and moving his hands over her breasts. He was urgent but still slow and sinuous in his movements, as though his eagerness made him more thorough. She felt drugged, stirred at some point within her he was moving to reach. She had a thick, feverish sense of something dreamlike and unearthly; then its strangeness made her oddly clear.

When Pauline went to work the next day, the stock boy at Gittelson's tried to joke with her about how pale and "fish-eyed" she looked. "Too much party last night. You got to watch it," he said. "You know what's the best thing for a hangover?" Pauline said she didn't know. "Bromo-Seltzer. You want me to get you a Bromo when I go out?" All day the stock boy made the sounds of a fizzing glass whenever he passed her; he kept doing it until, as he said, he "got a smile out of her."

Dewey was sleeping when she arrived home. He woke up an hour later and she fed him supper. He sat at the table in his undershirt, tearing at the bread in a way that reminded Pauline of her father. "What'd you do to this chicken?" he said. "It's all dry."

"The oven gets too hot," Pauline said.

"I can't eat it. You eat it if you think it's okay."

"I have my own piece."

"No, have another." He put a drumstick on her plate. "You need to practice chewing or you'll lose your front tooth some day like Adolfo. Of course his got knocked out. That's different, isn't it?"

"Very different."

"It's depressing eating with you," Dewey said. "Look at you working over the chicken bone. You're like a dog, you don't care what you eat."

"Yes, I do."

"This is you." Dewey twisted his mouth down on one side and made snapping noises.

Dewey slept on and off all through the next few days. He took long baths and he sat half dressed reading the paper. He was irritable if Pauline went out for any length of time (he said any cripple could do six errands in the time it took her to do one), but in the evenings she stopped at the candy store on the corner and made phone calls to Nita. Nita said, "You're getting so good at these sneak conversations. Maybe we should start leaving messages for each other under rocks."

"In lockers in railway stations," Pauline said. "That's how it's done." She wondered if she did like the intrigue of these calls. She understood perfectly well that the small triumph of doing something without Dewey's knowing was the most misleading kind of victory.

"I saw Peter," Nita said. "You know how much money was left in that bank account? He told me fifty dollars. Dewey ate it up fast, didn't he? Walter thinks it's hilarious – he says that's what happens when you ask a fox to guard the chicken coop, he says it serves everybody right."

"That's like what Dewey thinks." In his better moods Dewey did crow over how well he had done; he made sly remarks about how he had just exercised a little entrepreneurial initiative, and he guessed he had shown them all some of the newer management methods.

"Walter says Garrett ought to pay Dewey for having given him such a great educational experience," Nita said.

"I think he already did," Pauline said. She was about to make a comment about how instruction was really getting expensive nowadays, but she thought the conversation was already getting too brittle. It occurred to her that she was repelled, sometimes, by the idea that the purpose of experience was to provide something so wholesome and unpalatable as *lessons.* She liked it better thinking of experience as something to be acquired, like a wardrobe, a notable collection whose purpose was embellishment.

Nita said, "Is Dewey still hibernating? Walter thinks we should get him a citation from the *Wall Street Journal.* Walter has such a weird sense of humor."

"I'm glad someone's enjoying this."

"Oh, Walter finds a way. You can count on him for that at least. Do you think he's losing weight? I think he is."

Dewey kept the apartment dark while he

slept, and because there were no real doors between the rooms, Pauline read her book in the farthest corner of the kitchen. The low light and the straight chair made it hard to concentrate. Once, when Dewey was up, she tried asking him if he wanted to go out to see a movie, but he gave her a disgusted look and said, "What do you think?"

"You're like a troglodyte in a cave," Pauline said. She knew he wouldn't know what this was. "It's a very primitive form of human being."

There was an impulse in her to goad him into being as nasty as possible. She needed it on the record that he had said certain things, so that she could leave with a feeling of justice on her side. She wanted evidence tallied against him, as though the spoken word were always final proof.

"What did you say?" Dewey said.

"Forget it," Pauline said.

"No, I want to hear it again. I'm a what?"

"It's a kind of cave dweller. I just said that because you never go out."

"It sounds like one of Peter's words. Is it?"

"I don't know."

"Then why do you use it?"

"It fits."

"What did you say?" Dewey grabbed her by

the arm and jerked her to her feet. She tried to sit down again, but he wouldn't let her.

"Stop it!" Pauline yelled.

He mimicked her, whining in a falsetto, "Sto-op it." He wrenched her arm hard and she cried out. Then he was pulling her away from the kitchen toward the living room. She tried to hold her feet down on the floor to keep from moving but all she did was slide. She kept moving with him, no matter what she did. Under the archway to the living room the bump of the threshold made her stumble. He dragged her, letting her body scrape against the floor. He swayed so she knocked into walls. Pauline was shrieking; she listened to herself making pleading noises. She screamed "Stop" and "No" and "Help," and once she shouted "What are you doing?" as though he were a person you could ask questions. She sounded so shrill and futile. When her shoulder hit the wall near the couch, she could hear herself shriek again and she wondered who in the building could hear. She didn't want them to hear – even at the moment she wanted to erase what was happening – the worst part was a kind of final disappointment that this was in her life.

Dewey dragged her until she was kneeling by the sofa. He lifted her up under the arms – she thought he was trying to get her to stand, perhaps as an ending to the whole thing – but he threw her across the sofa head down and he held her face in the cushions.

"Stop it," she said. "I can't breathe."

"I'll show you caves," he said. "You want to see caves?"

Pauline kept trying to raise her head, but he was pressing her face down against the couch. She thought that if she could just move her face to the side, she could get enough air, but the cushions still smothered her when she swerved. Bunny's brother used to do this, Pauline remembered; he would hold Bunny's head down in the bed pillows until she gave way. She had felt sorry for Bunny, but it had seemed at the time only one out of the many humiliations of childhood.

Pauline's head was shoved so close to the cushions that when she panted she got the fabric of the cushions in her mouth – she was afraid she was stifling herself by trying to open her jaws for air. Dewey would have to let her go soon. She thought of people who died by drowning – how long could you go without breathing? – and then she had a surge of real panic. This was how it happened. She felt that wave of recognition that comes with the onset of horror, a sudden clear sense of having always known about this.

Her gasping was very loud inside her head – which made her think there must be a way to get air in through her ears, only she had never learned the way. It came to her as a terrible regret that she had never learned this. The lapse that couldn't be made up: she would be found later as she was now, forever caught, exposed. The accident that would be a permanent caption for her – she would be fixed in it, it would fix the meaning of what had gone before. Her windpipe was trembling as though it could get air from inside, as though it didn't know.

Dewey took his hand away, and she lifted her head. She gulped at the air – at first she was afraid the lungs in her chest might have jammed but they were pumping as they always did, automatic and normal.

"You all right?" Dewey said.

She sat up on the couch.

"Get up and walk around," Dewey said. "That's how you get your breath back after a run or something in sports."

"I don't want to walk," she said.

Dewey stroked her hair. "You get me so crazy sometimes."

She didn't mind his touching her, it was so usual, but she thought it was grotesque that he had gotten so fond all of a sudden. She felt sickened for both of them. He brought her a glass of water from the kitchen and she took it. The glass was from a set she'd bought at the five-and-ten, ugly yellow-green tumblers – mistakes from the first. It pleased her to think she would leave these behind when she left Dewey.

"Don't you want more water than that?" Dewey said. She could get plain fluted ones like Nita had. It was heartening to her that she was thinking ahead so quickly about practical matters.

8

The next day Pauline saw as she was getting dressed that she had bruises on her back from where Dewey had knocked her against the floor and the walls. She had bled in spots without knowing, and there were black-and-blue marks on her shoulders.

At work she had to be careful not to sit back in her chair too sharply, and she kept touching the tender spots through her blouse. It was odd to be walking around with this kind of thing at Gittelson's, as though she really had dropped now into a marginal class. She had a sense of having been involved in some appalling drama, remote from the office atmosphere, of having ventured to extremities, and there was a certain bitter pride in her about this.

When she looked in the mirror in the ladies' room, the marks were already getting more purple and turning yellow at the edges. She thought of Bunny, who must have seen this sort of thing tending all sorts of people in her settlement house. The thought of Bunny's ministrations made her feel a surge of pity for her own back.

On the way home from work she stopped at a pharmacy and picked out a bottle of all-purpose liniment. (The name *liniment* always made her think of that poem of Blake's, which she had misread when she was in high school: "What is it men in women do require?/ The lineaments of Gratified Desire.") "You shouldn't use this if you have cuts," the druggist said, while he was wrapping it. "You have broken skin anywhere?"

"I don't know," Pauline said. She knew this sounded peculiar; she almost wanted to have him guess what had happened or to intuit without saying. And he did give her a kind of anxious glance as he took her money, but perhaps he just had no patience with anyone who didn't know her own symptoms.

Leaving the pharmacy, she cut down a different street than usual, and she passed the Hotel Walpole, where Nita's friend Rose had a room. Rose always said that she had a great view, although the street didn't seem so special to look out on – perhaps she had a room in the back, over a courtyard. She had lived there for years and appeared to have no intention of moving someplace more settled or spacious. Rose was probably not very practical; she had a longtime involvement with a married lover who everyone said was never going to leave his wife. Nita said the trouble with Rose was that she was too lazy.

Pauline thought it would be interesting to live in a hotel – and easy – all you had to do was move in. She was struck by the simplicity of the idea. Perhaps Rose wanted to share, or she might know of a really small room that rented for not too much.

When Pauline walked into the apartment, Dewey was making dinner. He was mixing together some invented dish involving ground beef and macaroni, and he kept tasting it, smacking his lips and saying, "Not bad at all, if I do say so myself." Pauline ate her plateful with appropriate signs of gratitude. She was, in fact, thankful that she didn't have to cook. Dewey made up a long story about how he was going to make his fortune peddling hot lunches in the neighborhood. *Chew at Dewey's,* he would write on the pushcart.

"Where the swank bunch munches," Pauline said. She was aware that it was a mistake to talk with him like this; the worst part of it was that in helping him extend his joke about the lunch wagon, in thinking up names for the hypothetical concoctions he would serve, she was forgiving him. They were sitting over a meal the same way they always did – only with greater cheer, if anything – and there was nothing to mark the fact that he had crossed the line into irredeemable offense. For the first time she was afraid that she would never get away from him, that she had lost her strength and changed for good into someone lesser: that she had grown into her surroundings and this was her place now. Dewey was practicing his street cries as a vendor hawking his ptomaine specials; she did not think that he was charming, but she saw how he might sometimes really be so. When he took the plates away, she said, "I don't feel too good. I think I'm going to just go lie down."

She went to the bedroom and stripped down to her slip and got under the covers. She was almost asleep when Dewey came into the room. He sat on the bed and stroked her shoulder.

"Don't touch," she said. "I'm all sore there."

"Where?"

"All over," she said. "I was bleeding, you know." She felt that she was somehow, in her tone, overplaying this, milking her injuries.

"You got me so mad," he said.

She put her hands over her eyes. "I can't stay here any more," she said. "I have to move out sometime. You know that." She was afraid of what he would do as soon as she said this.

"I know," he said.

"I thought I could live at the Walpole. Rose Brody says it's nice."

"You don't want to live there. For someone like Rose it's fine. She doesn't care where she is."

"No, she really likes it."

"She's a joke. Floating around in those rags she wears for shawls. She looks like a harpy who thinks she's some kind of siren. She has eyes like a cow."

"I like her."

"Well, go and be like her if you want. Do what you want to do. Only you should think about what your situation is going to be. People aren't going to treat you the same as before. You have to face facts, a thing I know you don't like to do."

Her first thought was that people were going to be welcoming her more genuinely once she wasn't with Dewey any more, but that wasn't of course what he meant. He meant that as a girl left over from a "free union" that had been severed, she would slip in her standing to something perilously close to the image he imposed on Rose: weathered and wistful and cowlike, subject to bad luck and unchivalric intentions. It exasperated her to know he thought this. She didn't believe that he was right – his idea of wisdom was always to posit the worst in other people – but he would go on thinking that she had reduced herself in the public judgment, that he had exacted a great sacrifice from her by "taking" her, by sleeping with her. He would believe this no matter what she did.

The next morning was a Saturday. She and Dewey ate a late, slow breakfast, and then he settled in the living room with the newspapers he would spend all day reading. "I think I might go for a walk," Pauline said. "I don't get outside any more."

"Go and walk if you want," Dewey said. "Who's stopping you?"

It was an overcast day, in that stage of city autumn when the weather gets humid and chilly both at once. She walked through Little Italy, down past the courts where Dewey worked, through the deserted alleys of Wall Street, until she got to the dockyards and the harbor. It was supposed to be soothing to walk near water, and it did give her a sense of purpose to stand by the railing and look down at the currents; the water was a murky green up close, fading to a more decorous gray under the horizon. She noted the gradations of color from near to far – olive drab, pewter gray, oyster white – in an effort to absorb the vista with more intelligence. She wondered why painters found this sort of thing interesting – Peter, for instance – and whether the pleasure they got from this was purely abstract, whether it carried with it an apprehension of natural law that was useful in ordinary life.

She stayed until the wind got too strong, and then she walked back, keeping an eye out for To Rent signs in apartment windows; usually she saw a lot of these, but today there weren't any. She kept west of her own neighborhood, until she was a block from Nita's building. Nita wouldn't be out on her terrace in this weather, but she would be home, moving slowly through the day, and she would make hot malted milk if Pauline went there.

Nita answered the door wearing a yellow silk wrapper. Pauline was afraid she must have woken her up – it was almost two, but you never knew – or interrupted her with a lover – not that Nita had any lovers that Pauline knew about. "Oh, come on in, it's fine," Nita said. "I'm in sort of a hurry but not really."

"It's rotten out," Pauline said. "Very bleak. I'd stay in if I were you. Catch up on your mending or something."

"I could darn all my socks," Nita said, "if I wore socks."

"But could you do it without making them lumpy? That's the question. My mother used to do ours so it was like walking on wads of thread after she was through. Probably deformed my feet forever."

"Did you know Peter got married?" Nita said.

"Who did he marry?" She was acutely embarrassed in front of Nita; the whole world probably had known about this for a long time, but she was no longer part of the world. She had become shadowy or undesirable; even to Peter.

"Well, Marjorie, of course. The brunette with the helmet hairdo. The one who looks about twelve. You always liked her."

"Did they have a nice wedding? Did you go to the wedding?"

"Walter went. It was in Oshkosh or some place. Grand Rapids."

"I didn't know."

"They had some kind of honeymoon at a hunting lodge. They're back now, I saw them."

Pauline pictured Peter at the wedding, smiling behind his glasses, shaking hands with Marjorie's relatives. For Marjorie's sake he would do this – he would wear a cutaway coat and nod at people and be docile and cooperative, and he would find all this reasonable and inevitable. Pauline could imagine Dewey marrying her – once he had publicly referred to them as "engaged" – but she couldn't imagine him doing anything *for her sake.* In this she knew herself to be utterly different from Marjorie.

Nita said, "They got some very lavish presents. From relatives. And Walter gave them a painting that's worth really a lot, I think."

Pauline thought that Marjorie, who was so snappy and self-assured anyway, must feel that she had slipped very easily into her destiny. And it was a pleasant enough purpose to have in life, to be Peter's wife. Unlike Bunny, Pauline held no theory against marriage. And yet it always surprised her when people she knew got married – "so soon," as she phrased it to herself – although at home she had known girls well below her own age who were married, even then.

Nita had changed into a slip and was busy hooking her stockings. Walter was picking her up soon, she said, to go to a tea uptown that somebody was giving for the happy couple. "You could come too," she said. "I could lend you a dress."

"I would just spill something on it," Pauline

said. She was genuinely shocked that Nita would expect her to go some place uninvited. Nita of course believed that an extra girl, of the right age and personality, was always welcome; for herself, perhaps she was right.

For a while Pauline thought of leaving the city. Other people had packed up and sailed for Europe or moved to the country. The country seemed more formidable in a way but certainly more within reach. Walter's friend, the sculptor with the brushed-back haircut, was living in upstate New York, and Rose knew a couple who had a place year-round in Provincetown.

In conversations with Nita, Pauline complained about the noise of the El, she said she was sick of being jostled on the street at lunchtime, and she began to mind these things. She did feel put upon, tried by unfair stresses. And what was she here for? She had slipped from the old ties, she was on the periphery. Perhaps, in the country, she was about to be someone plainer and purer. Perhaps that was next, a house with printed curtains, quiet habits.

Nita also knew people who rented in the mountains, and she was ready to look for Pauline. (She said she would do anything so long as Pauline moved out of Dewey's.) Pauline did go so far as to bring up the subject with Dewey. "It'll teach you a lot," Dewey said. "You need more contact with out-of-door things. It'll make you not so spoiled."

The weather was by now getting cold – it was almost November. As she got wet and chilled just walking around in New York, the idea of living in a rural area began to seem more outlandish. She didn't like to imagine being away from heated apartments, nearby shopping. She thought there was something wrong with her that she could have wanted to immure herself in a bare landscape, without friends or promise of work. She was losing her grasp of the most obvious things; there was something wrong with her.

It was Nita, finally, who found her a place to move to in the city – an apartment on Bedford Street, next to where a friend of a friend lived. It had been vacant for weeks and had a smell of damp wood and old paper, like an attic. It *was* almost an attic, a fifth-floor walk-up whose cupboard-sized bedroom actually had an eaved ceiling on one side. From the window of this room you could lean out and see the roofs of other buildings. Walter said it reminded him of apartments in Europe.

Pauline felt panicked when she looked at the place, as though she were about to embark on something utterly foolhardy and had already gone too far to turn back. It was a nice apartment – "picturesque" she and Nita said, only half in jest – but she was overcome with a secret certainty that she was making a mistake in leaving Dewey. He had (whatever his reasons) chosen her, he had taken her in preference to all other people, he had liked her best; to everyone else, she was only secondary.

But the arrangements for moving went on and she let them. She went to the landlord's office, a woebegone chamber in a building in midtown, and signed the lease. She felt hazy and unwell the whole time. She didn't tell Dewey. He had been very genial lately, at his best really. He was working again at the courts, and he left each day looking crisp and resigned in his suit. She dropped hints. "Who'll cook this for you when I'm gone?" she would say, or "You can put that in the closet when I'm not here any more with all my stuff."

In the end, when she told him she was leaving for sure at the end of the month, he seemed to believe it had been his idea all along. "It's better for you," he said. "At first it won't be easy, you won't know what to do. But you'll make progress."

The day she left he wanted to carry the suitcases for her. She had not expected this and was quite horrified at the offer, although it seemed to be impossible to refuse without being ridiculously petulant. She hated the idea of his seeing the apartment. She had expected to disappear into it, to keep it inviolate of his appraisal. It had almost no furniture, only a cot bed the other tenant had left and an enameled metal kitchen table, with one chair, that the super had found for her in the basement.

Dewey was whistling when he walked through the door, showing his insouciance under the weight of the suitcases. He continued whistling while he opened one valise and began putting things away in the closet. "Some of these clothes should probably just get thrown out," he said. "Look at this jacket. How many decades have you had this?"

"Well, I wouldn't throw it *out.*" Pauline was sweeping the bare living room.

"What you should do is make the super paint the place. Get rid of that depressing garret look." Dewey fixed a broken chain on a window sash, and then he decided to fix the other windows, a project that took up a good part of the afternoon and involved trips to the hardware store. He made her look at each sash when he was done. "See, up and down, perfectly smooth."

Pauline was nervous around him; she applauded the windows with shrill fake enthusiasm. It was confusing that he was there, as though she hadn't understood something properly. Still, he was being helpful. He went out and got food for supper, and afterward he sat drinking from a flask while she scrubbed out the icebox.

"Gets you tired," she said, when she sat down finally. "Aren't you tired?"

"It's about that time." Dewey went into the bathroom. He was in there for several minutes, and then from the sounds she understood that he was washing himself to get ready for bed. When he came out, he took off all his clothes except for his shorts and his undershirt, and he lay flat on the bed, waiting for her. Even in silhouette, his shape on the bed looked active and factual, despite the fervor of her wishing him away. There was no getting rid of him until the morning; it was too late now.

She undressed quickly and put on her nightgown. When she got into bed, he pulled her next to him and began fondling her breasts. At first she lay still and made no response, but then as he was about to roll on top of her she turned away and slid to the other side of the bed, so that there was no contact between them (or as little contact as there could be in a cot bed). She had not expected to do this, but the instinct of avoidance was so strong in her that she was suddenly clear and forceful. Dewey said, "What's wrong?" and she didn't answer. Later he said, "Are you sure?" And then she could tell he had fallen asleep; she could hear his steady breathing in the room.

The bed was set at an angle aslant from the wall – she hadn't been able to decide how it should go so they'd left it that way – and she had a sense now that the bed was floating. It rose, unanchored to anything; it swayed in the dark. There was an awfulness in the room, from the bleakness of what had just happened. But Dewey would stay away from her now, he would know himself defeated. What seemed terrible to her was the way his physical eagerness for her had become hideous; an old simplicity had been broken.

Even when they had fought all the time she had found him (as she used to tell Nita) "tempting." The continuance of that desire had been a kind of verity to her, an essential truth underneath the imperfect form of her attraction to Dewey. Now she was no longer tempted to anything; a trait had left her; she felt as though her character had contracted and grown shallower.

Pauline, in the days following, spent long stretches of time reading the newspapers – as if she had taken over this job from Dewey. Gangsters had drowned a man in a burlap sack, a dead baby had been found in a garbage can, Sacco and Vanzetti were not getting a new trial no matter who else confessed to the robbery, bums in Battery Park were dying from drinking wood alcohol, whole villages in Asia were starving from famine. The cruelty of these reports blended with her sense of being newly exposed to everything, without advice or company.

The bareness of the apartment reminded her of her room at Mrs. Poganyi's. She was homesick for that time – it depressed her to find herself sinking into nostalgia. It seemed like an illusion – an error in logic – to think of certain periods as counting more, since all time passed at the same rate.

She had begun plucking her eyebrows again, and she wore, as much as possible, the one skirt that didn't look dowdy on her, although it was silk crepe and unseasonably light for winter. She kept it as fresh-looking as she could by sponging the soiled spots with benzine – until one night when she was cleaning it in a hurry before she went out, a cigarette ash fell on the wet fabric and a hole flamed through the front of the skirt. She wept then – the sudden spurt of fire had frightened her – and she was angry with herself for smoking a cigarette near dry-cleaning fluid. How was she ever going to manage to do anything if she didn't have more sense than that? It was the sort of thing her mother would have done (not that her mother smoked). And it was all made worse by knowing that it was ridiculous to cry over an article of clothing, that even her suffering had become small and ignominious.

At work Miss Pfeiffer was out a whole two weeks because her five-year-old niece had died of diphtheria. Pauline had never thought of Miss Pfeiffer as being bound by affection to anything so messy and soft as a small child. It was terrible to think of her secret familial tenderness and her grief. In her absence, Pauline sat at the front desk and stayed extra hours; she was tired from the pileup of work at Gittelson's and from a slow, pressing sense of discouragement. Sometimes she thought of contacting Dewey. She could leave a message by calling the candy store on his corner or she could send him a wire: THE JIG IS UP. LET'S BE FRIENDS AGAIN. Perhaps he had really been her one true friend.

She did remember how much she had wanted to get away from him, and out of respect for this sentiment she waited out the impulse to summon him. She missed having to cook for him, despite the fact that he had often criticized her cooking. Eating was more haphazard without him. Sometimes she ate out with Nita; there were different restaurants Nita liked to go to now, currently in favor and new to Pauline – places with black-lacquered woodwork, more designed and sleek, less cheaply cheerful than before. She eyed the men at different tables with twinges of interest – sudden little rises of erotic longing. But her sense of beginning again made her slightly cautious. A clean slate: she could take up with someone untainted by anything she already knew, a man who spoke another language or had habits formed in other circles.

She was walking home from work one night, on her own block, when she heard someone say, "You gonna fall on your nose you keep walking like that." She was startled – it was a moment before she recognized Adolfo. He walked with a cane, leaning and rocking, and his front tooth was gone – he looked gruesome and damaged – and then rakish, like a pirate, when he smiled. When he spoke, certain sounds came out as a lisp, as if he were making fun of someone.

"So you taking care of yourself all right?" he said.

Pauline said she was fine. If not for Dewey he would have stayed in bed longer, healed better, been less disfigured. She was ashamed to look at him. What had she done to help? She had acted as if none of it really mattered. "You okay?" she said.

"Sure. Too bad about you and Dewey. You couldn't work out your differences, huh? I always thought you were such a nice couple."

"Well, you know. That's how it goes sometimes."

"Without a license they can go take a walk whenever they want."

She had an impulse to offer him money, to make up for what Dewey had done. She supposed he wouldn't take it, even if she had any to offer.

"So you learned something – get a ring first. You'll probably find another fellow. I got confidence in you. Smile now – let me see you smile. Don't look mopey, that's the main thing. Nobody likes that."

Pauline said, "You look rested. You look good."

"The rest is over," he said. "I'm back to work."

"Where?"

"Vera's, where else? I been there nine years, I'm not leaving. Vera doesn't like my new look too much, but I wasn't getting tips just for my handsome appearance before. Customers ask what happened, I tell them they should see the other guy."

"They believe you?" She was thinking – a waiter with a cane? Maybe he didn't use the cane at work.

"I don't make it up – I tell them a story that's true, it's just not how I broke my leg. The guy I was fighting with – this is thirty years ago – I bet he doesn't have much of a lip even now. It doesn't grow back after certain things. I broke his nose in three places. You can hear when you do that. He was a mess. You should've seen. Nah, you wouldn't want to see stuff like that."

"Not me," Pauline said.

"Blood all around the eyes, he couldn't see for the blood. You don't want to hear."

"No." She didn't.

"I'm sorry."

"Well, you take very, very good care of yourself," she said.

"So go find another fellow fast," Adolfo said. "Just because one ditches you doesn't mean anything. You got time but hurry up, that's my advice."

Nita had begun an affair with Walter. She announced this to Pauline over supper one night – she was all slyness and mock embarrassment. "You know something else?" she said. "Fat men aren't so bad."

"I never said so."

"Also, Walter's not that fat. It's those Oxford bags he wears for trousers, they make him look wider. I'm trying to talk him into getting something a leetle more tailored."

Pauline supposed they would get married – that would be the end of all this. "It must be nice to be with someone you know so well."

"Well, it's very comfortable. I can just talk to him like a regular person."

It struck Pauline that none of the men she was drawn to was ever a regular person. She didn't associate sexual attraction with direct discourse – she wanted obliqueness, fleeting impressions, hints at hidden mutualities. All the same, she envied Nita now.

She saw Nita and Walter together not long after that, at a new speakeasy. Walter was fairly drunk by the time Pauline saw him – he had his arm around Nita and he was lifting her off the floor in a kind of one-handed bear hug. Nita was saying, "You're hiking up my dress, you're rumpling me," but she was laughing.

Later Walter stood at the bar, playing the match-stacking game with a group of other men, and Nita came over to the table where Pauline was sitting with Rose. "Walter likes his betting, you know," she said. "Look at him. His betting and his crossword puzzles. Yesterday he had me up all night looking up words for him in the dictionary. Till dawn." She seemed somewhat proud of this.

"Woman's work is never done," Rose said.

Nita seemed very happy at this time. She had developed a great interest in going to formal hotel dining rooms that had supper dancing – places Pauline never would have thought of choosing – and she referred to them by affectionate shortened forms of their names, which at first had to be translated for Pauline. Nita had gotten Walter to buy her an evening cloak, a great sweeping thing, blue-green velvet with a black and white silk lining. Walter referred to it as his walking deficit.

Nita still played violin at the restaurant, and in the midst of her new fondness for more conservative luxuries she decided there was a customer there who would be perfect for Pauline. He was a young business lawyer – quite good-looking, actually much better-looking than Dewey. On Nita's arranging, he took Pauline out to a play and to supper. Pauline didn't dislike him – he wasn't hard to talk to and he was intelligent, although he seemed a bit angry in advance over how she might regard him and he said things like "Of course I'm just one of your Wall Street stick-in-the-muds" or "A materialist like me would say." She wondered how Nita had thought they would suit each other and whether there was a plane of sheer personality on which they were supposed to find enjoyments in common. She let him kiss her at the end of the night – he seemed to think the evening had gone well – and she sank fully into the kiss, as though she were showing off for him.

Twice Dewey had been waiting for her outside the apartment when she'd come home from work. And he had gone upstairs with her, drunk the apricot brandy that Rose had given her as a house gift, talked about how he was thinking of being a news reporter after all his court experiences, and left only when she'd claimed unnamed places she had to go.

On the street she always glanced at the passing shapes of men, relieved when they weren't Dewey. It was amazing how many people looked like him. The capacity for variation within the same type of build and facial features was apparently very great. It made her feel how large the city was and how packed with multiple forms. After a while she began to hope that he had shipped out with the Merchant Marine after all, although there was no real chance of this – he had never talked about it himself; it had only been a rumor invented by other people. She didn't think it was wrong of her to want him to vanish over the horizon, but it worried her that she was so eager to never mention him again, she would have been happy to act as if he'd never happened. In this she was no better than Dewey, who was always stopping and starting over without a trace.

Nita was distinctly annoyed that Pauline hadn't liked the lawyer better, and then she was amused when Pauline took a mild fancy to an actor she met at one of Walter's dinner parties. He was a suavely quiet, slow-speaking sort of person, and they went out with Nita and Walter to a nightclub after the party. The club was in a big room, draped and tented with mauve-colored cloth; a band played light-tempoed jazz, and a woman in a white dress with silver flowers at her hip sang songs about men who had treated her badly. The actor spoke to Pauline in low tones about the crying need for new ideas in the theater; he used clichés with a blind assurance that made them sound solid and full of merit. Pauline liked it when he put his hand over hers; for a while his fingers tapped playfully on her wrist in time to the music. She felt happy in a thin, teenagey way.

"Isn't it nice here?" Nita said. She and Walter had just had an argument because she had ordered something called a pousse-café, a fussy concoction involving five liqueurs arranged in layers, held in suspension by their different weights. Walter said no serious drinker would be caught within miles of something like that, and he threatened to move to another table to preserve his reputation. Nita was now sipping from her glass with a look of delicate greed. Her expression was more languorous and dreamy than was characteristic of her, and it struck Pauline that Nita must feel that she was living more fully than she ever had. And it was all bound up with the spending of money. The sheer expense of things must be to her like a pushing away from old frontiers, a moving into wider experience.

Pauline tasted Nita's drink with close attention, making approving sounds. It had a full, subtle taste (maybe a little sweet), but she was aware that it didn't thrill her the way it did Nita. Being with Nita made her feel that it should; perhaps there was something stubbornly mediocre in her, unsusceptible. Pauline thought suddenly of her mother, who would have been utterly dumbfounded not only by the arcane mixture of liqueurs with their French names but by the glass, whose narrow bud-vase shape would have been so unlike anything she'd put to her lips before. It wasn't, Pauline thought, just from ignorance that her mother would have found all of this alien – the general arduousness of most of her life would have made it seem bafflingly childish to her.

Nita and Walter had another tiff about whether the waiter was Irish – they squabbled in little spurts, like pigeons. Pauline and the actor danced, moving around the floor in slow gliding shuffles. She felt dimly as though she were having a good time. The actor said, "You have a nose like a Renaissance painting, did anybody ever tell you that?"

She saw the actor, whose name was Alfred, several times after that. He had such an irrefutable handsomeness – a well-planed, even face – that it was pleasant just being in public with him.

But she was afraid the whole time of running into Dewey. She had a fear that Dewey might be lurking in the doorway waiting at the end of the night if she ever brought Alfred home. She didn't so much think of Alfred's shock as of the two men flailing at each other, Alfred turned snarling and abusive like Dewey.

Normally Alfred's features were untroubled, almost motionless; he was the sort of person who smiled knowingly. His mouth had a kind of healthy coolness to it when he kissed. At first she thought she was going to sleep with him – he was always very nice to her – but she liked him less and less each time. Still, in being with him she had a sense of getting on with things and moving forward.

She was sorry that she didn't end up with something like a miniature portrait of Alfred to keep, as she might have in another era. As it was, once they no longer saw each other, she had nothing to show for it. And since he had been (to her, at least) so colorless, finally, she retained very little of him.

The whole process seemed too wasteful. She didn't mind forgetting things – she rightly considered herself to have a modern elasticity of temperament – but what vanished out of thought couldn't be of use.

Nita said the important thing was to remain in circulation, although in her own life now she touted the joys of staying still; she seemed quite grateful to have found a resting place in Walter, free of jolts and rude surprises. No more to roam. The sort of peaceful setting in which there wasn't a constant strain to improvise, to rise to the occasion.

Now that she wasn't seeing Alfred any more, Pauline spent more time in the apartment. At home after work, she sewed. She made curtains and cushions and even a foolish-looking ruffle for the light fixture. She had frightened her family by admitting that she'd moved one more time – her father believed that she was fleeing to avoid rent bills – but they had let her take back fabric from the store. She had no sewing machine so she stitched by hand like a small girl with a sampler. It was slow work but steadying and soothing. When she went out into the street afterward it was hard to adjust her eyes to distances or to objects moving at the periphery of sight.

She was easily startled; once she thought a discarded heap of brown paper was a dog about to lunge at her, and she froze when a newspaper page blew across her path and grazed her ankles. There was, of course, no shortage of real things to be pained by in the neighborhood. Groups of children foraged through the garbage. Bums slept on the benches in a small park nearby; in winter they tried to cover themselves with flattened cardboard cartons. Once in the same park an old woman suddenly lifted her skirt at Pauline – she was naked underneath, and she kept flapping her skirt up and down; she was making faces and cackling, as though a lifetime of being asked to lift her skirt for sex had reduced her to a harpyish jeering. It's driven her crazy, Pauline thought. The woman turned her back and shook her rear end, as Pauline went farther down the street, and it occurred to Pauline then that she might be the one, after all, that the woman was jeering at.

9

Pauline could never get used to the fuss people made over Christmas. Nita spent enormous amounts of time shopping, and she thought it had been improvident of Pauline to drop Alfred so soon before the holidays. Nita planned to get a suit made for Walter as his present – something well-tailored in dark wool, which Pauline was sure he would hate.

Nita had gone to Macy's toy department with Walter to help him pick out a gift for his son. The son was ten years old and they sent him a red wagon – Pauline thought he was probably much too old for it, but Nita said he was just an ungrateful brat if he didn't go wild for the one Walter got for him, not a cheap item.

Walter's wife (they were almost divorced, Nita said; there were just some legal things that had to be done) had recently mailed him a copy of the boy's school picture, a gesture Walter considered in the worst possible taste.

"He resents that sort of thing; she should've known," Nita said. "The pull at the heart-strings."

They had no pity for the wife; she seemed so old to them. They both disapproved of her for falling back on methods that were so unattractive. And it was true that neither of them had ever had to resort to an appeal to responsibility.

Nita had decided that Walter should take her to the Ritz-Carlton for Christmas dinner, but Walter kept telling her they were going to a nice cafeteria instead. Nita had refused categorically to spend the day at anyone's house – she said it would only bring back terrible memories of her screamingly boring childhood in Wilkes-Barre – but in the evening she had consented to go to a big, dressy party given by some couple Walter had just met, and she wanted to take Pauline with them.

Pauline was surprised at how much she really couldn't bear this idea. It made her angry to think of working to keep up with a certain kind of conversation. It was Rose who saved her finally. Rose was very eager to have Pauline come to the country with her for Christmas. She had friends with a big house upstate – zillions of guests were coming and there would be lots of people there Pauline would like.

Pauline wasn't sure she *would* like them. (Ever since Dewey had spoken against Rose, Pauline had been afraid that Rose wasn't all that discriminating – with her fluttery wardrobe and her breezy amusement at everything, she was maybe too tolerant, too mild and forgiving. This of course made her easy to be with, certainly much easier than Nita.) Rose said they were going to roast a suckling pig in the fireplace, and this finally won Pauline over; it sounded so rollicking and medieval.

It was a pretty ride up on the train, with the Hudson visible outside the window for most of the way, very close and rippling with light. At the station where they got off, everything looked bleak and bare. The ground was all frozen puddles and dingy patches of snow. They took a taxi through the cold, quiet town and past it, down a dirt road. At one point the driver seemed to be turning directly into the woods – they were on a drive that was hardly more than a bridle path. The driver, exposed in his front seat, had to keep pushing away the branches that snapped at him from the sides. Pauline was excited then, elated at going so deep into the pinewoods to a place so secluded, and she gave Rose a pleased look. The taxi stopped suddenly, almost before they saw the house.

The house was painted barn red and had ripped screens on the front porch; someone had hung a stuffed deer's head on the door, with plaid ribbons on the antlers for Christmas decorations.

When they rang the bell, they could hear the sound of a baby crying from inside. A girl of about six opened the door for them. "I'm being the butler," she said. "Did you know that?"

"Aren't you Jeeves?" Rose said. "You look just like Jeeves."

"I'm *Martha.*"

"She works cheap but she's noisy," a man behind her said. Rose was busy embracing people. A Christmas tree took up a good part of the living room, and Pauline almost fell against it when Rose made a sudden turn. The guests were a mixed group – dressed in everything from tiered chiffon to rusty wools – and they were older, on the whole, than Pauline was used to.

A very pretty woman in an apron walked by carrying the baby who'd been crying when they'd come in. Pauline said, "Calmed down now, has it?"

"For a minute. Are you going to be a good boy now? Yes, you are."

"He's very handsome."

"He is, isn't he? You can hold him, if you like."

Pauline wasn't really eager to hold the baby – from the years with Solly she had a definite fear that he was going to pee on her through his diapers – but she took him and tried to walk through the crowded room jiggling him against her shoulder to keep him from crying.

"He likes that," a man said. "Wants to see what's happening."

Carrying the baby evidently made her very approachable. A couple came over to admire him – she had to explain that he wasn't hers – and she ended up having a long talk with them about whether orphans could ever be happy in later life. Pauline said, "Why not? It's a free country," but the other woman said that the affection of substitute parents was always inadequate. "Great people have been orphans," Pauline said. "Poe was an orphan."

She realized as she said this that he wasn't a good example of serenity in later life, but a man who had just joined them said, "She's right. Don't argue with history, Frances." He was a thick-necked man in his thirties, with a heavy, old-fashioned mustache and beautiful strong teeth. "And Harold agrees with me," he said, patting the baby's arm.

The baby's mother was in no apparent hurry

to take him back, and he fell asleep quite sweetly in Pauline's lap when she sat down. The man said, "There he is. The first one to pass out at the party." She felt a little funny using the baby as a prop, like those women who walked dogs to meet men. She noticed that holding the baby made her feel like someone very kindly and reliable. It was quite relaxing, the sensation of being that sort of person.

Someone in the kitchen was banging a pot with a spoon – this was meant to be the dinner gong. The mother came finally to take the baby away, and the man with the mustache, who said his name was Mack, stayed with her as they went in to dinner. He had a nice, courtly way of guiding her to her seat with his hand at her back. Rose, who was at the other end of the table, waved and mouthed the question, How was she doing? and Pauline made a round OK sign. She looked down at the long table, where people were passing dishes of food and cutting up portions for children, and there was a small rush of sadness in her; she was touched at their wholesomeness.

Mack kept piling things on her plate – he was like a playful uncle – he tried to make her take two kinds of soup, extra dumplings, biscuits on the side. Everyone rose and applauded when the suckling pig was brought in on a platter. (Pauline thought it looked disgustingly lifelike, with the apple in its mouth.) There was a contest between two of the men about who could carve better, and they had a mock duel with the carving set. Martha, the six-year-old, thought this was so funny that she got the hiccups. Pauline showed her how to take nine gulps of water from the wrong side of the glass – one of the few remedies from her mother that really worked – but the girl kept giggling before she could get past the first few gulps.

Mack tried to put a giant wedge of pork on her plate but she stopped him. She'd been eating nonkosher food since she left home – she loved shellfish and she didn't mind bacon and once she had even eaten an Italian sausage at a street fair – but fresh pork was still something she couldn't get down; it would've been like eating opossum or camel meat, too alien to be palatable. Mack said he understood and he got her the apple for her plate instead. "My father's like that," he said. "He follows all these health regimens – malted barley and raw vegetables, keeping the temple of the body sacred – and he used to read a lot of Shaw. No feasting on the carcasses of dead animals."

She saw that he had assumed she was a vegetarian. It would be too difficult now to explain that she wasn't without insulting his father.

"I think it's nice to be answerable for everything you do," he said. "To know that you're not sinning with your dinner. I think that's what my father found rewarding about it. Of course, it's a very self-conscious way to live. Chewing every morsel of food twenty times – that's what he does now, it's his latest routine."

"But it's not really possible, the not sinning. I mean you can't go through a whole meal without doing an injury in a way. You're always taking it out of someone else's mouth, aren't you?" She was surprised at what she seemed to be so certain about.

"Oh, I don't know," he said.

"Did they make you chew your food twenty times too?" Pauline said.

"Oh, no, they let me be a noble savage. I had an easy time of it as a kid, a very progressive childhood."

"And look how well you turned out," Pauline said.

"Did I?" He flashed her a half smile from under his mustache – he was really very dazzling when he tried to look sly.

After dinner everyone sat in the living room, a little stupefied from all the food, drinking the brandy that Rose had had the foresight to bring. Martha played "It Came Upon a Midnight Clear" over and over on the piano. Mack said his house was farther down the road, but in the summer with the windows open he could stand in his front yard and hear Martha practicing. "Not from inside, though," he said. "The house is stone. It's like being inside a giant cistern."

"Do you work around here?" Pauline said.

"Well, I don't do anything really. Along those lines. You mean a job – is that what you meant?"

"A job, yes." She sounded too abrupt, like her father.

"For a while I taught Latin and Greek at a boys' boarding school, but I never really meant to make a career out of it."

"I took Latin." She was afraid then that he was going to address something to her in the language and expect her to answer, like Miss Oughton.

"Did you?" he said. "I might have known."

"I've forgotten it all, I think."

"It would come back if you needed it."

When would I need it? Pauline thought. But maybe you did have a need to consult certain authors, the way you might need to do physical exercise or to visit the seashore.

Mack said he was working on a new translation from Epictetus. "It's wonderful working up here. Sometimes when I get snowed in I don't see another living thing for days at a time. It's very peaceful." Pauline wondered if this was meant as light sarcasm but he looked perfectly earnest. And it was nice to think of him sitting over his Epictetus in a room like a rock cavern with white at the windows.

She told him about Miss Oughton and how she used to drill them about things like how many foot soldiers in a legion, how many tribunes in the government. Mack, it turned out, had never gone to high school, had never gone to any school before college. His parents – his father especially – had taught him and his brothers, sometimes they had had tutors, and they had all read a great deal at will. Pauline had never heard of anything like this; it was quite staggering to her, a childhood so emptied of ordinary schooldays. She felt, in looking at him, a faintly superior sense of her own vitality, as though he'd just told her he'd spent his youth as a convalescent. There was a glamour in it too, though, the privilege of that privacy.

The woman whose baby Pauline had held announced that they needed someone to go out to the shed for more firewood. "Want to come with me, just to get a little fresh air?" Mack said. Pauline had no desire at all to go out in the cold but she said yes out of being pleased that he asked.

"Me too. I'm going too," Martha said.

It was still early evening – the sky was a bright, back-lighted blue. Pauline was relieved that it wasn't darker, although they were only going across the yard. She had never really been any place more countrified than the Jersey shore or a Newark reservoir, and she was uneasy, wary of hidden animal life in the trees or in the dirt.

"I can stay up late tonight," Martha said. "I could stay up as late as I want. Did you know that?"

"No," Pauline said.

"I've been up late a lot."

"You do seem very alert."

"Alice Leidecker always has to go to bed early. Her parents think she's a baby. How old do you think I look?"

"Forty-two," Mack said.

"No, really." Too bad, Pauline thought, that she couldn't tell Martha to get lost the way she could Solly, and Martha was too little to take a hint. Her chaperonage made Pauline feel distinctly deprived; Mack's figure walking next to her seemed all the more silent and electric.

They had reached the shed. Mack handed

Martha a stack of branches to carry back. "The birch'll give off a nice smell when it burns," he said.

"I used to know a song about birches," Pauline said. "In Russian. My aunt taught me. I don't really know what the words mean, but it's something about birches."

"You look Russian. The cheekbones."

"I'm not really."

"Are you going back tonight? Do you have to go back? Or are you staying over?"

She was surprised, caught off guard – for him to suggest (as he seemed about to do) that she stay the night with him indicated that he had a completely different nature than she had thought, more sexual and more impatient. It was a little arrogant of him not to expect that he had to spend more time with her first. But there was something very forthright about the suddenness – for a moment she had a kind of pleasurable shock at the audacity of it.

"I'm supposed to stay over at the house with Rose."

Martha was walking ahead of them, singing a song about a little green frog on a log in a bog.

"That's good. I was hoping," he said. "So you'll be here tomorrow."

"For a while. In the morning at least." She got over being disappointed almost at once –

she was extremely relieved that she hadn't said anything to give away what she'd thought he meant. But she felt as if she were a rougher sort of person than he was, bulkier and less delicate. She had the natural desire to eradicate this difference between them, to modify and subvert him.

She and Rose were given Martha's room to sleep in – Martha was excited about their being there and she kept rushing in to show them her doll collection until she was finally carted off to her parents' room to sleep.

Rose said, "Well, you did all right for yourself, didn't you? Is he nice? He looks nice."

"I hope he's not too nice."

"With a little coaching I'm sure he'll be fine." They were both undressing as they spoke, undoing hooks and rolling down stockings.

"I think he's kind of a hermit. He stays in all the time and translates. He's a Greek and Latin specialist."

"Well, there you are. His mind is probably seething. Probably reading dirty poems all day about orgies and Nubian slave girls."

"I'll have to ask."

"He probably can't even say some of that stuff in English. It's probably too complicated."

"Maybe he can draw me pictures."

Rose had lit a cigarette and she was sitting on the bed in her underwear. Pauline had never asked Rose's age – she was probably around thirty, with those straggly bits of gray and a tiredness around the eyes. But her figure was perfectly slender and matter-of-fact, no different from Pauline's. For some reason Pauline found this depressing – not that she wished Rose a more matronly shape, but she had always thought of thirty as a stage far enough away to produce marked alterations of some sort. And here was Rose, fresh, unfaded, still waiting.

Rose was moving Martha's dolls off the bed. "She's got so many toys," Pauline said. "I didn't have this many toys."

"They all do now," Rose said. "My friend's kid is even younger. He's always buying her stuff." By friend she meant her lover, the one who was married. Pauline already knew something about him – not facts exactly but the bits of behavior that Rose was always having to interpret. Pauline had by now told her things about Alfred and about Dewey. It was impossible not to talk about men; Pauline didn't mind this – it seemed to her as substantial a field of inquiry as anything, and she was still at an age where nearly all intensities attached to sex.

Rose, lying next to her in Martha's bed, fell asleep within minutes; Pauline listened to her breathing and thought of Mack. She had such a strong sense of his being nearby, as though he were somewhere in the house instead of up the road. She imagined him coming to the room, and Rose sleeping through it all.

Her idea about Mack (it seemed essential to have at least a hypothesis) was that he was very good, very staunch and true-blue, the sort of person who expected himself to behave decently at all times. She was a little worried about his being too unworldly, despite his age – but there was a great longing in her for something pacific and still. She thought of Nita and how she was thriving now because of Walter.

Mack was there when she went down to breakfast. Martha and the baby were making a racket, the baby's father was singing "Jingle Bells" in a goofy voice to distract them, and the mother was at the stove. "You better turn down the heat or the eggs'll get all dry," Mack was saying.

"Happy Boxing Day, all," Rose said.

"It's freezing," Martha said. "Don't you think it's freezing in the house?"

"My nose is an icicle," Rose said. "My behind has turned into two snowballs."

"Watch it," Mack said. "Little pitchers."

"Don't be so stuffy, Mack," the mother said. "It isn't necessary."

"What ravishing six-year-old whose name begins with M is going to drink all her milk today?" the father said. Pauline was bringing the plates to the table.

Mack was not pleased with the way the eggs turned out. He seemed stern today; maybe he'd been jollier than usual the night before from the drinking. His sternness irked her, made her want to change him at once, make him more affable. She hovered over him, taking his plate when he was done, asking him if he wanted more coffee. She was as seductively attentive as she could be with other people present (even so she was probably making a spectacle of herself), and he liked it; by the end of the meal he was conversing amiably about itchy woolen underwear and heating problems in old houses. "Nobody thinks a fireplace takes any trouble to maintain but it does," Mack said.

"It would be fun to be a chimney sweep, don't you think?" Pauline said. She was saying whatever came into her head. They had shut out the others – who else but two sexually interested people would go on talking about clogged smoke ducts? He offered to show Pauline how he had rebuilt the fireplace at his house.

Rose said, "Go ahead. I'm not in a hurry."

Pauline chattered on the way to the house, talking about how it was really healthier to sleep in a cold room (a thing she actively disbelieved) and how she'd never gotten sick the whole winter she lived at Mrs. Poganyi's. From the outside, Mack's house was like a lumpy stone fortress; inside it was plastered and ordinary, small rooms with dusty windows.

He did show her the fireplace – he had done something minor about changing the flue – and then he laughed and said, "You didn't really want to see that." He was reaching out his arms, about to embrace her as he said this – she thought it was ungallant of him to laugh at her for being willing – but she was enormously glad that they were holding each other finally; this part seemed at least simple and clear.

She was very sure of herself, very calm. It surprised her how quickly they moved through the beginning stages – he was quite deft and hasty once he got started; the more aroused she was, the more everything seemed faultless and straightforward and smooth: she knew utterly how to do this. Later, when they were lying down, it struck her that he was unusually graceful, a thing you wouldn't guess to look at him. In a sense, of course, the whole thing was very abstract – he was like the silhouette of a man, a figure moving behind the light, not so singular, almost without a name, despite the intensely specific immediacy of touch. She didn't mind this, it didn't bother her that it wasn't more "personal"; it seemed elevated and featureless. For some reason she kept thinking of the beach, despite the cold – of lying on the beach.

When they were almost asleep in his bedroom afterward (who would have guessed that he had a flannel coverlet with pictures of horses on it, a childhood leftover?), she said, "The light in this room is so nice."

She was very happy and relaxed; it was the most relaxed she had been with him. He said, "I'm so glad you're here." She was sorry they had to get up so she could leave. When they were dressing she could tell he was watching her. She moved easily, stepping into her clothes, still very sure.

On the train ride home Rose had the good sense not to talk to her. She must have seen that Pauline was in that state of reverie and self-congratulation that is too powerful to be interrupted easily. Pauline, although she was too far gone to emerge, felt strange having such highly colored reminiscences with another person present.

She was looking forward to giving the news to Nita – Nita was such a great booster now of the whole concept of forming a couple. She phoned Nita directly from the train station, after she'd said good-bye to Rose. "Well, I had a happy holiday," Pauline said. "Very festive. How did your Christmas go?"

"What Christmas?" Nita said.

"The one yesterday."

"Well, I don't know really. It wasn't on the calendar. I suppose there were people who went to church or exchanged presents in their crass American way. Personally I was taken to a cafeteria. To Rexford's. Walter likes Rexford's."

"For dinner? Why did he do that?"

"He's cheap."

"No, he isn't. He isn't usually."

"He *did* it to save *money.*" It was not a good idea to disagree with Nita now. "He's a very seedy person. I didn't know how seedy he was."

Pauline personally didn't think of cafeterias as a humiliation to eat in. She and Bunny had a favorite one in downtown Newark, where they had liked the huckleberry pie and the mosaic floor. For Nita, though, and for Christmas dinner, it had been mean of Walter.

"I stood in line – I was wearing my beaded crepe in Rexford's, he let me get dressed up –

and I got a sliced turkey plate with two vegetables and I handed it to the last person in line and I left. I did not make a scene until Walter ran after me in the street. It was his own fault."

"What kind of scene?"

"Some shouting. I pushed him once but he didn't fall or anything. Many people had some extra holiday entertainment for free. He followed me home later and he tried to make up. He tried to play on my emotions. He brought me a fairly ugly silver cigarette case that he had just gotten somewhere and then we went back to his house and I threw it out the window."

Pauline remembered the sofa cushions that another woman had once reportedly thrown out Walter's window at a party – Pauline had an image of multiple falling objects raining down from the apartment, the overflow of repeated and violent angers. She said something to Nita about how the street under Walter's windows should be declared a danger zone; fortunately Nita thought this was funny.

She seemed in the mood to joke; whenever Pauline said anything directly sympathetic, Nita bristled and got sarcastic ("Mr. Worm" or "Blubber-boy" was how she referred to Walter). Pauline joined in the general blaze of disparagement – it was the least she could do out of loyalty, especially since her own current state was so vastly preferable. She had never been up when Nita was down before; it surprised her that Nita was subject to changes in circumstance. It made Pauline feel more cheerful about her own history, but she wasn't fully prepared to believe that no one was immune to reversals of fortune, and secretly she thought less of Nita for it.

In the weeks to come, she tried not to use Nita too much as an audience for reports about Mack. Nita wasn't all that interested anyway. When she went to dinner with Pauline she was either raging or spiritless; she was distracted by the process of reclaiming items she had left behind in Walter's apartment.

Nita kept forgetting objects she later decided were important – bottles of talcum powder, a broom – and every time she went back there was either a fight or the start of a reconciliation. Once after she'd gone back for some towels she stayed for a week. "It was a very *interesting* week," Nita said when Pauline saw her later. "It's very wearing. It's too exhausting."

All the same Nita did get told everything. She called Mack "your peaceful farmer." (He had said to Pauline that he was like Virgil in the *Georgics,* retiring to the countryside in his post-youthful years – not that Mack was that old.) He did seem peaceful to Pauline. When she went to visit him she always had to bring something to read while he worked, and she spent the days of the weekend in a haze of mild eyestrain, squinting by the fireplace.

Mack tried to coax her into trying to read Latin again but she refused flat out. She liked it when he stopped for tea, as he did several times an afternoon. He was amazed at how hot she could drink tea. She showed him the Russian trick of taking it with a lump of sugar behind the teeth. She had never thought of tea as a beverage that was refreshing, but in the stony cold of the house its heat and its tannic clarity had a brightening effect, a pleasantness associated with childhood or with the teas in English novels. They were very companionable, warming their hands near the teakettle and crunching their Vienna wafers.

Mack would never come to the city to see her. He said it was too loud and too ugly and too full of people. Now when she went home she noticed how noisy and rushed it was.

It was difficult telling him about New York things anyway. She had to repeat and explain the most obvious parts, so that every story was distorted or withered in the telling. For instance when she talked about Nita, Nita sounded shallow or vicious, and when she tried to adjust this ("she's really fun"), she seemed to be bragging about what a colorful, amusing character her little friend Nita was.

Many customs were also foreign to him. He didn't know that marijuana was used by non-gangsters or that bad liquor was called panther piss or that sex could occur during menstruation without infection. He shook his head when she mentioned all this; he looked amused and doubtful. Once she tried describing the costume she had worn to be a flame in the revue for Dean White's magazine – first the dimensions of the skirt sounded ridiculously provocative, and then when she explained it again she bored him with the dressmaking details.

She seemed to be boasting when she described something as simple as one of Walter's dinners – which she had gone to pretty commonly before Nita's break with him – any funny episodes became like cartoons of cosmopolite archness, and her own narratives were clichéd and inexact. And yet it was too hard not to talk about these things – she was stuck up there in Mack's house, huddled uncutely in his old jacket, with chafed cheeks and a runny nose, and there was no sign that she had ever known anything else unless she talked about it. It annoyed her that she spoke so clumsily; she had a sense of self-betrayal, of hurting her own feelings.

Mack sometimes liked to tease her by saying things like “Any friend of yours?” when there was an article in the news about bootleggers arrested, or “You should know about that” when the cat went into heat. Sometimes he was very understanding; he would pat her shoulder while she was talking, as though she had been through something much worse than she really had.

10

When Pauline saw her family again, Solly had changed a lot. He was almost fifteen now, skinny and smart-alecky. His great enthusiasm was military history, and he showed off at the dinner table, expounding on his latest insight into the campaigns of Napoleon. "Nobody knew that before you, right?" Pauline's father said. Solly's manner of explaining – a dogged and condescending patience – and his utter belief in the importance of his subject reminded her of Mack.

At dinner her father was in a bad mood – at one point he smacked his hand on the table to make them all be quiet for the rest of the meal. Pauline reported this to Mack later – she referred to her father as "a real pill," surely one of the milder ways she might have described him – and Mack was taken aback, shocked at this open scorn for a parent. Pauline thought he failed to understand her father's temperament; he seemed to think no one had ever made a sufficient effort with her father or tried to reason with him properly. Pauline said, "Listen, you can't change the leopard's spots," which only came out sounding like another of her crudities of feeling.

She hadn't mentioned Mack to her family – they would have asked questions and found out from his surname alone that he was part of the unsafe gentile world. (And Mack was so safe, he was the embodiment of safety.) She told them she was going to the country sometimes now on weekends with friends, but that only impressed them as an odd thing to do in winter. They had always lived in cities; her father resented the out-of-doors, he was annoyed by most kinds of weather, and her mother was too timid to venture even into parks.

Pauline herself was starting to feel proprietary about the particular corner of the Hudson Valley where Mack lived. She had read a book about the Indians once resident in the region – not that they were current neighbors, but it satisfied her to see what Mack said were hickory trees after reading that the Algonquin diet had included hickory nuts.

Even so she had been trying to get Mack to go out more. There was a roadhouse outside town where Pauline had heard you could get liquor just by asking for it – Rose's friends went there when they could get someone to babysit for Martha and Harold. It was a dank, high-ceilinged place where old men sat together and young men in sports jackets came in with girls dressed up to look fast (they probably *were* fast). To Pauline it seemed cheerful, like a wayfarer's inn, an outpost of sociability. She suspected that Mack secretly liked it – he talked more when they were there. Once he told her a long story about a woman he'd gone with in college; he had almost been engaged to her but they had quarreled about a play they'd seen together and afterward they had drifted apart. Pauline was surprised at how well he remembered, for something that had happened fifteen years ago. She wasn't jealous – the relationship sounded to her as though it had been fairly slight and casual really, but so little else had happened to him that he had pondered it into significance.

Once, another time when they were at the roadhouse, he had looked over at a man who was belting down a jigger of whiskey and said, "See how his profile is? He looks just like Louis the Fourteenth, don't you think?" Since the man lacked long ringlets, Pauline couldn't see the resemblance, but it pleased her that Mack had thought of this, that he was on such familiar terms mentally with the major figures of European history. Another time, a woman who was very drunk stopped at their table and muttered at them for several minutes, and Mack lit her cigarette for her with such beautiful politeness that Pauline had a pang of sudden happiness at being with him.

She tried to get him to stay out at the roadhouse as late as possible. She liked the early morning hours and the feel of a bar thinning out at closing. She was at her most alert late at night. In the day they both carried with them the vague grogginess of new lovers. Mack was surprised at the way their afternoon teas so often trailed off directly into bed; he had expected her to be more retiring or more fragile.

They had only had a few arguments – one about whether aluminum pots should ever be cleaned with scouring powder and one about the mechanization of labor in the twentieth century. Mack hated all machines and thought they always did more harm than good, but Pauline said had he ever made a shirt by hand? Had he ever plowed a field on foot?

They hardly ever saw other people, except in the roadhouse or at the store. Pauline was surprised to find that Mack wasn't all that friendly with Rose's friends. He thought Martha was a brat and he said they were flighty, they lived on credit, they racked up bills at the local store and then made jokes about it. Pauline said feeding a family always cost more than you planned, but Mack thought their fiscal irresponsibility was all the worse for their being parents. He had an annoyingly Thoreau-like view, Pauline thought, of people's ability to do without money.

Pauline was always low on money herself these days. Gittelson had given her only a two-dollar raise at the beginning of the year, and the train trips to see Mack were eating into her salary. Had she been Nita, she would have gotten the ticket money out of Mack, but to ask him for it was offensive to her, like being a hooker or a nagging wife. She made cracks to Rose about how it was so typical of her that being with men always made her poorer while everybody else managed to lean on the male sex as the source of miscellaneous extra luxuries.

Rose was a good person to complain to; she was used to bouts of being broke herself. She did illustrations for fashion ads in the paper and there were slow periods, like now right after the holidays. She was full of advice on budgeting. She went in for what Pauline thought were peculiar economies. She would fast all day and then eat a wedge of Camembert for supper; she went out in winter in an old, thin velvet coat and a fur hat (you were warm, she said, as long as your head was warm). When there was no work at all she passed the time in her hotel room sketching still-lifes of breakfast rolls and wine bottles; she never minded anything and she was never bored or resentful.

She was also the only one of Pauline's friends that Mack had met. (It was probably just as well that he didn't know Nita.) He thought Rose was "endearing," a phrase you would only use, Pauline felt, about someone you didn't think was very bright, and Rose was perfectly intelligent.

Mack liked to give the impression of being extremely fastidious about whom he spent his time with. (There was an implied compliment to Pauline in this, of course.) He apparently did not require much other company beside hers. But Pauline frequently felt very bottled up just being with him – it was harder to be lively with only one person watching.

So Pauline was glad when she heard a man's voice call out her name at the roadhouse. They were there on a Saturday night, when the place was as crowded as it ever got. A group of teenage boys were telling dirty jokes, a man showing off for his wife was blowing smoke rings, and when Pauline turned around she saw Garrett leaning against a wall. "Pauline," he said. "Little Miss Samuels."

He was wearing a cream-colored overcoat, a little dressy for the surroundings. Pauline hadn't seen him since the days with Dewey – he looked healthier, more fleshed out – or maybe he only looked pinkish the way he did when he was halfway into his drinking. "Well, well, well," he said. "Of all people." Perhaps he hated her. (He certainly hated Dewey.) "Do you live here now?"

"Oh, no. I just visit my friend who lives here." He and Mack shook hands. "I can't believe it," she said.

"Well, believe it," Garrett said.

Garrett said he was on his way down to the city after a week at his family's place in the Adirondacks. "You can't drive in the cold unless you stop a lot. A car needs gas, a human needs alcohol."

Mack lifted his glass. "This'll warm you up." He was being hearty tonight.

"I hate the cold. It's one thing about the mountains," Garrett said. "I notice it every time I go there in winter." He chuckled to himself as though this were a bit of real iconoclasm on his part. "You come here often?" he said. "This a favorite spot of yours?"

"Not really," Mack said.

"You get a real taste of country life here, don't you? Quite the suave crowd."

Mack snorted. "They're all right," Pauline said. The man at the bar was still blowing smoke rings; his wife, who was fat, was leaning on his shoulder. Two men in overalls sat blank-faced next to them, staring straight ahead.

"You know what it is?" Garrett said. "Look at the shapes of those heads. It's inbreeding. It's not their fault. It's just a degeneration that happens."

"They don't look degenerate to me," Pauline said. "They look normal."

"Why don't you go ask them where they get their hair cut? That domed effect would be sweet on you."

"You need a rusty scissors and a bowl to get the look right," Mack said.

"They're not bothering you," Pauline said.

The high school boys across the room were having another outbreak of hilarity. One of them kept repeating the punch line, slapping the wall of the booth. "Look at that boy's teeth," Garrett said. "He looks like a horse."

"He's not a horse," Pauline said.

"Go talk to him," Garrett said. "He's kind of your type."

It surprised Pauline that Garrett's distaste for the people in the roadhouse (his class hatred, Bunny would call it) was so strong. And Mack was joining in. The crowd in the bar seemed altogether ordinary to her, grotesque only insofar as any crowd can be grotesque. In a sense of course she wasn't one of them either. If she had walked into that roadhouse followed by her parents, with their accents and with the mournful old-world cut of their clothes, the place might well have gone silent; the bartender would've found an excuse not to serve them. Or if she had come alone, as a woman she would've been subject to overtures that carried a heavy element of scorn, if not danger. But the men in the room did not look like horses to her; they looked fully like humans. That was the least, the very least, that was required of her.

"Perhaps she should go neigh at him," Mack said.

"I used to have a horse I really liked," Garrett said. "You keep a horse up here?"

"Oh, no. Too expensive."

"They eat a lot. Oats. Hay. That's not what'll eat through your cash, though. It's certain kinds of people that do that. Isn't that right, Pauline?"

"Sometimes."

"She's so pretty. Isn't she pretty?"

"*I* think so," Mack said, a bit huffily.

"She used to live with a swindler, did you know that?"

"I'm not going to answer that," Mack said.

"Oh, well, it's public knowledge, I'm not slandering her. He had a phony magazine and he got people to give money to it. Pauline was sort of the lure. So you'd believe in his artistic purpose. Dewey was totally illiterate, but when you went to their house Pauline was always sitting there in the corner reading away." It struck her as especially violating that Garrett remembered her this way, since this was the one activity in which she never thought of anyone observing her. "He was more an athletic type," Garrett said. "When I stayed overnight on the couch I could hear them going at it in the next room. For a lot of women, criminals have sex appeal."

"That's enough," Pauline said.

"That's a nice dress, Pauline. Did Dewey get you that?"

"No."

"I don't object to your wearing nice dresses. It isn't that. What I want to know is who's going to pay me back the money," Garrett said. "That's what I'm asking."

"It's Dewey who took it. I never had any

money. I don't have any now. Go ask Dewey. Why are you asking me?" Pauline could tell that this sounded shrill and weak. Mack was wincing; he had a cold, pinched expression.

"I'm sorry it happened," she said to Garrett. This was very true but she said it somewhat bitingly so it seemed insincere or sarcastic. And then she put out her hand – she was surprised herself that she did this – and she and Garrett shook hands. The ceremoniousness of this made it a good cue to leave, and she and Mack made their way out not long after.

Mack had known in a vague way that she'd been involved before with a sort of caddish type. Now he said grimly, "Well, this was interesting."

"He left out the part about Adolfo," Pauline said. This was the heart of the matter, as far as she was concerned – Adolfo's broken leg, his missing tooth, his lost income – it was necessary to tell the fuller version. She told it flatly, as though she were a witness in a trial, one of those worldly, well-dressed women in detective stories who show great coolness in front of the judge. And she did feel cool, narrating it as a string of facts. The telling spilled out on itself, an audible form of remorse. Actually, she felt defiant about it – it was her own business – only she wasn't dignified enough to keep silent.

"That's a charming tale," Mack said. They were in his car, moving slowly along the dark, snow-banked road. "I suppose," Mack said, "that the thing is to keep your eye on the main chance. That's what the smart-money crowd does."

"What smart-money crowd?" Pauline said.

"Your friends," he said. "Rose, Nita, the whole lovely group." He shook his head and laughed soundlessly to himself. She had a great desire to push him out the car door into the snow.

"You're getting it wrong," she said. "You don't have the slightest idea about any of this."

"Yes," he said, "I'm sure I don't."

He seemed satisfied, as though the whole thing confirmed a belief he had held for years about the corruption inherent in most other members of his species. It was certainly possible that he had nothing comparable in his past, that he had managed to avoid the experience of disappointing himself. He had not been tried and found wanting; he had hardly been tried at all. She thought of him as a kind of innocent, although he was thirty-five, a grown man with gray in his mustache and a thickening jawline. She had a grudge against his innocence, which had made him harsh, a champion of unchallenged dogma. How did he know what he knew? He had the intolerance of the untraveled, and he was as unforgiving as an adolescent.

In the morning he argued about how she cooked the eggs. "They're worthless when they're overcooked," he said.

"Eat them or don't eat them. It's your business, brother."

"I'm not usually called brother. My name is Mack."

"Oh, for Christ's sake." She thought for a moment he was going to chide her for taking the name of the Lord in vain, but he didn't.

"Well, I can't eat them this way." He was still harping on the eggs. "And there's no milk for the coffee. What happened to the milk? We didn't get any?"

"I always forget you don't get it delivered," she said. "There's no milkman, right?"

"And it's a good thing," he said, "with you around."

Coming from Mack, this was a considerable insult. She wouldn't answer – he had such scorn for the proverbial antics of the randy housewife and the milkman – Pauline was indignant, suddenly loyal to all bawdiness.

She got up and went into the other room, to

sit by the fire with a back section of a day-old newspaper. "That's friendly," Mack said. "Don't say excuse me or anything."

"I'm reading. I do read, despite what they say."

"You must find the *Sentinel* fascinating. Reading the ads for horse serum?"

"I'm riveted."

"I see."

"Maybe you don't think horses should be inoculated," Pauline said. "Too modern."

"I'm not opposed to things of advantage."

"Ain't that the truth?"

Her voice was deeper than usual and she was speaking the way she might speak with Nita or in bars (overdoing it a little, even). Her usual manner with Mack was drier, more like his own (he didn't like girls to be slangy). It was nice to revert, reassuring to hear. Perhaps it was what she would sound like in the future.

They read in separate rooms until the afternoon, when Pauline said she was going for a walk. She would go around to the farm at the end of the road, where they usually bought milk, and bring back a bottle.

"You sure you want to go in the cold?"

"I'm in the mood. I need some money, though."

"I thought I gave you some before."

"It got spent for the cider." He couldn't think she was a gold digger for the milk money: that was too silly. Still, she felt very awkward; she was smiling crookedly at him.

"I only have a twenty," he said.

"I'll take it. Hah, hah, you won't see me again."

He did not think this was funny – he looked miserable as he handed the bill to her. Pauline made a great show of sticking it into her bosom like a dance hall girl.

When she came back with the milk she put the water on to boil and she set out the tea things. "That looks sweet," Mack said. She brought out a bottle of whiskey from the cupboard to spike their tea with.

"Rose used to tell fortunes from tea leaves. She told mine once," Pauline said.

"I hate that. It's such a racket."

"She didn't do it for *money*. She's an *artist*. She didn't go around with earrings and a shawl sitting in storefronts. Is that what you thought?"

Mack shrugged.

"Well, I was going to tell you what she told me, but now there's no point."

"What did she tell you?"

"She said I would live a long life." This did

sound pointless. Pauline poured another slug of whiskey in her tea, out of sullenness. "I liked it when she told me that."

"I'm sure she was right," Mack said. "You always seem so strong and healthy."

"Do I?" She wasn't sure how she felt about this.

"You were probably worried about your state of health then. From the kind of life you were leading. It's understandable."

"What life? I had just come to New York."

"It's been good for you to be here," Mack said. "Away from there. You look so much better – well, not just better, I mean much calmer – than when we first met. You were like a little nervous mouse then."

"I was?"

"You know. You talked fast, you couldn't eat – at that dinner you practically tossed your plate in the air every time I put food on it." He winked. "And look at you now."

"Look at *you,*" she said. "You hadn't crawled out from under a rock for years until you met me."

He was surprised that she had gotten so testy; she was so volatile, he said. They quarreled all afternoon – it was their longest tea ever, Mack noted at the end. In the early evening he drove her to the train station. "Are you upset?" he said. She was annoyed by the question – she was much too full of animosity to be upset. She had also drunk a fair amount of rye in her repeated cupfuls of tea, and she was in a clear and merciless frame of mind.

"Don't fret," she said (a somewhat artificial phrase for her), and they kissed good-bye. It was a normal, full kiss but with a faint rhythm of mutual suspicion in it.

She liked being somewhat drunk riding the train. She couldn't see much out the windows in the dark – there were the occasional blurry lights of stations passing. She might have been anywhere (it was just the kind of thing she liked); it was a great relief to be away from Mack.

When Mack called later in the week, she said she wouldn't come to the country this time. It was too tiring; maybe he would like to come to the city. "The light fantastic," she said. "The gaiety, the throngs." He was phoning her at work, and she broke off from the conversation a few times to answer people in the office. "Go chase yourself, George," she said to the stock boy. She told Mack that if he couldn't decide then about coming in, he should call her back when he knew.

It was Friday by the time he called again.

While she was talking, the stock boy kept walking by her desk singing "I love my baby, my baby loves me," which of course seemed to typify everything peppy that Mack was so remote from. This was unfair of her. Mack often sang jokey little tunes – old Broadway ditties and parodies of hymns with made-up verses – but still she thought of him now as hopelessly dour and stodgy. It was humiliating to her that she had involved herself with someone so old-maidish and conservative.

Mack thought it was out of sheer spite that she was denying herself the peace of a visit to his quiet valley – whereas, in addition to spite, she was sick of the cold and the quiet and the long train trip. "You always say you love the train trip," he said. He was triumphant, having found yet another sign of deception in her. He wouldn't come; they were very stubborn with each other. She felt that she had not been stubborn enough with him before.

At work Pauline flirted with the stock boy. She said things to get his attention each time he went by the desk, calling him Georgie-Porgie even. "Why don't you come into the stockroom and see my etchings?" he said.

"Don't tempt me," she said. He looked startled, afraid she was serious.

On the way home she stopped at the Italian

grocery on her street. The owner was complaining that he had lost money betting on a fight. "The wrong guy won. Am I a fool or what?"

"Nobody can tell how these things are going to turn out," Pauline said. "If you could tell before, there'd be nothing to bet on."

He took this as a real piece of consolation. "The truth," he said. She felt very citified and nimble.

For a week there were phone calls back and forth with Mack. She had gotten very uncompromising, he said. Sometimes, in between the calls, she would begin to relent a little. She would picture him – bearish, suffering, wincing at the phone – confused by her, genuinely baffled. But she got angry again when she spoke to him. He agreed finally to come to New York as proof that he was the more obliging one.

She took him to Tony's for dinner. There was no one she knew there – the place had apparently gone out of favor – and it was filled that night with college-students. The veal piccata was oily and underseasoned, and the waiter was indifferent when she made friendly remarks. Mack looked miserable at being there and hardly spoke.

Afterward they went to the Elephants' Graveyard. Pauline was afraid this might be another mistake – she hadn't been there for a long time. Walter was at the bar. He gave her one of his hugs, rocking her off the floor. "Pauline, Pauline, dream of a dream." His eyes were very small in his face from drinking. She wasn't sure that it was appropriate to be friendly with him since she was (always and forever) Nita's ally, but it was nice being greeted with such enthusiasm. "You look so sweet tonight," he said.

"That's me," she said. "Sweet all over."

Walter wanted to buy them drinks, but Mack said they were going to sit down in the back somewhere. "Desert me," Walter said. "The hell with you."

The back room had an especially beery smell. "I've gotten some bad hangovers from this place," Pauline said. "Once I took a bath that lasted the whole day. I couldn't get out of the tub."

"Who are you waving to?" Mack said. A friend of Peter's had come out of the men's room.

"Someone I know. He's gone now. You can't see him."

Pauline ordered a Manhattan when the waiter showed up. "You never drink them," Mack said.

"Yes, I do. For the color. I thought it would

go well with my outfit. A potable accessory, don't you think that's a good idea? Red is a very primary color. The important countries on maps are always red."

"Why are you being so silly tonight?" Mack said.

"For Christ's sake. Don't be unbearable."

Someone had broken a glass in the front room and there was the sound of applause, and then another glass falling, and more cheering. "Very merry tonight, aren't they?" the waiter said, passing their table.

Walter came into the back room singing. He stuck his chest out at Pauline. *"Toreador-o, la-la, la-la, la. . . ."* Pauline put her hands on her ears. "I need you," Walter said. "The bartender refuses to believe I can stand on one foot and balance a glass of brandy on my head. Great sums of money are riding on this."

"Oh, Walter," she said. "It's so *hack*neyed."

"Don't be difficult," Walter said. "We need a reliable person to observe and judge – someone fair-minded like yourself, the soul of honor."

"No bribes, that's right," Pauline said. "I'll be right back," she said to Mack.

The bartender, as it turned out, had decided to prohibit Walter from any more tricks with glasses, but Pauline was given a drink for what

Walter called her putative good-sportsmanship. Walter's rowdy moods were not her favorite side of him, but she was glad that Mack was at least getting some proof that a world of social gaiety and freedom really existed and that she had some part in it.

"Nobody appreciates my glass stunt," Walter said. "My dog likes it. He likes to see a human do tricks."

"Rabbits out of hats are probably his favorite," Pauline said.

"I wonder if Houdini had a dog," someone said.

"I admired Houdini so much," a woman said. "Do you think he's dead? I don't think he's dead."

"Perhaps he's come back as Walter's dog," a man said.

There was a discussion about what life form you'd want to come back as – a woman wanted to be Lake Michigan and someone wanted to be the entire population of Tuscany – and then Pauline got sidetracked into a debate about reincarnation, which did not even interest her but which she had difficulty drawing away from.

When Pauline went into the back room, Mack was gone. It was chilling to see the empty table – the sting of his rebuke. He had left money by the glass; he had taken his coat and hat. She stiffened, as though he had just yelled at her. She was immediately miserable. In a way she didn't blame him, only it had been so petulant and dramatic of him. There were people she knew in the room.

He had never been to her apartment, although he had the address; it seemed unlikely that he would go there. He had probably taken a taxi to the railroad station. In a huff: she could imagine him sitting stern-faced in the cab. She felt deserted then, insulted.

Even in the rudeness of it, though, his going was something like the lightening of a burden. She went back into the front room. A man was trying to explain how Houdini had trained himself to breathe under water. Everyone at the bar made up breathing exercises. When she left much later, no one asked what had happened to her friend, and she couldn't tell what anyone noticed.

It was only when she was back in her apartment that the situation suddenly struck her as agonizing. The place was cleaner than it had been in months, with all the objects on the table and dresser arranged at right angles and a bottle of real Scotch by the sink in the kitchen. She had tied a stocking around the neck of the bottle for a ribbon. It was embarrassing to look at. Her strongest feeling was, in fact, a kind of profound embarrassment. The entire evening was shoddy, she was sorry that she had ever taken up with Mack, she felt grossly mistreated, and she had a distinct sense of having behaved badly. Her life looked formless, without order and without standards.

She considered opening the bottle of Scotch for herself, but the thought of its smell was unappealing after all the Manhattans. Once at a party at Walter's, Dewey had told her that she reeked of Scotch. She was outraged now, thinking of him saying that.

She was sick of all the affronts that had fallen on her in the course of romance. The whole thing seemed full of degradations. (And none of it for love either – it was one thing to be a fool for love – she had not even liked Dewey.)

At least, she thought, I *know* more than Mack does. She had done more, been through more. She contemplated some of the more extreme episodes in her life with considerable secret pride, as though she had been a reporter sent on colorful assignments. She felt very superior to him in this. The glow of this thought did not last very long – she was still smarting from the ugly clumsiness of the evening and she had a general feeling of having compromised herself for a long time in unnamed ways. She leaned very heavily on this idea of *knowing* – but what was it? It was so airy and inexact an accomplishment, and perhaps not even directly useful.

11

At work on Monday she was dull and slow, weighed down with blank mournfulness over Mack. When she was in this kind of flat mood, it was satisfying to sort and file things, to find receipts. It was almost interesting then – the names on the invoices, the lists of goods sold. Other days she hated it more. She minded the time lost to it, the days gone (the Days of Her Youth). She also minded Mr. Gittelson, who was always patting her cheek and pinching her nose and docking her pay when she wasn't on time.

Late in the morning, just when she was getting hungry for lunch, Mr. Gittelson came around to her corner. "I have a beautiful surprise for you," he said. "Come into my office, you have to see."

It was probably just a new sample he meant, but she was wary.

"Could you guess?" he said.

In the seat by Gittelson's desk was her father.

"I gave some orders for the ribbon," he said. "So I came, here I am."

Mr. Gittelson said, "I told him you're a lovely girl only sometimes you sleep too late in the morning, right?"

It was so startling to see her father there. In outline he didn't look that different from any of the men who might be in Gittelson's office – jobbers, salesmen – but his face was too vivid to her, too known, as though she had caught herself talking out loud.

"I was thinking about lunch," her father said. "You're hungry?"

When they walked out through the office together, the stock boy gave Pauline a look. Perhaps he thought she was cozying up to one of the out-of-town buyers. Miss Pfeiffer said, "You're going out now?"

"You have to stay?" her father said. "Stay in, I'll go."

"Is it all right?" Pauline said to Miss Pfeiffer.

Her father was at the door already. "Stay. Go. Just let me know." Pauline couldn't stand it. Miss Pfeiffer said she could go now if she kept it short.

Pauline took him to Schapira's Home Dairy Restaurant on Thirty-first Street. "It looks clean," her father said. "You come here at night too?"

"Oh, no," she said. "I go places near where I live. With my friends."

"That's nice. You go with friends."

"Often."

"Your friends don't cook – you have to go out?"

"I cook sometimes. I made boiled pike one time, they liked it."

A long while passed while her father ate without speaking, the way he did at home. It made her think of Dewey, the silences at meals during the time he wasn't talking, after he had given up the bankbook to Garrett. That was the worst time, she thought. That time is over. She felt with confidence that the most excruciating disasters of her life were finally behind her. In her stubbornness – which was accentuated by being with her father – and in the natural limits of her prescience, she could imagine nothing worse.

"My friends like my cooking," she said. "Nita can't cook at all. Well, maybe fudge. She does fudge well. Rose could cook if she had a kitchen, I think so. She has that kind of personality."

Her father grunted. She dug into her vegetables with sour cream, an enormous portion which her father would yell at her for ordering if she didn't finish.

"How's the store?"

"All right," he said. "Solly helps more now. He's a know-it-all is his problem."

"He is," Pauline said.

"So I'll come back tonight when you're through," her father said. "You can show me your house, before I go back."

For the rest of the afternoon Pauline walked through her apartment mentally, trying to remember what she had left out, what was exposed. It pained her to think of his looking at things – the Scotch with the stocking around it, the ruffled light fixture, the kitchen table with one chair. She had always thought they would send Solly if someone came to see. Still, there was nothing she could do about it.

When her father came at the end of the day she took him on the El, to save the thirty-minute walk. He seemed too old for doing all those blocks on foot, although he was only fifty. In her apartment building, going up the five flights of stairs, she had a wild hope that he would tire and turn back.

She pulled the cord to switch on the light fixture as they went inside. "You want some tea?" she said. "I have tea." He walked through the living room to the bedroom, he opened the door to the bathroom, he looked into the kitchen. "Very small," he said.

"Sit down," she said. "There's a chair."

He was still moving through the rooms like a browser in a store. "If you have bugs," he said, "you should put out boric acid on a potato cut in half."

"I don't have bugs," Pauline said. This was a lie.

She lit the gas and put some water on to boil, to give her something to do while he went on with his inspection of the rooms. Hadn't she outlived this sort of thing already? Wasn't she through with all this? Her rooms looked cramped and dark now, cluttered, embellished unsuccessfully.

"I'm not staying," he said. "I just wanted to look."

"I have Swee-touch-nee," she said. "You like that kind."

"I'm going," he said. He put an arm around one of her shoulders quickly, by way of good-bye, a form of gesture Nita always called a quarter embrace.

At least he hadn't come while she was at Dewey's; it occurred to her after he left to be thankful for that. He wouldn't tell them much at home, whatever he reported; you could never really get information out of him. He would say a few vague things to keep her mother from being any more fretful than she was. But he could come back next week if he decided to – couldn't he? – he could come back any time he wanted.

Mack had once asked her how good Nita really was at the violin. Pauline had said, "Oh, very good, I think," although actually she didn't think that and Nita had certainly never said it. Still, Pauline was sorry she hadn't told her father she had a friend who was a violinist.

Ever since Nita and Walter had broken up, Nita had been practicing five and six hours a day. She played the same pieces over and over, some études her teacher in Wilkes-Barre had given her. The rash came back on her neck, and she wore cake makeup that smeared the handkerchief she tucked under her chin when she played at work.

She was not a person who enjoyed being alone, and she often had people over when she was practicing. Pauline would sit and flip through magazines, waiting for her to finish. Nita looked workmanlike moving her bow, not earnest but fixed on the task. She said she wasn't interested in getting jobs in better places or advancing professionally – she claimed not to like the sound of the instrument. She practiced, she said, because it was one of those urges, like cleaning the house or going shopping, that took hold of you and made you not want to do anything else.

A neighbor complained of the noise, but Nita played louder whenever he banged on the floor. She got cramps in her hand – from bad technique, she said – an early sign of tendonitis, which she believed she could work out by playing more. She would have kept on, but she played at work with a bandage she had contrived out of crossed strips of grosgrain ribbon – the manager of the restaurant said she looked like a boxer without his gloves, and he made her take a week off.

It was not a good week to have off. It was the beginning of March, blustery and cold. She had no money to go away, and she had just lost her one hobby. For a while she talked about getting Walter to lend her some money so she could go to France. She was at a stage where she was impatient with a lot of the things that had diverted her before. There was a French singer in a bar on Cornelia Street, and Nita coaxed Pauline into going there to hear her all the time. Pauline made attempts to translate phrases from the songs. *L'amour est un orage.*

The singer was not a young woman, and when she sang the lyrics to her songs about lost love, she adopted a particular expression of melancholy wisdom – resolute but misty-eyed. She stared into the audience, attempting to convey how well, all too well, she knew the things she was singing about, trying to remind them of their own share in this same knowledge. Coaxed, Pauline thought of Mack and of Dewey; she was aware of Nita sitting next to her, and how they fit into this atmosphere of regretted romances. The torch singer was asking what good it did any of them.

Sometimes the singer did songs like "Varsity Drag" in French. She had to rush to make the lines fit.

"Pack a ukelele when you go to France," Pauline said. "You'll be a big hit."

"I'd never take an instrument. Tony Goodwin had his whole trunk stolen between Le Havre and Paris."

"One of the risks of travel," Pauline said, although she had never been farther away than Pennsylvania.

"It's the same here. It's worse. Rose had her fur hat stolen on the street. Some kids came up and grabbed it off her head. Did you know that?"

"That's horrible."

"Three or four kids. They took it and ran. They tried to take her purse but they couldn't get it."

"Where did this happen?" Pauline knew

when she said this that she was pretending that only certain blocks had danger in them, spots where only someone a little foolish or inattentive like Rose would walk. Whereas there was no spot on earth without the possibility of menace. In this respect at least her parents had been right, with their constant suspicions of other people's intentions.

She did think that Rose was the last person who deserved to have anything stolen: she was so ungreedy herself, so content with little. And she had really been very devoted to the hat – a beaver cloche with a band of gray lamb. It was her one impressive garment. "Poor Rose," Pauline said.

"She's so *stubborn,*" Nita said. "She won't buy anything else because she says it's too late in the season. She's in mourning, like people who won't get another pet after one dies. So she's running around hatless; the wind is whistling through her ears."

"She'll catch her death," Pauline said. She was kidding, but they had both grown up with the idea that hats were worn at least partly for medical reasons. "I could lend her my old green felt. Do you think she would wear it?"

"No," Nita said.

The French singer was repeating the same

repertoire they had heard before – one jaunty street ballad to three gurgling torch songs. Nita was restless; she decided they might as well go to Vera's. She said this with some degree of resignation, but it was clear that she believed that real life was going on at Vera's without them, like the tree falling in the forest. You could only stay away so long.

Pauline also believed this, but she was no longer completely comfortable at Vera's or the other places. And being awkward there made her sentimental about the past, an emotion she considered more or less humiliating at her age. Walking up the stairs to Vera's made her think of the words to a song Bunny used to play on the piano, bowed with the burden of the years.

At the top of the stairs, through the kitchen door, she could see the cook carrying a pot between the stove and the sink – he was yelling something to one of the waiters (not Adolfo, someone younger) – she had a sense of everything happening at a fast, glib pace, on a schedule of urgency. There was the noise of voices from the next room, which also seemed very fast and loud. This was exactly what made her uncomfortable in Vera's – things going too quickly, too mercilessly, to get hold of. You needed a lightness of heart, a thoughtless surety, to keep up.

She and Nita hung their coats on the wall outside the main room. Some of the pegs were chipped and loose – Mack should be here, she thought, he's so good at fixing things. She had a moment of missing him, a quick daydream of Mack.

"I hate March," Nita said. "I hate all months."

"It's one right after another," Pauline said.

Nita was not going to be lively (in her black moods she was intransigent and unpleasable), and there was no one else in the room Pauline knew well enough to talk to, although there were plenty of people she knew by sight; it was distracting to notice them out of the corner of her eye. Vera, the owner, stood in the corner with her arms crossed, a buxom woman in a man's shirt and tie. She nodded hello to Nita; Pauline waved, but Vera had turned away by then. She was watching two men who were chasing the waiter, trying to play tag with him. They bobbed past the tables, ducked behind pillars. Vera, who didn't drink herself, looked sardonic and said nothing. Pauline thought that Vera really wanted people to act like that, that in her own stone-faced way she encouraged it.

"Here comes the Rose," Nita said. "The Rose in bloom."

Rose did look blithe and blooming, or at least

flushed. She was swooping down on them – her hair all flyaway and electric – leaning over them in her fluttering, light-bodied way. She hadn't *seen* them in so long. "This is my friend," she said. He looked nineteen or twenty, very collegiate, and he was holding Rose's hand. He corrected her on his last name; they had apparently just met. "How's your country life?" Rose asked.

"I've abandoned it," Pauline said. "I've decided to go in for feverish dissipation and low companions instead."

"Oh, that again," Rose said. She had a cough that snuffed out the last consonants – she was laughing at the same time, so there was a final wheezing effect, like an old person's cough.

"For crying out loud," Nita said. "Get a hat, will you?"

"I'm fine."

"She should be home in bed," Nita said, looking straight at the boy. "She doesn't take care of herself."

"I do," Rose said. "I've been drinking hot lemonade all day and putting mustard plasters on my chest."

"That's disgusting," Nita said. Pauline made a prune face.

"Oh, no, it's the best thing," Rose said. "It always works."

"I'll watch her very carefully," the boy said, and Rose led him back to their table.

"See what happens?" Nita said. "She ditched Mr. Married finally, and look at her today."

"She's free to make a fool of herself in a new way entirely," Pauline said. This came out sounding much sharper than she'd expected – she was surprised at this leak of something bitter-spirited from her: to jeer at Rose, of all people.

A man at a table near them was haranguing his date. "We don't *have* to come here. There's no law that says." The woman stroked his cheek and leaned her head on his shoulder. She blotted her beet-colored lipstick on his collar. "Why did you *do* that?" he said. "You're always doing things like that."

"I bet the logs are wet," Pauline said, thinking of Mack. "It's very smoky. I bet they store their wood someplace where it's damp."

"In Paris they don't have central heating a lot of places," Nita said. "Did you know that?"

"Those girls who do the can-can must get chilly."

There was the sound of someone beating a metal gong. Vera was standing by the fireplace, hitting a copper pot with a spoon. She banged over and over; at first there was a ripple of laughter and a surge of talk – people were asking each other what she was doing. The lights went on and off, which was the usual sign to get out for closing. People groaned and booed. "It's *early*," someone yelled.

"You all have to leave," Vera said. "Are you listening to me? There's a fire in the kitchen. Walk, do not run. It's not serious."

"Not again," somebody yelled. "It's old hat, Vera."

There's going to be a stampede, Pauline thought. She was much more afraid of being trampled than of the fire itself, which couldn't, she thought, spread that fast (she was still thinking vaguely of wet wood). The waiters were herding people out, getting them to line up. "Is it for the insurance?" a woman said. "Is that why she does this?" One man walked out with a teacup and saucer in his hand. Someone yelled, "Oh, that Vera. *Any*thing to get her name in the papers."

The hallway was foggy with smoke. Pauline had been in this hallway a hundred times – it seemed so unlikely a spot for anything serious to happen. People behind Pauline were pushing. You could breathe but it was like putting sand into your lungs. Nita was handing her someone's coat from the row of hooks – Nita had taken one for herself and put it over her head. Pauline tried to do this too but the coat kept slipping – it was a man's heavy overcoat – and she was holding on to Nita with one hand. Her eyes were tearing from the smoke. She was afraid someone would trip if she dropped it so she toted it under her arm. Her nose ran, and when she touched it her hand came away with black on it. She thought she kept hearing Rose's barking cough behind her, but it might have been anyone.

On the stairs a woman was shouting, "Don't push, we're almost there, don't push." Pauline lost hold of Nita. People were crushing against her from the back. A man who was being shoved toward them actually said, "Excuse me." She heard Nita say, "Don't mention it."

Pauline had gotten over her terror at being at the mercy of other people's behavior, her certainty that they would close ranks against her, that she would be the one to slip to the bottom of the pile. Past the landing there was more room. Somebody made a joke about being ticklish. Now the crowd no longer seemed menacing, they seemed comradely – they were not even a crowd really, only a group of perhaps forty pressing down the stairs with her to the open door and the street.

They stood on the sidewalk in the cold. People milled around in groups, thronging the street. A couple sat on the hood of a parked car, drinking out of a flask. She and Nita were both in men's coats down to their ankles. They could hear the sirens, wailing very loud as they got closer. When the first fire truck turned the corner, people clapped and cheered. Somebody whistled through his fingers. A man with a booming voice started singing, "Oh, say can you see/ By the dawn's early light," and people joined in. They sang in a rowdy, garbled way – they kept it going for several lines. Whatever fright they had felt had been over fast (and not necessary, as it turned out) – as a group they felt celebratory and valiant, pleased at the way they had behaved.

The firemen filed into the building – there were a great many of them, more than could be needed, Pauline thought. They stomped through the doorway in their rubber boots, hauling a line of canvas hose from the truck. Some hazy smoke was coming from the doorway and blackish puffs rose from the windows. Pauline kept thinking the firemen were going to be angry when they discovered how small a fire it was.

Passersby were already gathering around asking what had happened, and Pauline heard a man explaining that something had flared up in the kitchen. She could tell how proud he was to have information. And she too was already eager to tell about it, glad she had gone there tonight. Even in the worst part on the stairs there had been a wild thrill of interest.

One of the fire trucks was leaving. Vera came out of the building carrying a pile of coats. Pauline took off the man's overcoat – she felt guilty for having put it on. The coats in the pile were soaking wet from the hoses. A couple shook theirs out, joking and sprinkling each other.

Rose was there – she came walking toward Pauline, arm in arm with her collegiate friend. "When he heard the gong he thought it was a raid," Rose said. "He was *so* disappointed."

Pauline scrounged through the pile for her own coat – she was afraid that someone had taken it, her one expensive piece of clothing. When she found it, it was somehow shabbier than she'd remembered, mangled and soggy now.

"Who got hurt?" Rose said. "Somebody got hurt."

The firemen were coming out of the building with a man on a stretcher. Pauline could see part of the head – black hair with gray in it – and the feet sticking out of the blanket. They set him down on the sidewalk and one of the firemen knelt next to him, unpacking what looked like a suitcase; he drew out of it a rubber mask and he clamped the mask over the man's nose and mouth. Pauline wondered whether there was a finite amount of air in the case.

"That's what they do," a man behind Pauline was saying. "See that? That's the procedure."

"It's one of the firemen," someone said. "I bet it is."

Perhaps it was; the fireman who knelt over him showed an intentness that might be personal. It seemed bizarre to Pauline that children always wanted to be firemen. It was more dangerous than any other job, grueling and full of the sight of other people's miseries. She couldn't remember at what age Solly had been old enough not to love fires.

The men were hoisting the stretcher into an ambulance, sliding it through the back like cargo. Vera sat in front with the driver; she looked businesslike and grim.

All around Pauline people were asking each other questions. There was a new theory that the injured man was the cook, but the cook was black and Pauline had glimpsed enough to know the man on the stretcher was a white man. "I've seen burn wounds in the war," a man said. "You ever see anybody really burned? You don't want to see it. This fellow wasn't burned."

Pauline looked back at the building, which

was still smoking slightly, wafts of black trailing out the second-story windows. She hated the building – she understood why firemen like to smash these places, hacking doors and axing through walls. She hated the restaurant, with its cell of a kitchen too small for the volume of business and with its tables crowded so close together – a spark from the fireplace had once burned a hole in her stocking; she was surprised there hadn't been worse fires before now – and she hated, in a fuddled, unreasoning way, the heat of the crowds, all the people coming to mingle together, the friction of their physical presence.

Nita ran after one of the firemen as he was going back into the building. "Who was it?" she said. The fireman shook his head – he didn't know or he wasn't talking. She went to the fire truck and yelled to one of the men; he shouted something down to her.

"A waiter," Nita said, when she was close to Pauline. "He thinks his name was Rudolfo."

"Adolfo," Pauline said. "Don't you think that's who he means? What are the other waiters' names?"

Neither of them knew. Jimmy, they thought, maybe a Henry. "He meant Adolfo," Pauline said.

"Christ," Nita said.

"I forgot about Adolfo," Pauline said.

She was horrified at this, at what had happened while he had slipped from her mind like a lost umbrella. She *had* thought of him on the way into the restaurant, but she hadn't remembered him at all during the fire. She couldn't get over this.

He wasn't burned, a man had said that. "Do you think he's all right?" she asked Nita, although she knew Nita didn't know. She felt too young all of a sudden to know how to behave.

The crowd began to break up. People were edging away, moving slowly as if they'd been chastised. She wanted Nita to ask if there was something they should stay to help with. The firemen were telling people to go home, and Nita said they were both in the way standing there. "Time to call it a night," she said. She steered Pauline by the elbow. "We look like the Wreck of the Hesperus," she said. "All we need is a little seaweed around our collars."

At work the next day Pauline told the stock boy about her "trial by fire" – even Miss Pfeiffer was interested. "Someone got hurt but they said he was okay," Pauline said. "The color of the smoke was so much darker than I would have expected."

It wasn't until the afternoon that she got the phone call from Nita. Nita had been crying – her voice was nasal and weak. "You were right. Not Rudolfo, Adolfo," she said. He had gotten out of the restaurant with everyone else and then he had gone back in to get his shoes. He always kept his street shoes in the back of the kitchen; he wore his old ones for work.

"He died," Nita said.

"I know," Pauline said. She meant that she had known from Nita's voice. She was trying to say something steadying.

"He was always so dapper," Nita said. "He wanted his good pair of shoes." It was true that he had been careful about his appearance, tonic on his hair and starch in his shirts – Pauline hadn't known that Nita noticed. She wouldn't have expected her to be crying for Adolfo – when had they ever had a conversation? – but Nita had strict fidelities and her own points of honor. She was ardent when an event fell into the realm of things for which she had feeling.

"He was fifty-four, did you know that?" Nita said. "He was very youthful." He had tried to help the cook put out the fire, but it was a grease fire and pouring water on it had made it worse. Pauline could picture him, baffled at the rippling of the flames. Salt, he should've used salt: any housewife would know.

"Will you come to the funeral with me?" Nita said. "I want to go."

Are we invited? Pauline thought. She was afraid they didn't belong, they hadn't known him well enough. She thought that it might be too showy of Nita to think they should go. Or perhaps not – maybe it was the staunch and upright thing. Adolfo would've liked it, the young girls in the church for him.

"Somebody I know died," Pauline said when she got off the phone. This was to explain – you were not supposed to be on the phone for more than a minute if it was a personal call – and also to announce a gravity of mood in case anyone was about to talk to her. She knew that it would be a partial lie to say that she would miss Adolfo – when had she ever sought out his company? – but the idea of him gone was a mean surprise. He had sacrificed himself for his shoes – he had gone back in without thinking, he had made a mistake. People who had never known him would know this about him. When had he known what he'd done by going back? It must be like drowning or choking – to be "overcome" by smoke – the rush of realization and then the giving up to it. She didn't know him enough to guess what he would've wanted more time to finish, what he must have thought he'd left undone. The idea of "finishing" meant, of course, a shape you thought your allotted time would assume, all the wastes made use of as spaces in a pattern. Possibly this was another form of vanity: we learn from our mistakes, Pauline thought, frequently things which are never applicable again. Adolfo had learned never to go back for his shoes.

People closer to her than Adolfo had died, before this. Her Aunt Peshie, the one who had taught her the song about birches (really a great-aunt), had died of heart failure, and in school a girl had died of pneumonia in the fifth grade. At the classmate's funeral another girl had sobbed very loudly all through the service and had wailed, "She looks like an angel," at the sight of the figure in the coffin; Pauline had thought this was a terrible way to behave. At Peshie's (where Pauline had been truly anguished – Peshie had been her one relative who liked to play with children), the family had hugged each other afterward and murmured, "What a life she led. No picnic, I tell you." In each case Pauline had felt, among other things, a sense of importance in being at the funeral, a pride that this thing had touched her life. Going to Adolfo's she felt like an imposter, trying to cadge some of the event's importance for herself.

Nita wore the black crepe dress she had worn playing the violin in the revue for Dean White's magazine two years before. The service was in an old, darkened-brick church on a side street in the south Village. When they went in, there were very few people in the pews – two old women whispering in Italian, a couple with a small boy, a very tall black man who was the cook at Vera's, and Vera herself in an odd gray costume that was like an elongated gym smock. Dewey was not there. Maybe he was out of town by now; maybe he hadn't heard or hadn't cared. There was no one there who looked like him. She realized then how much she didn't want to see him; she was frightened that he might mock her even there. She was still glancing toward the door, waiting to see who was coming, when she saw that the priest was walking down the aisle past her, intoning something. She was afraid of not knowing what to do, of doing something "against her religion," of kneeling in compliance or receiving Communion by mistake. One of the pallbearers was another waiter from Vera's, expressionless under his shouldered load.

She had known, of course, that the chanting would be in Latin, but it stirred her to hear ordinary people speaking out responses apparently as familiar to them as any household sayings. She could pick out occasional words. *Et lux perpetua luceat.* They used a soft Italianate *c* – it was all much more rolling than the clipped, hard pronunciation Miss Oughton had taught. The priest had a strong oratorical tenor. It was probably the first time, Pauline thought, that she had "used" her Latin. She had refused to let Mack review it with her, she had been saving it. It seemed right that it should be for this, as though the language – stony, classical, half understood – was designed for mourning, for anything elevated and indistinct.

She did not think of Adolfo directly until the priest began his sermon. The priest made a mistake quoting from a poem; he attributed it to Tennyson when it was really Longfellow. This struck Pauline as being the sort of thing that would happen to Adolfo even at the last – his name would be mispronounced, he would be laid out in clothes he had hated.

It seemed bitter to her. But then Adolfo in his own time had been good at adapting to random events made permanent, had in fact made something of a career of it – he lived in the same hotel room he had checked into casually twenty years before, he went around without the front tooth he was meaning to get fixed when he got some money. Now all those things were his life. She didn't care so much that he had been disappointed – who wasn't disappointed? – but that his life had the quality of still being unformed.

While people lined up for Communion, the cook kept looking down at the church floor, and Pauline copied this. Adolfo had called the cook "our jungle bunny" in conversations with Dewey. There were ways that Adolfo would not have gotten better, things that age would not have corrected. But the cook had overlooked it; a certain amount could be overlooked, was always overlooked at funerals.

For a moment Pauline thought the cook was really closing one eye as he stared down – as if he *were* trying to overlook things, to discern a shape in the whole experiment of Adolfo's life by squinting sideways at it.

It was possible, of course, that the cook had tears in his eyes; that had not occurred to her at first. As far as she knew, the cook had not been what you could call Adolfo's friend. (Pauline counted eight people at the funeral, including the child, and at least half of them had never seen Adolfo outside a restaurant.) Perhaps the cook's tears, if they were tears, were not from friendship but from something purer, not personal.

She had heard Adolfo describe in detail the contusions on the faces of boxers he'd fought with. He had been very proud of the damage he'd done. It comforted her now to think of his faults, because she couldn't stand there without feeling remorse for certain undefined things in her own past, the funeral had cast an unmistakable tone of regret on everything, and this was not yet an uplifting feeling; she was waiting for it to become so.

The woman with the small child reached over and put her hand on the boy's arm to stop him from fidgeting. She kept him and herself as motionless as possible. Her broad back (you could see through her dress how tightly laced she was into her corset) was rigid and respectful. Pauline saw in everyone else in the room the same solemnity of posture. They wanted to quiet themselves, to be still in the face of Adolfo's stillness – as if by mimicking they could comprehend – but the effort was too much for them; they stirred, they shifted their weights.

The priest was wiping out the inside of the chalice, an act that reminded Pauline of something Adolfo might do in the restaurant, as though the priest were honoring him in the gesture. What order of monks was it that had to do menial labor in the monastery as a form of worship? The priest swirled the cloth around with a bit of a flourish, which made it seem even more like waiter's work, like a gold-lit version of Adolfo on the job.

During the blessing, the small boy stood with his head up and stared at the altar. And then they were all filing out of the church, following the pallbearers, and the service was over.

On the steps of the church one of the old women stopped to rewrap the shawl around her head. She looked like Queen Victoria, Pauline thought, but with a beakier nose. The other woman spoke to her in a fast, voluble murmur. One of them might have been Adolfo's mother; there was no difference in their expressions.

Miss Oughton had said that modern Italians weren't direct descendants of the Romans but of some other peoples, diluted mixtures; this was to explain the disparity between the lofty Romans and an immigrant group known to be so noisy and emotional. Pauline didn't see now that the Romans had behaved so nobly – parading captives through those triumphal arches they were so proud of, making slaves, crushing revolts, pitching camp, and laying waste to. She was disgusted when she thought of these things, as though they bothered her newly, were freshly offensive.

The old women got into a car. Pauline and Nita had decided in advance not to go to the cemetery, and they slipped away from the group.

Nita waved good-bye to Vera. "Thank you for coming with me," Nita said.

"Well, don't thank me for that," Pauline said. They spoke in very soft voices; they were both tired now in a way that made them gentle.

12
(Spring, 1927)

Vera's reopened for business the weekend after Adolfo's funeral. They had put a big metal-cased door on the kitchen, which was supposed to make it safer. The sound of the door slapping shut reminded Pauline of the fire doors in the halls in her high school. Vera's was crowded on the night of its opening – people had missed being able to go there – there were lines on the stairs to get in. Pauline thought Adolfo would've like that, he would've liked the idea of the place continuing, out of the eternal necessity for it. But for Pauline it was too close and noisy, too full of people she didn't know how to behave with.

At the height of the evening she got separated from Nita, who went off to talk to Peter and Marjorie, and then when Ernest came in and Pauline got up to greet him, the man turned out not to be Ernest at all and she lost her seat at the table. She leaned against a wall. A man standing next to her was wearing a coat indoors, a fur coat in April. Pauline thought he was one of the most affected-looking people she had ever seen. "You have intelligent eyes," he said. "It's very unusual for me to like brunettes." She listened to him talk about his childhood in Virginia, about cats he had owned. She couldn't think how to get rid of him. By the time she left she was leaden-eyed and exhausted. She wouldn't let him walk her or take her in a cab, although it was colder outside and drizzling rain. She tied her scarf under her chin like a babushka and walked to a newsstand to get a paper to use as an umbrella (her mother always did that).

A woman in a red hat was in front of her at the newsstand, taking too long getting out her change. Pauline edged behind her to get her to hurry up. And she saw that it was Bunny.

She looked good in red, more spirited than she ever had before, despite the fact that the coat was shapeless and too long. They called out one another's names and threw their arms around each other, blocking the newsstand from another customer.

"I can't believe it," Bunny said.

"Ha," Pauline said. "It's you." She should

not have put that scarf on her head. "Well, Miss Roberta," she said, "what are you *doing* here?"

"I just came to see some people. I can't believe I'm just meeting you here like this."

"Well, how's the settlement house business?"

"I'm working someplace else now with indigent alcoholic cases."

"That's wonderful."

"It's a job," Bunny said. Pauline was glad a bunch of old rummies had the benefit of Bunny; Bunny would be nice to them. In a way, she thought, Bunny was more fearless than she was. It occurred to her to admire Bunny.

"So you're still filing at the ribbon place?" Bunny said. This question did not at first make sense to Pauline. In the noise of the rain, which had gotten heavier, it took her a second to make out the words. She and Bunny were huddled under the awning of the newsstand.

"Oh, yes, still there."

"Do you think it's going to keep raining?" Bunny said. "I was on my way to a party for the Young People's Socialist League, but I don't think I want to go now."

"It'll stop."

"You like New York?" Bunny said. "It's not too hectic?"

"Oh, well," Pauline said. "I manage to control my rampant social life."

"I knew you would like it. You always liked those things. You have your own apartment?"

"Now I do. I was living with someone for a while."

"Me too," Bunny said. "Well, not really living with."

Some men would see Bunny as having sex appeal, in a languid, round-eyed way. She had an ardent nature. It had always shown itself in her principles, in the heated logic of her arguments. She had been silly and imitative and frequently right. Often Pauline thought of things Bunny had said – quotes from Gorky and Marx – as though by having known Bunny she had advanced these opinions herself.

"You like Philadelphia?" Pauline said.

"It's okay. I have activities. You know, YPSL, the Sacco-Vanzetti Defense Committee."

"That's a good committee. You help with that? That's good."

"A little." Bunny gave her crooked half smile, proud of herself but careful to convey that she was on the slower fringes of things.

The rain was beginning to let up, as Pauline had said (she was glad to have been proved right, as though New York weather were within her expertise).

"I should show up at the party," Bunny said.

"You don't want to go, do you?" Pauline said she didn't think so, but she walked part of the way with Bunny, since her house was in the same direction Bunny was going. Bunny didn't seem to be afraid of being on the street at night, even when they passed a man sleeping on the steps of a building and the man moaned and lurched suddenly in his sleep; Pauline jumped back but she didn't. Bunny on the job saw more alarming things all the time, certainly worse drunks; Bunny wasn't some innocent.

"See my shoes?" Bunny said. "You always said my shoes were oafish but I still like this kind." Pauline still thought they were oafish but she had at least learned not to say everything. "You were mean to me sometimes," Bunny said.

"I know." Pauline was somehow surprised that Bunny knew, although she had complained at the time. Pauline hadn't meant to deliberately torment Bunny but she had been callous; she had been always afraid that Bunny was going to disgrace her. She was not happy at the picture of herself at a certain age, unfocused and wildly out of shape.

"How's Murray?" Pauline said. "What happened to him?"

"He's in France," Bunny said. "He lives there now. He doesn't speak any French, though – don't you think that's peculiar?"

"Yes," Pauline said. "I'd learn French if it were me." Pauline had stopped; they were standing by her corner. "*Voici* the street I live on," she said. Bunny gazed down it dutifully. "It was great to see you," Pauline said. "You look great."

"I thought you would be different," Bunny said. "I thought you would be more glamorous."

"Oh, well," Pauline said – she pretended to find the very idea of this funny – and they kissed good-bye.

In the days afterward she kept thinking that New York had become too repetitious for her. She was curious again about France – how could Murray get there and she couldn't? She looked at her Baudelaire again, the perfumed landscapes, the stylized languor. She bought a copy of a French magazine – the ads were the easiest to translate. It was slightly disappointing not to be able to buy the products. Rose said that French tooth powder tasted like burnt vanilla.

Rose had been sick for a week – she had missed Adolfo's funeral because she was laid up in bed with a bad cold. On the night of the fire she had gone off in her wet coat to show the college boy a speakeasy with dancing that was open all night; for a day or so afterward she had mistaken her fever for the ache of a bad hangover.

"She's so dumb sometimes," Nita said. Rose's dumbness, in Nita's eyes, consisted in the first place of exposing herself to germs for the sake of some person in pants. (Nita had spells of being very haughty on the subject.) She thought that Rose fell in love too easily, although Pauline wouldn't have described Rose's latest fling that way; Pauline was always surprised at how freely people used those terms. She herself was careful not to use them, quite scrupulous really. She wouldn't say that she had ever been in love (although sometimes Dewey had made her say it). She was wary about taking the phrase in vain, not because she was "saving herself" – on the contrary she might be said to be blithely throwing herself away – but because she prided herself in making fine distinctions; it upset her, actually, that there was no accurate terminology for the sort of attractions she had had. She was losing her memory of certain things for lack of a mental wording for them – her old, fitful attraction to Ernest, which had had some of the swoon and longing properly associated with love, and her surges of interest in certain men seen in passing or talked to at parties.

However it was true that Rose was impractical – Nita was right about that part of it. Rose was enough to make anyone impatient at times. For her cold she was following a regimen of hot baths with cold showers right after. She wouldn't eat, or she ate things like raw oatmeal and dried figs, and she drank hot salt water. She acted amused when they told her she was going to give herself pneumonia or tuberculosis if she kept this up. She had done all this before, it was the best thing, she would lend them the books if they didn't believe her.

She couldn't do any cooking in her hotel room anyway; the best she could do was to boil water over one of the sconces by the mantel that still had a gas jet that worked. Rose's hotel room showed all through it her efforts to adapt its features to a fuller existence than they were meant to provide. She had draped every surface with a paisley scarf or a piece of cross-stitched embroidery. When friends visited her, she knelt in her kimono and served tea on a trunk covered with one of those Cuban shawls she wore. A few of her dresses always hung along one section of ceiling molding, by way of brightening the wall.

In a way she had succeeded; it was pleasant to sit there with her. She had good afternoon sun from the window that looked over the back yard, and at the end of the afternoons she had the fading shrimp-bisque color of city sunsets. She was very appreciative of the sunsets. The room, when she guided you through it, seemed unusually fortunate and well-situated.

Nita tried to bring her cold broiled steaks to build up her blood, but Rose said red meat wasn't good for you if you were sick. Also she said she didn't believe that large animals that could live for years should be killed for her personal benefit. She had never said this before and Pauline thought of her hiding this opinion, not letting anyone know, perhaps eating nut loaf and carrots in private.

Nita was worried about Rose's cold showers. Rose did seem to believe in heroic measures, rigorous techniques to attack disease and give it no quarter. In a way Pauline was impressed by Rose's courage – Rose didn't mind subjecting her body to rude shocks or denying herself normal comforts. Nita said Rose liked the whole principle of self-punishment, but even allowing for that, there was a physical bravery in it. Pauline wasn't sure, for herself, whether she cared about being physically brave. Still, you never knew what was going to be required of you.

Actually the cold showers seemed to be helping. Pauline's theory was that colds got better in their own time no matter what you did. Solly had gotten colds a lot during one phase of his childhood. Once when she was home alone taking care of him he had disobeyed her by getting up from his bed to watch something out the window, and she had made him stand by the open window for an hour in his underwear. And he had gotten well anyway; he had gone to school the next day. She had been mean to Solly sometimes – irresistibly, in an aimless exercise of power. She had been like Dewey. It surprised her to remember herself like that.

She wouldn't have seen Rose again for a while if she hadn't passed a drugstore with a metal bottle labeled *poudre dentrifrice* in the window. She bought one for Rose and one for herself. The label on the back was all extravagant and poetic claims in French about the health of the teeth, the beauty of the mouth.

It was a warm evening, and she was surprised when Rose answered the door with a blanket wrapped around her. Rose was huddled under it and her eyes were glazed. Pauline thought about whether Rose took drugs (Walter liked opium); perhaps her cold had been no cold at all.

"I'm better," Rose said. Her voice didn't sound normal; it sounded distant and thin. "I was so hot this morning. I think that's over, that part."

Pauline showed her the tooth powder and Rose said she hadn't seen any of that in a long time. She was less enthusiastic than Pauline had expected. She lay back on the bed and shivered a little; she still had the blanket wrapped around her. "Do you mind – could you just get me a glass of water from the sink?" she said.

This was so un-Rose like, this request to be waited on, that Pauline knew then that she was truly sick.

"I'm so thirsty," Rose said. "It's good for you to drink water though, isn't it?"

Pauline put her hand on Rose's forehead, not that she could really tell a fever that way. "Keep drinking," she said. "It's legal."

Rose coughed and sputtered some of it up. Pauline took the glass away.

Rose said, "Do you miss Mack ever?"

"Not really," Pauline said. "Not personally, I don't think."

"I miss my friend," Rose said.

She meant her married lover. Pauline couldn't imagine that he had ever been much help when Rose was sick. "We used to talk a lot about politics," Rose said. "He was very astute, he was good to talk to about that."

"Do you want tea?" Pauline said.

Rose shook her head. This shaking motion

continued bizarrely into a great shudder, her head kicked back, and then she was shivering so violently that the bedstead rattled. "Are you all right?" Pauline said. Rose rolled her eyes toward Pauline; her teeth were chattering. The shivering went on for a long time, as long as ten minutes, during which Pauline rubbed Rose's arms to get some warmth into her, piled coats on the bed, and finally began making tea. "I've got the pot over the flame, I'm holding it," she kept saying. "Is this right? It's almost boiling, I can hear it."

"Thank you," Rose said a few times, through her teeth, and, "Don't worry."

When the shivering stopped, Rose was still afraid to drink the tea for fear of spilling it on herself. What did she need the tea for anyway? Pauline saw that she was bothering Rose about the tea to no purpose – she didn't know what she should be doing. She was alone with Rose, and Rose was not sick in a minor normal way. Pauline was frightened for both of them. She felt the weight of Rose's solitude, her days alone in the room. She was sorry for Rose until it occurred to her that if she herself were sick she would be no better off. On the other hand she was younger and healthier than Rose, she thought, with some vanity. She wondered how Adolfo had managed with his leg.

Rose had more color in her face and she said she felt better. "You have to eat," Pauline decided. "When did you eat? If you're shivering and coughing you should be eating more than usual, you're using up your strength." Perhaps this was true. Did Rose want a chicken sandwich? Maybe some applesauce?

"If you're going out," Rose said. "Maybe you could get me some Unguentine." Rose had burned herself with the mustard plaster. She showed Pauline the patches of blistering skin between her breasts. She hadn't meant to leave the plaster on so long but she had fallen asleep.

"You dumb cluck," Pauline said. Rose said it wasn't so bad, they used to do that on purpose, blister people to drive out the toxic fluids. "That was in the Dark Ages, for crying out loud," Pauline said. Rose didn't know anything about what to do either; her body was wallowing in their ignorance.

I should get a doctor, Pauline thought (she didn't know any doctors except in Newark). Instead she went out and called Nita, and she came back with a chicken sandwich, which she made Rose eat half of before she left.

The doctor Nita called didn't come till the next day. When Pauline got there in the evening, Rose was imitating the doctor's accent, which she said was like the Katzenjammer Kids. Nita said he probably spoke perfect English but was just overwhelmed from getting a peek at Rose's naked chest. Rose was flushed tonight, sweaty and overexcited.

"She's got pee-neu-monie," Nita said.

"I have to go on a soft diet," Rose said. "Don't you think that's insulting for an adult?"

Pauline tried to see from Nita's face how serious this was. Nita gave her one quick glance: not good. Rose's one worry was about the doctor coming again. She didn't want the hotel to know she had something as bad as pneumonia. She was sure they would take her room away. Nita kept saying they *couldn't* throw her out on the street, but Rose thought that she had disqualified herself by falling below a certain level of health. She seemed to think of the hotel as a great blessing rightly bestowed only on the fit. Everybody wanted her room anyway because of the view. She was not sensible on the subject and had to be led off onto other topics.

It was less frightening with Nita there. Still, when Rose was coughing Nita and Pauline both turned away – they couldn't look at each other. Nita left early – they arranged that she would come in the mornings and Pauline would stay on after supper. Pauline was pleased to have something definite apportioned to her. She washed some cups and saucers and rinsed out Rose's nightgowns and then she got the idea that maybe Rose would like to be read to. Rose wanted to hear something from the newspaper. Pauline went down to get a paper, and then she read Rose two articles about the sentencing in the Sacco-Vanzetti case and a feature about April in Central Park. At the end Rose was asleep.

Pauline was satisfied to see this; the atmosphere of reading aloud had made her feel peaceful too. She was full of plans for things she would do for Rose – she would buy her a bed jacket, she would air the room, she would make puddings, she would surprise her with flowers. She had spent her childhood reading books about these things – all the novels where orphaned families lived inventively in terrible poverty, crippled boys were tended by ragged but sweet-tempered sisters, and acts of considerable heroism were performed by children no older than herself at the time. She knew perfectly well that these had been sentimental stories – some of them, when she thought of them now, were downright grotesque – highly dated and beginning to be old-fashioned even then, but there was something in them also which was not purely sentimental and which she had not encountered elsewhere in her childhood. She had been very hurt as a child when her father had made fun of those books. They had given her a taste of a particular kind of glory and left her with secret moral longings.

Nita thought they should get in touch with Rose's parents. She said she felt funny that only Rose's friends knew how she was. The doctor said it wasn't a grave case, but who knew about this doctor anyway?

"It's no good telling them," Rose said. In the first place she wasn't that sick and in the second place there was never any point in bothering them with news. Not that her relations with them weren't cordial – she had a picture of them, a portrait taken in a studio in Wausau, Wisconsin. They were older than you would think – the mother was broad and white-haired and the father had a long, shrunken face. Their eyes had come out pale and moony in the photo; they both look transfixed. There was a brother who lived at home. The father had been in a long gloomy spell some years ago and he had been too timid to do much since then; moving cars made him run. Her mother believed he had weakened his constitution by eating green fruit.

There was plenty Pauline hadn't known before about Rose; in a way they didn't know each other that well. Yet they were intimates – they had told each other strong and indelible details about their private lives, their sexual experiences; they had counseled each other. And Rose was not surprised that Pauline and Nita were the ones in the room with her now, sitting on her bed watching her. She would've been with them if they had been sick (probably coaxing them to drink that miserable hot lemonade of hers). They were bound to each other, for now, not only by the usual ties of friendship but by their shared lots and their understanding (perfectly clear and grim) of how it would go for them without each other.

The next time Pauline came, Rose said she was better, she was well rested, she had been sleeping all the time. She had put on, presumably for Pauline's visit, a pearl rope necklace and a blouse that she wore as a bed jacket. She looked odd, Pauline thought.

Rose said she had been thinking all day about Sacco and Vanzetti. She had had a dream that the air in the room was burning her up, and when she woke up, she realized that she had stolen the idea from Vanzetti, who'd had a violent delusional fit a few years ago about the burning atmosphere in his cell – he had tried to barricade himself and he had smashed furniture. "He was preimagining the electric chair," Rose said. "It's so obvious now." Her eyes teared up.

Pauline, to her own surprise, also got teary. Usually she thought it was not fair in some way that of all the unjustly confined prisoners in the world, people liked Sacco and Vanzetti because they were more eloquent; they could convey what it was like to be in prison. They would probably be dead by July – they had been sentenced now, after seven years. Actually, unlike almost everybody else on both sides, she liked them because they were anarchists.

And she was teary because they reminded her, in a way, of Adolfo. Adolfo would have been insulted by this comparison. He was certainly no radical and he would've considered himself socially several cuts above the level of a shoemaker or a fish peddler. But they reminded her of Adolfo in the way no one listened to them. She pictured Vanzetti gesticulating on street corners, streams of people hurrying past his speeches, and she thought of Adolfo trying to yuk it up with customers or muttering to himself in the kitchen, that vivacity expended in empty space.

Rose was coughing. Pauline thought that pneumonia must be like a kind of claustrophobia within the body, a threat of the lungs closing off and no air getting in – an exitless confinement like Vanzetti's, and like Adolfo's last minutes in the smoky kitchen. Prisoners always longed for things they had barely noticed before. Rose hacked and struggled, marshaling her strength in the simple desire for air.

Pauline tried to arrange the pillows under her so that she could sit up straighter. Nita was much better at this, more deft and better at intuiting what Rose really wanted. Pauline tended to care for her by rote – did she want water? tea? a window opened? Nita was better at thinking of items to bring – silly postcards, an embroidered pillowcase. But Pauline had more staying power. Nita bustled off to her lunch job after a few hours with Rose in the morning, but Pauline's visits began at supper and went on into the night, when Rose was at her worst.

In the night Rose's fever went up; she still had fits of shivering and she breathed in a wheezy, rapid way; she would grunt suddenly when the breathing hurt her. When she slept, the jolts of her own grunting woke her up. "We could maybe have the doctor in again," Pauline said.

Rose said, "I can't believe you would do that." She was angry then – Pauline had never seen her angry. It was the room – she didn't want to have to give up the room. She had been there for years; her things were there; she had arranged everything the way she liked it. Pauline wondered whether all this was because Rose wanted to make sure her friend could find her if he came looking, but Rose didn't say anything about him. It was the *time* she had been in the room; she was very emphatic about the strength of her sentiment based on a sort of depth of occupancy. "I was here before I even started drawing for the *Journal,*" she said. Pauline thought it was nice that Rose felt such an attachment to certain years of her life there (which could hardly have been all pleasant); she seemed to be insisting on their value. Still it startled Pauline that Rose pictured a continuing future in the hotel. So they would all go on as they were, was that it? For herself, Pauline was used to thinking of her current condition as more or less provisional, an introduction to something not invented yet and not really imagined.

"Maybe we can have the doctor show up in disguise," Pauline said. "Camouflage his black bag as a hatbox or something."

Rose didn't laugh. She said, "Don't *talk* about it," and she was getting hoarse and querulous.

Pauline made Nita come with her the next night. By that time Nita had talked to the doctor, who said that Rose was approaching a "crisis"; they should call him if certain symptoms appeared.

"Like what?" Pauline said.

"Turning blue," Nita said.

"No, really," Pauline said. But Nita was serious. It was hard now to tell what could be joked about and what couldn't. Rose was not blue (surely this was a metaphor – how would they know when she approached what was meant by this color?). She was pale and her face was hollowed in parts and swollen in others; she was not herself. She lay without talking to them. When they asked her things she answered in one word and closed her eyes. She seemed to be concentrating on her breathing. Nita said, "Are you warm enough or do you want another blanket?" "Warm," Rose said. Pauline had never seen anyone this sick before. She saw how the downward curl of Rose's mouth was like the sketches done of Keats at his bedside, and then she was ashamed of noticing, of *making comparisons* at such a time. And yet it was not out of heartlessness that she wanted to see, to see clearly. She breathed evenly to try to guide Rose.

Nita tried to give her the hot lemonade she

liked, but she made them take the cup away. Rose grunted, a sound of small pain lower than the range of her real voice; in real life she would have begged their pardon.

Nita and Pauline whispered in the corner to each other. Nita thought they should both stay the night; one of them could sleep on the floor and the other one on a chair. Pauline felt a surge of gratitude toward Nita for thinking of this. She was so relieved that they would be doing the right thing it made her believe for a minute that nothing perilous could happen as long as someone was keeping vigil. She smoothed the blanket around Rose's feet; she went around the bed tucking in corners.

Nita turned out the light. Rose made a murmuring noise – perhaps she was saying good night to them. They sat waiting to hear if they could tell when she was asleep. Nita said, "Here," and passed a roll of caramels to Pauline; they chewed in the dark, as though they were at the movies or around a campfire. "To keep our strength up," Nita said. Pauline at that moment did feel their strength, their solid forms in the hotel room and their small careful movements.

Nita got up to wash at Rose's sink. Through the window there was a noise of voices from the courtyard underneath – some old men were standing outside drinking and telling stories. They weren't loud enough to wake Rose, and Pauline thought they were a good omen; their distant sociability was soothing in the room.

"It's nice here at night," Pauline said. She did like Rose's room at night – she had noticed this before in the evenings alone with her. There was a pleasure in staying, a clarity of mind about being in the right place.

Later they heard Rose wake up. She opened her eyes and saw Nita curled up under a shawl on the chair. Nita waved. "All the company passed out," she said. Rose made a little snorting laugh.

When Pauline woke up in the middle of the night, the room was quiet. She was on the floor, with a pillow under her head, and she saw everything from below; the dark columns of the legs of Rose's bed were at eye level. A glass light fixture glimmered overhead; she felt as though she were lying on the deck of a ship. She got up to see how Rose was. She stood as near to the bed as she could, but it was too dark – she could only make out the hump of Rose's body under the covers and the pale blur that was her profile. How could she keep watch if she couldn't see? It struck her as crazy now, what they had thought they could do. She tried to see if Rose's chest was moving under the covers – there seemed to be a motion but perhaps it was a trick of perception, like the vibrations of color people see in total darkness. She stood for a long time, trying to discern what noise or motion was Rose's, waiting, knowing that she was far outside the small realm of what she knew, and hoping that here and now this time she would not be caught out.

In the morning Rose said, "Gads, who was that snoring?" Pauline didn't think that any of them had snored. What sound had come buzzing up through Rose's ears? "I'm just kidding," Rose said. "For Pete's sake. Trying to inject a little humor here."

And she was willing to eat a soft-boiled egg for breakfast. "Isn't that a stirring sight?" Nita said. "Look at how she dribbles that yolk on her chin. It makes my heart spasmodic with joy."

"You eat too," Rose said, in her cracked sick-voice.

Pauline and Nita shared a bowl of shredded wheat with some slightly sour milk that had been left out on the sill. "I have a little sister," Pauline sang softly, "Tries very hard to sleep./ She chews on Father's whiskers/ And thinks they're shredded wheat." She was actually singing out of happiness at hearing Rose talk in whole sentences.

"Don't sing," Nita said. "It's not sporting when you're in a room with someone who can't get up and leave."

"I could leave," Rose said. "I feel better."

Rose had of course announced that she was better every day since she'd gotten sick. But she *wasn't* as bad as she'd been last night. (Unless she was going to waver: better, worse, better, worse.) Still, she seemed with them again; swelled and dried, but herself.

"You don't see me practicing my violin here," Nita said.

"She'd love it," Pauline said. "It would feel so good when you stopped."

They tried to get Rose back to sleep again after breakfast, but she wasn't tired, she said. She wanted them to wash her hair. They had to bend her head into a basin, soap her down like a dog, and try to rinse her off without slopping all the water on the bed. "Aren't you going to work?" Nita said, when they were wrapping the towel around Rose's head. The bed was all soggy on one side, and they sat Rose in a chair with a blanket on her while they changed the sheets. Pauline had assumed she wasn't going to work – it was nine thirty already; if she went she would be leaving Rose alone all through the lunchtime hours while Nita was off playing. Nita's opinion, which she had to whisper and signal, was that Rose would sleep only if they both went away – she was all worked up today.

If Pauline left at once, she could get to Gittelson's before ten and they wouldn't dock her more than an hour's pay. Rose was putting on bracelets, layers on both arms, and she insisted on making Pauline wear a china-bead one for the office. "It looks so nice on you, Pauline, Pauline," she said.

When Pauline walked out into the sudden light of the street, she was conscious that she had slept badly on a wooden floor, that she was wearing the same clothes she had had on since yesterday, and that her own hair needed washing. She was not alert; she let people jostle her. She felt that she had poured her strength into Rose, although she knew that this was not quite true – she was envious of Rose's being able to sleep for the rest of the day. She shuffled, exaggerating the signs of fatigue in her walk. At work she would have to let Miss Pfeiffer know why she was late; she would not make an issue of it but she would tell them: a sick friend. This would be a shallow and reductive summary, like any traveler's report; already the extremes of the night had a visionary quality. The bracelet clinked, a souvenir.

As it turned out, Miss Pfeiffer was not even there, a truly unusual circumstance. Pauline couldn't remember her ever missing work, except after her niece's death. The bookkeeper was at the front desk, trying to cope with the switchboard.

Pauline slipped to her corner in the back, hoping no one would see her and yell at her. The place seemed under-patrolled today. George the stock boy was sitting on a carton sneaking a look at the sports page. Pauline made him stretch out his arm so she could see the front page – something about the health of the economy in one of the headlines. The news, she thought, was always rife with figures of speech about sickness and decline and recovery. In fourth grade her teacher had lectured them about the War and blamed it on the Ottoman Empire, which she said was called the Sick Man of Europe, as though a difficult patient had caused some kind of family havoc. Still, to think of Rose's "crisis" and her "turning point" was for Pauline to feel that she had in the course of things participated in the vocabulary of the race.

There were stacks of invoices waiting for her to file them. She tried to be efficient and fast, so no one would ask her to stay late. She was doing pretty well, she thought, keeping up a good pace. She worked while George went to lunch; the office was quiet. George came back with a printed flyer, which he waved at her. "A present," he said. "Right up your alley."

"If it's a sale, I can't afford it," she said. The flyer said: RALLY IN UNION SQUARE. THE PEOPLE WILL BE HEARD. SACCO AND VANZETTI MUST NOT DIE.

"Oh, I was going to go," Pauline said. She meant she had been thinking about doing *something*. She wondered if Bunny had anything to do with planning this.

"You know what I don't understand?" George said. She hated it when they argued politics. "How many times did they try to get a new trial and get turned down? A lot, right?"

"Seven," Pauline said, reading from the flyer.

"How could they stand that? You think you're going to live, you think you're going to die. Live, die, live, die, et cetera."

"What are you asking me?" she said. "How they could stand it? They stood it, that's it."

"I'm not asking you anything," he said. "It was a rhetorical question."

"They stood it. That's what some people do."

On her late lunch break Pauline went out to smoke a cigarette on a park bench. She didn't smoke outside in public normally, but today she wanted to. The bench was not in a real park, but in a triangle of dirt with one skinny tree. She was very tired once she sat down. It was Murray who had first taught her to smoke in high school. Murray had said it relaxed you. Pauline pictured the blue line of the smoke, taken in, diffusing through the body, making it lighter. She liked the thought of some inner expansion taking place from what she took in, the burning matter transformed. To smoke and think this now made her feel braced for the rest of the day, steadfast.

In the afternoon at Gittelson's she did some of the bookkeeper's job, sitting at the adding machine. She had to work a crank to make the paper roll each time, and the work was physical enough to keep her alert. She worried about how Rose was – Rose couldn't phone for help unless she went down to the lobby – she would probably rather die than do that and have them see how she was. Nita would be there by three-thirty or quarter to four. Pauline was jumpy until that time came, restless to leave.

In the evening when she went to Rose's, the room smelled of cologne. Rose had given herself a sponge bath and doused herself with some strong flowery scent, jasmine or tuberose, and she had put drops of it on the sheets and blankets.

"Smells like a whorehouse in here, doesn't it?" Nita said.

"Spring is here," Rose said. They seemed to be very short with each other. Pauline took this as a good sign, since Nita would've had to stay agreeable if Rose weren't better.

"They're just some kinds of perfume I don't like," Nita said.

"Otherwise it's like a cell here," Rose said. "I shouldn't say cell. Vanzetti is in a real cell."

"She has a crush on him," Nita said. "An ethical crush."

Pauline showed them the flyer the stock boy had given her. This turned out to be unwise – Rose announced right away that she wanted to go to the rally. "It's this *Saturday*," Nita said. "You're not going anywhere."

"We'll go for you," Pauline said (too brightly – not even Rose was going to fall for that).

"Well, *I'm* going," Nita said. It surprised Pauline that Nita was so eager. Nita said the whole thing made her want to bomb the judge personally. "It would give me great pleasure to see him blown to pieces."

"Don't be disappointed, they're not doing

that at the rally," Pauline said. There was a real question, of course, about what they *were* doing. Shouting into the wind? Then – fleetingly – she was happy about the rally, full of the feeling that if Rose could be better, Sacco and Vanzetti could be saved.

Rose said, "I really like Vanzetti."

Pauline knew why she liked him; they had talked about it. Rose's friend had said Vanzetti was the perfect example of a worker more intelligent than anyone wanted him to be. Pauline, having come somewhat late into all this, liked him because of what he had said before the court at the end, that he had never committed a real crime, *"though some sins."* This seemed to her so unflinching in its acknowledgment of things – which no one had asked him about – that he was privately ashamed of; he was so insistent on explaining just which sort of innocence he could claim. It gave her a particular kind of fellow feeling with him.

"Rose," Nita said, "for Christ's sake, stop making that noise with the straw." Pauline had brought a milkshake for Rose, which she was sipping with discouraging slowness. Nita said it probably tasted like soap from the scent in the room.

"You take it," Rose said. "I don't want it any more."

"I don't want it."

Rose coughed for a while, to back up her point, and she closed her eyes, weary with them.

Nita said the rally was going to be a real fresh-air outing for them after all the time spent in Rose's closet of a room with that one crummy window. When they got to Union Square on Saturday, it was already too crowded for them to get very close to the platforms – there were throngs of people spread out on the grounds and out to the sidewalk, people standing on benches, and blocks of people standing in rows holding banners. PERSECUTION OF WORKERS MUST STOP. *Garment Workers for Justice.* TODAY IT IS SACCO AND VANZETTI; TOMORROW WHO? The closer they got, the more massive the crowd looked. Pauline felt personally triumphant to be joining a gathering that was already so successful. She was sorry they had gotten there late – the speeches had already started, she had missed things, possibly the most important parts had gone on without her. On the platform nearest them a man in a black suit was shouting to be heard; from different sides they could hear the blurred ringing of other speeches being given from other platforms. The black-suited man had to hurl himself forward with each phrase to get volume.

"I can't understand a word he's saying," Nita said. "He's not talking English."

Pauline could understand him fine because he was speaking Yiddish – she had forgotten for a moment that Nita didn't understand. "The powerless are hated and feared," Pauline said. "That's what he's saying. That's kind of a literal translation."

Nita wanted to move – a woman was speaking in English on the other side. "Our mother tongue," Nita said.

"I like it here. It's like being in a giant train station." Pauline said the speakers were rotating from platform to platform, and if they waited the English speaker would come to them. But the next one to mount the podium was an old man who held forth in Italian.

She thought about Rose's "crush" on Vanzetti. Vanzetti was good-looking – the eyes, the mustache – even if he'd gotten balder in his time in prison. Rose said anarchists treated their women well (Rose would believe that). Perhaps they would be a good match, he and Rose. It was odd to be thinking of romance at a time like this – not that it was inappropriate, she thought firmly, as though she were defending Rose's right to happiness (not to mention Vanzetti's), but it seemed on the wrong scale, too particular and specific for the event at hand.

The old man was using impassioned gestures and a spitting manner of delivery; Pauline was quite taken with him. "I can't stand it," Nita said.

"Well, go then," Pauline said. "Go move somewhere without me."

She was mortified that they were having a fight at a time like this. But Nita said, "Look for me at the southwest corner in an hour." Pauline thought it was ingenious of her to think of this; sometimes Nita didn't get mad when you would expect her to.

After Nita left, the crowd felt different; she was packed in closer with them, more similar to them. The old Italian went from the fiery phase of his speech to something more wailing and grief-stricken. All around Pauline, people who were surely not Italian and who could not have understood what he was saying, stood watching him, respectful and even moved. Mostly they looked patient – Pauline thought about the high intentions that had brought them there, that made them wait; she had, with them, a feeling of holding something at bay by simply standing there.

When the woman who was giving her speech in English finally got to the platform, the words at first were too blunt and direct. Pauline disagreed with her about the jury being just a bunch of bigots. She was disappointed – the woman's speech was too unintelligent and it was weakened by cant phrases. The woman was saying that the governor's committee was "too stupid to see its nose in front of its face," a phrase Dewey would have used. Pauline was indignant at the resemblance. She was angry at the woman; she felt so strongly that the speech should be more solemn. Pauline saw then how sure she herself was that Sacco and Vanzetti were going to die.

The woman broke into a suddenly sincere sentence about what had happened since the "terrible accident" of Sacco's and Vanzetti's arrest. "They were taken by surprise," she said, "seven years ago, and what did they do? They didn't yield to fear." (Pauline knew this was not strictly true, they had both had crazy spells in jail – Sacco had beat his head against the wall, Vanzetti had had his fits about the air burning him up – but it was close enough to be true.) "In jail all that time, with all their reading and brooding and waiting, they rose to their fates." The crowd burst into a round of clapping, thunderous once it really got started. Pauline clapped and then, when a cheer started, she was shouting too. She felt buoyed up, floating – she was only standing up and making a noise with a lot of people – but in that long shout she had the sense of expansion people feel in the face of great vistas out-of-doors. In the din she couldn't hear her own shout, and she had the odd temporary freedom of doing without her own personality.

After that she kept looking around for Bunny. She wanted Bunny to know she was there. Would she have come from Philadelphia? Pauline thought it would make them both happy to see each other, give them a feeling of reprise and order. But it was impossible to see far enough into the mass to pick out a face more than a few feet away. And Bunny was short, easily hidden.

She didn't think she would ever find Nita either. Someone was halfway through a speech in German, of which she understood bits and pieces, when she spotted Nita just where she was supposed to be, on the sidewalk waving to her. With Nita were two men, a sandy-haired blond with a pug nose whom she recognized from Vera's and a thin man in a brown hat. She had not thought about people from Vera's or Anselm's or the Elephants' Graveyard being here, although if Nita was, lots of the others were bound to be. Not all – some of them wouldn't be at a worker's rally. (Walter had once asked if she soaked her feet in hot water after a long day at the office, and he had asked her in a jeering way; he had been making fun of her for having that kind of job. She had been surprised at that – class snobbery in Bohemia. But then she had expected her own ratings of people, based on taste and flair and currency of style, to reign just as rigidly.) She had almost forgotten about Vera's, so the sight of the men startled her.

"Are you having a good time?" Pauline said. She knew this was a somewhat brainless question, but she needed to know if Nita was going to want to leave right then.

"Did you see the lawyer from Hungary?" Nita said. "On the other side? He was very wonderful."

"I'd like to climb a tree and really see how many people are here," one of the men said.

"Oh, lift me up," Nita said. "I'll sit on your shoulders and count."

Pauline was amazed at the modesty with which Nita managed to get herself hoisted up. The thin man helped, lifting her by the elbows – she was so nimble no one got more than a glimpse of her garters. Still it was quite bold of her to be straddling the blond man's neck like that – perhaps he was a new interest.

"Billions," Nita said. "I see billions. It won't

do any good for those poor suckers, but it's a very great sight." They let her slide down. The blond man offered to take Pauline up too, but Pauline said she could get a sense of it from where she was.

"Aren't you glad we learned not to be afraid of crowds?" Nita said.

Pauline couldn't recall that either of them had ever really been afraid of crowds – a good part of the time they liked large groups, the cells of city life – but she thought that Nita meant that they weren't too delicate, that they were hardened and sturdy enough so that they weren't going to fall down at their posts. This was also to say that she intended to stay through to the rest of the rally with Pauline.

It was late in the day when they got to Rose's room. They had let the men buy them coffee at a soda shop off Union Square, and they had all walked west together, bone tired and with a sense of having spent themselves well. Nita was doing a lot of whispering with the blond man before they said good-bye in front of Rose's hotel.

Rose was in bed – she applauded when she saw Nita and Pauline in the doorway. "It's the army of the righteous, back from walking the face of the earth." She had put on a head scarf fastened with a brooch above one ear, and she looked like a very skinny girl playing a pirate in a comic opera. "So how was it?" she said.

"It was huge," Pauline said. "You wouldn't believe how many people."

"I bet my friend was there," Rose said.

"Probably everybody you ever knew was there," Nita said.

For a moment Rose looked sad to hear this. They had come in with all this rush and flurry from the outside world; they were too excited. Rose was propped up with pillows, waiting for them. They had forgotten her till now.

She had made them a punch out of rum and tepid milk. Pauline thought it was the kind of thing Byron might have revived himself with on his travels. "How many do you think were there?" Rose said.

"Zillions," Nita said.

"She had a unique view," Pauline said.

"I saw somebody's hat up in a tree. He threw it and he couldn't get it down."

"Why do people throw things when they get excited?" Rose said. "It's an urge, isn't it?"

"What tree?" Pauline said. "I didn't see."

Rose said, "Tell me something better about it. What was the crowd like?" She twisted in the bed, angry at it, stretching her feet against the bedstead.

"Very varied," Nita said.

They weren't doing a good job of telling her about it. Along with the punch there was a plate of buttered soda crackers. Rose had been moving around much more than she should have been. She had that gloss in her eyes that she got with a fever. She's not that much better, Pauline thought. Why did we think she could get better that fast? "I'm hot," Rose said. When she took off the blouse she wore as a bed jacket, her shoulders under the straps of her nightgown were spindly and birdlike.

"Did you eat?" Pauline said.

"I'm eating a cracker now," Rose said. She was tall, taller than Pauline, and when she sat upright her shoulders looked square. Pauline appraised them, gauging their boniness. She was thinking of how much had passed through Rose's frame. Rose still had something of a hard time breathing – you could see by the way she lifted her chin, putting muscle into the effort.

On the wall above the bed was a watercolor that Rose had done, one of her still-lifes of a wine bottle and a roll. Nita said even in the picture the roll looked stale. It did look inedible, like a yellow-brown stone. Around the roll there were dashes of brush strokes – Rose had pictured the air as full of speckles and vibrations – crowded with threatening, random motion. Pauline had looked at the picture many times before, and the menace of that storming background was connected in her mind with people giving each other hot tea and the sense of being encamped there.

Rose decided now that she wanted the window open. It was a casement window and it stuck at the top, so that to get it open you had to stand on a chair and push at the corner and pray you didn't fling yourself outside when it finally unjammed. Nita and Rose were both quite brave about doing it. Pauline said she would do it this time. Nita held her feet. She got a good grip on Pauline's ankles; her hands, with their nails kept short for violin playing, were surprisingly strong.

While Pauline was pressing on the pane, she saw straight down to the bottom of the courtyard and she had a twinge of real vertigo – why had she volunteered for this? The window gave way suddenly; it squawked and swung open. Pauline braced herself, with her palms on the wall, and then she had to reach around and hook the window outside so it didn't flap. The chair under her wobbled. Once it was done she was very pleased with herself, hopping down off the chair, but it made her especially admire Rose and Nita, who always did it so casually.

The wind came through in a cool, pleasant gush of air. The light in the room had dimmed and gotten shadowy, but Rose wanted to wait before they turned on the lamp. The line of her dresses hanging against the wall looked frieze-like; the skirt of a limp crepe one near the window stirred slightly. In the dimming light the white of the walls was dappled and the varnished woodwork had a dark watery sheen. Nita had gone back to sitting on the edge of the bed; she was settled sideways, drinking her cloudy white punch out of a teacup. Rose was saying something about the breeze – she liked the breeze from that window – her voice was still thin and raspy and Nita had to lean forward to hear – and Pauline stood for a minute watching them.